Rosie Goes to War

Rosie
Goes to
War

ALISON KNIGHT

Published by Accent Press Ltd

ISBN 9781783752515

Published by Accent Press Ltd – 2016

CHAPTER ONE

Mum can never understand why I don't like going to Gran's house. She doesn't see the shadows, or hear the whispers. She says I'm just being stroppy, and I don't respect the older generation. But it isn't that at all. Gran's cool. She laughs a lot, she's addicted to her telly, and doesn't mind if I stay up late. And, she doesn't nag.

Seriously, I love my Gran, but her house gives me the creeps. Sometimes, it's like there's two houses in one place. The one everyone sees is sunny and warm, full of plants and family photos and odd cooking smells. The other one, that's hiding inside it, is dingy and cold, where there are other people just out of sight. You can hear them in the next room, or see them out of the corner of your eye. At least, I can. Mum can't. And if Gran notices, it doesn't seem to bother her.

'Mind the wind don't change while you've got that sour look on your face, our Rosie,' says Gran, plonking down a mug of tea in front of me, 'or you'll be stuck that like for ever. You won't get no handsome boys chasing after you then.'

I feel myself go red at Gran's words. 'Boys don't chase after me,' I say. 'They like girls with big boobs,' I say, thinking of some people I know from school. Oh my God! Did I just say that to my gran?

'Not much change there then,' laughs Gran. 'It was the same when I was a girl. Mind you, the war changed all that. Them lads in uniform were happy for some attention from anything in a skirt. Frightened, they were, that Hitler would do for 'em before they got into a girl's knickers. I was fighting them all off in the end, 'cept my Billy of course. God rest his soul.'

'Too much information, thanks.' I just can't picture my grandmother as a girl. I mean, she's in her nineties – although, as Dad always says, pretty spry. Still, it's really old. Eewww!

1

'Don't you go all prissy on me, our Rosie. I know what it's like to be fifteen.'

I try not to roll my eyes.

'I was working by then,' Gran goes on. 'After our mum died, me and Nelly had the house to ourselves, what with Dad being away in the war. Had some adventures, we did. Nelly'll tell you when she gets here. We didn't sit around sulking because there weren't no interweb.'

Huh! Gran and her sister had it all right then – no school, and no parents telling them they're not old enough to be left alone for a few weeks, which I am, I don't care what Mum says.

Not that it matters where I am this summer: it's still going to be worst one ever. I wanted to go on holiday with my bestie, or rather ex-bestie Jessica. Her family's staying in a villa with a pool in Italy. They'd invited me to go with them, and it was going to be great because her brother Luke was going with his mate Simon, who I've fancied just about all my life. I saved up and bought a sexy bikini that was guaranteed to impress him.

Then what happens? I catch Jess snogging Simon. Yeah, really. I mean, she's always known how I feel about him. How could she do that to me? And I can't believe he is so shallow that he's snogged her when he was pretending he was interested in me just a couple of days before. I'm not sure I want a boyfriend who plays around like that. And then I had the embarrassment of Luke asking me out. I mean seriously – Jessie's brother? I've known him for ever, he's like a brother to me. He was probably motivated by pity anyway, but it was really awkward, turning him down. I couldn't go on holiday with them after that, could I? I told Mum and Dad I'd stay at home.

But no, my parents are off on a jolly to France because Dad's got to fix a computer system that's playing up over there, and they reckon I'm too young to stay home alone and made me come to Gran's instead. It's so not fair! And now her scary sister Nelly is coming to stay too. It just gets worse and worse.

'It's the internet, Gran,' I say. 'And I'm not sulking.' Well, maybe I am, but I reckon I've got reason to. 'I'm just bored, that's all. If you had proper Wi-Fi I could talk to my friends.' I can't use my mobile, because I stupidly forgot to pack the charger. I'll have to go out and buy another one soon. The battery's nearly dead and I'll die if I can't text anyone.

'Well I haven't, and I'm jolly glad. You ought to be out and about, making new friends, not sitting here all pale and quiet. In my day, we made our own entertainment.'

Here we go again. Another lecture on the good old days.

'I'd be up town, going to the picture-house, or to see a show. If me old knees weren't so bad, I'd go with you now. Loved it up town, I did.'

Gran always calls central London 'up town'. I quite fancy going there myself. Jess went to Covent Garden once, and she said it was wicked, with street performers and nice shops and stuff. I won't admit it to Gran, but I'm a bit scared of getting buses on my own. So I shrug, playing it cool. 'It's not the same these days. I'd probably get mugged.'

'Gor blimey! What's the matter with you? I've never in all my days been mugged, and I reckon them toe-rags what do that sort of thing will pick on the likes of me, not you. The cowardly little so-and-so's will go for the easy target, not a fit young thing who can scream and beat 'em off.'

'If someone comes after me with a knife, Gran, I'll just hand over my purse and phone. Nothing's worth getting killed for.'

'Neither is it right to give in to the likes of them. If you don't do nothing else, my girl, you run. You've got a good pair of long legs on you, and most of them muggers are drugged up or drunk, so you'll leave 'em standing.'

I laugh. 'How did we go from me being bored to dealing with muggers?'

'Well, I dunno. Something to do with you being too scared to leave the house, I think.' Gran's eyes twinkle behind her purple-rimmed glasses. 'So, are you getting the bus up town or not?'

She's got me. 'I suppose so. But didn't you say you wanted me to help you this morning?'

Gran looks confused for a minute. She does that a lot. Then she tuts.

''Course I did. It won't take long. We need to sort out

Nelly's room before she gets here.'

It looks like Gran has been using her sister's old room as a dump – there's stuff everywhere. It's probably quite big when you clear all the junk out. But right now it's making me feel weird. The sun's shining through the window, but it's freezing in here. One minute there's wallpaper with little lemon flowers on. The next, I swear, it all merges into plain, dingy, green paint. It's making me feel dizzy.

'What's the matter with the walls?' I ask.

'What walls, love?'

'There.' I point at a spot of dark green that looks like a big smudge on the pale wallpaper.

Gran peers at it, scrunching up her eyes, then she shrugs and shakes her head. 'I can't see nothing, darling. Is there an air bubble under the paper?'

I rub my eyes. Maybe I've got something wrong with my sight? I don't think so, though. I had my usual eye-test not long ago and I'm fine. I look at Gran, wondering if she's in denial. After all, it can't be easy, living in this house. It's beyond weird. 'Must have been something in my eye,' I say. 'So what do we need to do?'

'That'll be all the dust in here,' says Gran. 'I'd better get the Hoover.'

'I'll get it,' I say, glad to get out of here for a minute.

'Oh, ta. Get the Pledge and a couple of dusters while you're at it, love.'

'OK.' I run downstairs, trying to think up excuses to stay out of there.

It takes us an hour to sort out the room, which behaves itself for once and looks like normal. When most of the junk has been put away, it's quite nice. The wallpaper is pretty, in a vintage sort of way. The pale lemon curtains match the cover Gran throws over the duvet. I'm just straightening it for her when I stub my toe on something under the bed.

'Ow!' I hop around a bit, the pain bringing tears to my eyes. Gran fusses over me until I get embarrassed and calm down. I lift up the corner of the bedcover and glare at the object that attacked me. It's a suitcase – brown leather, dead old looking.

'What you got there, love? Let's have a look.' I pick it up – Oh my God, it's heavy – and put it on the bed.

Gran looks at the label. 'Well, I never did. I forgot all about her.'

Before I can ask what she means, the doorbell rings and Nelly arrives.

I must stop calling my great-aunt that. It's Gran's fault. She always calls her Nelly, even though her sister doesn't like it. I don't see her much, but I remember the last time I did. She told me off: 'My name is Eleanor,' she'd said, looking down her nose at me. 'Only my foolish sister insists on using that ridiculous nickname.' It made me feel stupid, like when Mrs Sparks, my History teacher, tells me off for not paying attention – which happens a lot. I suppose it's not surprising that Great-aunt Ne … Eleanor used to be a head teacher at a huge school in London. She probably trained at the same place as Mrs Sparks. They're both seriously scary.

I volunteer to put the kettle on. I'm a bit shy round Great-aunt Eleanor. She's quite posh, not like Gran. It's hard to see that they're sisters, really. I use the cups and saucers instead of mugs, find some biscuits, and put it all on a nice tray to take into the lounge, where they're talking.

'Here she is, Nelly, hasn't she grown?'

I put the tray down on the coffee table and wish Gran would stop embarrassing me. Of course I've grown – last time Great-aunt Eleanor saw me, I was about ten. I'm nearly sixteen now.

'Oh, you've forgotten the sugar, love,' said Gran.

I always forget the sugar – no one takes it our house. 'Sorry. I'll get it.'

'No, you sit down and talk to your auntie. I'll get it.' Gran leaves us to it.

Great-aunt Eleanor doesn't say anything at first, she just looks at me all funny. I'm starting to wonder whether I've got a spot on my nose or something.

'You're Rosie. May's granddaughter,' she says at last.

'Yes.'

'You remind me of someone.'

Gran comes in the with sugar bowl.

'Who does she look like, May?'

'Well, she's got her dad's colouring – brown hair, green eyes. But she don't really look like him.'

Eleanor is staring at me with that funny look again. 'That's not what I mean,' she says. 'There's something very familiar about her, but I can't put my finger on it. It is very annoying.'

Gran peers at me, puzzled. Then she shakes her head and puts a hand to her mouth. 'What am I thinking? I forgot the spoons. We can't have no sugar if we ain't got no spoons.'

I laugh as Gran goes off to the get them. What is she like?

Eleanor carries on frowning at me, so I stop laughing. She's really freaking me out. I resist the urge to check my nose. Instead I check my teeth with my tongue, in case there's something stuck there. But it feels like I'm sticking my tongue out at her without opening my mouth, which must look rude, so I stop.

Between the two sisters, I'd have said that Gran looked like the crazy one, with her purple glasses, matching blouse and silver dangly earrings. Apparently she used to have dark hair like mine, but hers is just a ball of silver frizz now. On the other hand, Great-aunt Eleanor is the complete opposite – gold-rimmed half-moon glasses perched on her nose, her white hair pulled back into a tight bun, and a single, neat string of pearls over a lavender twin-set. Yep, definitely scary.

'Here we are,' Gran comes in with the teaspoons. I breathe a sigh of relief as she takes the attention off me.

While they chat, I'm thinking I should be able to escape soon. I still have to get a new phone charger, so that's a good excuse to go out. I hope old Nelly won't stay long if she's going to stare at me like that all the time. It's a bit rude, really. I'd be in loads of trouble if I did it. I must remember to call her Great-aunt Eleanor as well, otherwise I'll be for it, like last time. Just as I'm psyching myself up to interrupt them, Gran spoils it by pointing at me.

'Our Rosie's doing ever so well at school, Nelly. She's

doing loads of them GCSEs. I reckon she's got your brains.'

'Gran,' I say. 'It's no big deal.' Oh God, this is so embarrassing. I do all right at school, but I'm not one of the nerdy girls who are going to get all A-stars or anything.

'Do you like school?' asks Great-aunt Eleanor.

'Yeah, it's OK,' I say, sounding a bit sulky. I hate the way she's looking at me, like she's going to give me a test or something. 'I'll probably stay on for A-levels.' But only because I don't know what else to do.

Gran is ever so impressed. 'Good for you, girl. You'll go far, like Nelly. Me, I was glad to leave school. I never was much cop at lessons. Nelly hated having to leave school at fourteen, didn't you, love?'

Great-aunt Eleanor nods.

'But our poor old Dad couldn't afford to keep her there after Mum died,' Gran went on. 'He needed Nelly out earning, to help pay the bills. She got her qualifications after the war. Did evening classes, didn't you?'

Again, Great-aunt Eleanor nods, then takes a sip of her tea, her little finger raised, like she's having tea with the Queen.

Gran is on a roll now. 'In them days there wasn't much money about – you've heard of the Great Depression, have you?' I haven't, but before I can say so, Gran goes on. 'Before the war, there was so many men out of work.' She shakes her head, looking all tragic. 'That's why our dad joined the Merchant Navy. It meant leaving us girls on our own, but it was steady money and he got fed and watered while he was at sea. That's how he managed to pay for this house. Reckoned it was a good thing to own the roof over your head. 'Course, we nearly lost it in the Blitz, didn't we, Nelly?'

I nibble on a biscuit, not knowing what to say. I can normally talk to Gran, no problem. But her sister's too scary. But good old Gran likes to chat, so she just carries on.

'Ooh, Nelly, I nearly forgot. You'll never guess what me and Rosie found under your old bed upstairs.'

'I suppose I won't,' she says, lifting her cup to her lips. 'So why don't you tell me?'

'Queenie's suitcase!' said Gran.

Great-aunt Eleanor blinks. Then she very carefully lowers her cup back onto the saucer, and puts them both on the coffee table. 'It's still here? I thought we'd thrown it out years ago.'

'I know you wanted to,' says Gran. 'But don't you remember? Bill said we couldn't chuck it out because it wasn't ours. He reckoned she might come back for it one day.'

'That's ridiculous. Even if she survived the bombing, she'd never have come back. Not after what she did.'

This is getting interesting. 'Who's Queenie?' I ask.

'A spy,' says Great-aunt Eleanor.

'No,' says Gran, smiling. 'She was a bit odd – downright daft sometimes – but she couldn't have been a spy. She was a girl who stayed with us for a bit in the war.'

'She wasn't as stupid as she appeared. I think she was very cunning. She was far too vague about where she came from, and she disappeared without a trace.'

Gran sighs. 'The poor girl didn't stand a chance. We should never have let her go out on her own that night. '

'It was her own fault,' says her sister. 'She managed to upset everyone. I'm sure it was deliberate. I'm convinced she'd completed whatever mission she had, and used our argument as an excuse to escape back to wherever she'd come from.'

'Oh, for goodness sake,' Gran laughs. 'What good would a fifteen-year-old girl be as a spy? There weren't no war secrets in our house.'

'No, indeed, but she came to work with us at the factory, didn't she? She could have been spying there.'

'Blimey, Nelly, what would Hitler have needed to know about the seams on sailors' trousers? Their inside-leg measurements? She never got good enough to do more than the basic stuff.'

Great-aunt Eleanor sniffs. I try not to smile. This is great. Whoever Queenie was, she'd caused a stir.

'Maybe not,' Great-aunt Eleanor goes on. 'But she certainly got friendly with the young men around here, in and out of uniform, as you well know.'

Gran tuts and waves a hand at her sister. 'Are you still cross about that? After all these years? Come on, love, I'm sure she didn't mean no harm. It all worked out in the end, didn't it?'

'What happened?' I ask.

'She stole her man,' Great-aunt Eleanor points at Gran.

Gran laughs. 'Oh, God help us. She did me a favour. Besides, it was seventy-odd years ago, Nell. It's all water under the bridge. Here, Rosie, nip up and bring that suitcase down, love. We'll have a look.'

CHAPTER TWO

I run upstairs for the suitcase. As I go into the bedroom to get it, the walls start doing their funny stuff again. The bedcover is dark red now, and there's brown lino on the floor instead of the beige carpet. But the case is still there on the bed, so I grab it. I nearly fall down the stairs rushing to get back to Gran and normality.

Great-aunt Eleanor opens the case. Inside are clothes, shoes, a gas mask, and some old notebooks. Gran picks up a buff-coloured booklet.

'Ooh, look! It's an old ration book. I don't miss the food from them days, do you, Nelly? There was hardly anything nice in the shops, and what you got wasn't enough to keep a mouse fed. We had no trouble keeping our figures, did we?' She pats her belly. 'Now we can eat what we like, we always have to watch the scales.'

'You're not fat, Gran,' I laugh. I hope I'll be like Gran, but it's not likely, worse luck. I'm already taller than her. I'll probably end up more like Mum's side of the family. They're what Dad calls 'substantial women'.

'I'm not as skinny as I used to be, our Rosie. Like a stick insect, I was. No curves, just straight up and down.'

'And what you lacked in inches, you made up for in chatter,' says Eleanor. 'What else have you got there, May?' She rummages in the suitcase and finds some papers. I reckon that woman needs to chill out. Doesn't she ever smile?

The papers don't look very interesting. I'd rather look at the clothes. They're all neatly folded, and some of them are wrapped in tissue paper.

I take out a pretty blue cardigan. I'm careful, because I'm worried it might fall to bits since it's been in that suitcase for so long. It was obviously hand-knitted, and has some lovely pearl

11

buttons. It feels so soft, but it smells so horrible it makes me cough.

'Eeoogh, that stinks!'

'Mothballs,' says Great-aunt Eleanor, still looking at the papers.

'They keep the bugs out, love,' says Gran. 'These are good quality clothes and mothballs keep 'em safe. Otherwise the moths'll eat their way through this lot.'

I shiver at the thought of insects crawling around in the suitcase

'Right. Nice.'

I lay the cardigan carefully over the back of a chair, and pick up the next thing – an old-fashioned cotton nightdress. It's white, with tiny flowers embroidered in pinks and purples around the neckline. It stinks as well, but I turn my head away, and take a deep breath before I hold it up against me. It covers me from neck to toe.

'Oh, wow! Did people really wear stuff like this?' I ask.

Gran smiles and nods. 'Ah, that's lovely,' she says. 'And cosy too. We didn't have no central heating back then. A nice long nighty was just the thing to keep your bum from getting frostbite.'

'Gran!' I laugh. What is she like?

'Well, it's true. Blooming freezing, this old house was. We had big candlewick dressing gowns too, and bed socks. Didn't we, Nell?'

'Mmm?' Great-aunt Eleanor was busy studying the papers, but looked up when Gran said her name. 'Bed socks. Yes.'

She's staring at me again. I feel cold all of a sudden. I turn round and stuff the nightdress back into the case.

Gran tuts. 'No, come here, Rosie. Don't do it like that, love. Let me fold it proper.' She picks it up and sorts it out. But before she puts it back she gets all the other stuff out. 'You should try some of these on.' She picks up a tweed skirt, shakes the creases out and passes it to me. 'I reckon they're about your size.'

I hold the skirt against me. It's a lot longer than I usually wear, ending below my knees.

'An excellent idea,' says Great-aunt Eleanor. 'I believe the fashion these days is for "retro."' She makes quote marks in the air. 'Your grandmother will be able to style your hair as well.'

Gran nods, clapping her hands together. 'Ooh, yes! I used to love hairdressing, didn't I, Nelly? With all that long dark hair, I can give you some really fancy do's. It'll be fun.'

I'm not so sure. This feels freaky. 'Actually, it's vintage.' I say. 'And it's not my sort of thing, thanks.'

Gran looks disappointed, making me feel mean. I really don't want to play dressing up with a load of old clothes. But I don't want to upset Gran either. Great-aunt Eleanor just looks annoyed.

'Nonsense,' she says. 'Just about everything you young girls wear these days is a copy of fashions your mothers wore in the 60s and 70s. You might at least try these on.'

I want to stick my tongue out at her for real now, but don't dare. Instead, I bite my lip. It just feels wrong, that's all.

'You don't have to if you don't want to, love,' says Gran, making me feel even worse. What else can I do?

'Oh, all right,' I say. 'I'll give it a go.'

Immediately, Gran cheers up, and old Nelly nods, satisfied. I pick up a pale pink blouse to go with the skirt. With any luck they won't fit.

The skirt and blouse do fit, perfectly. I can't believe it. I go and show the old women, trying not to gag as I get a waft of *Eau de Mothballs* as I move. They're in the kitchen, brewing more tea. Gran fusses over me, while Great-aunt Eleanor watches, all narrow-eyed. I pretend not to notice, because she's freaking me out again. The sooner I can get my jeans back on, the better.

'Come on then,' says Gran, 'Let's do your hair. It's a shame I got rid of me old curlers. I could've made you look like a film star.'

I sit on the kitchen chair that Gran has put in the middle of the room and let her fuss. Her hands are a lot stronger than I expect, and I can't help yelping in pain as she yanks a comb through my hair and sticks it with a shed-load of pins.

'Sorry, love. Nearly there.'

'Here,' says Great-aunt Eleanor. 'Put these on.' She kneels down, quite flexible considering how old she is, and slides some shoes onto my feet. Again, a perfect fit. I shiver and the walls of the kitchen wobble for a second then go back to normal. This is getting really weird. Or maybe Gran's been overdoing the hair pulling a bit and my eyes have gone wonky. I lift up my feet to get a look at the shoes. Black leather, plain like a court shoe, chunky heel. Not my usual style.

At last Gran is satisfied, and I'm allowed to stand up. The heels on the shoes are quite high, and I wobble a bit as I walk into the hall to look at myself in the big mirror on the coat stand. The silky lining of the skirt rustles against my legs as I move, and the heels make me walk differently. It feels quite sexy.

The old women follow me. I smile as I imagine walking down a catwalk, with loads of people watching and thinking how gorgeous I am. Yeah, right.

'Wow!' I look like someone out of a black-and-white film! My hair, which is usually frizzy as anything, looks great. I put a hand up and feel how smooth it is.

'That's a French pleat,' says Gran. 'Very elegant.'

The clothes, which still smell of those awful mothballs, give me some curves. I look about twenty-five, in a vintage, Paloma Faith kind of way.

Gran and Great-aunt Eleanor crowd behind me at the mirror. But when I look at our reflection, I don't see two old women. Instead there are two girls, one blonde, one dark, and both are dressed like me. My mouth drops open, I can feel my heart start to race. It's impossible. It's like looking through a window, except I can still see myself clearly reflected, right between them.

'You need a bit of red lipstick,' says the dark girl.

I blink. The girls disappear, and Gran's smiling at me in the mirror where the dark girl stood. Great-aunt Eleanor is glaring at me from where the blonde was. I blink again and for a split second the girls are there, and I want to scream but I can't, and before I can do anything they morph back into Gran and Eleanor.

'Ooh, don't you look lovely!' Gran coos.

I'm too shocked to say anything at first, then I just blurt out, 'Red lipstick?'

'Yes, love. I used to have a lovely one from Max Factor,' says Gran. 'It would've been perfect.'

Great-aunt Eleanor jumps, like she's had electric shock or something.

'That's it!' says Great-aunt Eleanor. 'Of course!'

'Ooh, that's a good idea,' says Gran. 'I might still have some somewhere.'

I look sideways at Gran. She can't be serious. I doubt if she's worn red lipstick in my lifetime. I dread to think what sort of bacteria might be growing on some old tube she's had for years.

'Perhaps not,' I say.

'Well, if you're sure?' she says. 'I could probably find it.'

'For goodness sake, May,' Great-aunt Eleanor snaps.

I look at her reflection, relieved she's not gone blonde again. Did Eleanor see the girls as well? Before I get a chance to ask her, she gets a hard look in her eyes and pokes me in the back.

'Hey!'

'Nelly!' Gran looks shocked.

'I knew it,' says Great-aunt Eleanor. 'So you're back, are you? I don't know how you did it, but you've got a lot of explaining to do, young lady.'

I shake my head, unable to speak as my throat has closed up. I'm feeling dizzy and think I'm going to pass out. I'm too frightened to blink again in case those girls come back, so I must be looking a bit googly-eyed but I can't help myself.

'What are you on about, Nelly?' asks Gran. 'You're not making sense, love.'

'Can't you see?' Eleanor grabs my chin and shakes it. I watch the reflection of my head wobble from side to side. 'This is Queenie.'

I get a funny feeling in my stomach. What is she on about?

'Of course it isn't. This is Rosie, Nelly, and you know it. Don't go saying daft things like that.' She prises Eleanor's fingers off my chin. I rub my jaw; I'm sure she's left a bruise.

'I know who we think she is, May, but look at her. Just look!' Eleanor waves a hand in my direction and I duck out of the way before she can attack me again. 'The clothes, the hair. All she needs is a coat of your Max Factor red lipstick and we have Queenie standing here again.'

I feel sick at the mention of the lipstick.

I look in the mirror again. Both of the old women are glaring at each other. However crazy they are, I prefer them to those strange girls. I don't know where they came from, or who they are, and I hope I never see them again. What is it about this house that makes everything so flipping weird?

Gran lays a gentle hand on her sister's shoulder. 'Even if she does look a bit like her, it's not Queenie, Nelly. If she was here, she'd be old like us now, wouldn't she? This is my grand-daughter, Rosie, remember?'

'Don't treat me like an idiot. I know exactly who this is. But as you clearly won't see what's in front of your own eyes, we must agree to disagree.' Great-aunt Eleanor is glaring at Gran who huffs a bit but doesn't argue. Eleanor turns to look at me again. I want to squirm, but don't dare. 'Queenie caused a lot of upset in this house, and then disappeared without trace. Everyone said she was dead, but I wasn't so sure. And you, young lady, look remarkably like her.'

Out of the corner of my eye, I can see Gran shaking her head and looking upset.

'I can't help how I look,' I say, my voice squeaking because Great-aunt Eleanor is so much like old Mrs Sparks when I haven't done my History homework right. She's always glaring at me over her glasses like Eleanor's doing now. It's so not fair. 'You two dressed me up like this.' I look back as calmly as I can. I'm still too frightened to blink. That seems to annoy Eleanor even more.

'Yes we did.' She turns away. 'Has that kettle boiled yet, May? A woman can die of thirst around here waiting to be offered another cup of tea.'

As Great-aunt Eleanor stalks down the hall to the kitchen; Gran touches my cheek. 'Don't worry, love. Nelly's feeling her age a bit.' I nod. She must be right. Great-aunt Eleanor is even older than Gran. 'She gets confused sometimes,' Gran goes on. 'I think seeing you in that get-up made her think she was still a girl. I suppose Queenie did look a bit like you, but she's long gone.' Gran shakes her head. 'So sad.'

I follow Gran into the kitchen, wondering what's 'so sad' – what happened to the girl, or the fact that her sister has probably got dementia or something? Maybe I'm going mad too. I have no idea what just happened out there. Did I really see two girls where Gran and Eleanor should have been? If I was anywhere else but Gran's house, I'd have said someone had was playing some sick joke with a trick mirror. But not here.

I feel shaky as I sit down at the kitchen table. The smell coming from the clothes doesn't help. I hope I'm not going to throw up.

'You all right, darlin'?' asks Gran.

'Yeah, I'm OK,' I say, waving a hand in front of my face. 'Mothballs. They're making me feel a bit sick.'

'I never did like that pong,' says Gran with a sympathetic smile. 'But you get used to it.'

'Are you sure that's all?' asks Great-aunt Eleanor, eyeing me with distrust. 'You're looking decidedly peaky.'

I swallow hard, resisting the urge to blurt out what I think I've just seen. It's all so freaky, I feel like crying. If I tell them about all the weird things that happen to me in this house, like the wallpaper and the mirror and stuff, they'll probably think I'm on drugs or something.

'I think I just need some fresh air,' I say. 'I've got to buy a phone charger anyway, so I'll head over to Oxford Street.'

'Good idea, love. You can get the bus from the end of the road. Takes you straight there.'

'I'd better get changed,' I say. 'I don't want to get these clothes dirty.' And I don't want to be seen in them in public. What if I see someone fit?

I head for the stairs, trying not to look in the hall-stand mirror as I pass. Big mistake. I'm so busy avoiding the mirror, I forget to breathe through my mouth and inhale a huge lungful of that awful mothball smell. I sneeze, hard, and then I can't stop. With streaming eyes, I stumble and catch the heel of my shoe on something. The next thing I know my head's slammed against the hall stand. I don't have a chance to call out before everything goes black.

CHAPTER THREE

What is going on?

I remember the smell of mothballs got so bad I started sneezing, and then I lost my balance in those stupid shoes. My head really hurts. Did I knock myself out? How stupid am I?

I open my eyes, but nothing happens. Seriously, everything is black. I can't see a thing. Oh my God – am I blind? How will I get my make-up right? I could end up looking like a panda and I wouldn't know. No, wait – I put a hand out. I'm caught in something. It feels rough, like a horse blanket, and it smells like one too. Ugh! It's revolting. Where the hell did that come from? I've got to get it off before I vomit. I start to pull it away from me and see a chink of light.

'Oi, you. Stay still,' a female voice orders. 'Ain't you done enough damage?'

I don't care, I'm getting this thing shifted at last! Yes! Result! But hang on a minute, who said that?

It's definitely not Gran or Great-aunt Eleanor. It's a girl's voice. How did she get in here? Did she chuck this over me? Maybe I didn't fall. Maybe she sneaked up and caught me by surprise. But now I'm on to her I can take another girl, I reckon. If I have to. And if she's thinking of hurting my Gran, then I definitely will have to. And where is Gran? I've got to make sure she's OK.

I pull harder. I've got to get this thing off me. I don't know who she is, but I'm ready for a fight. Gran's put the radio on in the kitchen, and obviously hasn't heard a thing. I could be being attacked at her own front door and the stupid old bat hasn't even noticed.

'I said stay still.' The girl thumps me on the back. 'For God's sake, you'll rip it.'

As if I bloody care. I move again and there's a tearing

sound, then I'm blinking in the light. There's spots in front of my eyes and I can't see clearly at first. A stranger in a dressing-gown is standing over me. Yeah, I know – a dressing gown? Definitely a crazy person. She's angry, but I don't care, because I'm furious.

'What are you doing here?' I ask her. 'You leave my gran alone!'

She glares down at me, and I realise she's got the advantage as she's standing up and I'm still in a heap on the floor. I push the torn blanket away and get up. Whoa, dizzy! I've got to take these shoes off in a minute, they're downright flipping dangerous. But right now they make me taller than her, so I stand up straight and glare back.

She ignores my question and points a scarlet-tipped finger at me. 'Who the bloody hell are you?'

Oh. My. God. She's the blonde from the mirror. She's right here in front of me. Did she come out of the mirror? No, that's a stupid idea. It's not possible. But wasn't seeing her and the other girl in the mirror impossible too? I feel like my head's going to explode.

I take a step back and my shoe makes a clicking sound on the floor. I look down. I'm standing on a sea of brown lino. It can't be, or I have seriously lost my mind. Where's the carpet gone? And the walls – the colour's different, a sort of cat's poo yellow at the bottom and a nasty beige at the top. And where did that old glass light fitting come from? What happened to Gran's uplighter? The only thing that's still here is the old hall stand with the mirror.

I feel sick. I've seen Gran's hall like this before, but only for a nanosecond, before it disappeared again. It was like a dream. But this looks solid, permanent. I take another step back, because I can tell you I am seriously freaked now. Did she pull me through the mirror? No, that's ridiculous.

The back of my leg comes up against something hard. The suitcase.

'Well? Come on,' she says, following me until she's glaring into my face. 'I asked you a question.'

'I'm Rosie,' I whisper, getting scared now. What is going

on?

The girl spots the suitcase and bends down to look at the label. '"Miss R. Smith,".'. Well, why didn't you say so, instead of making all this fuss? It's about time you got here. Me and my sister have been waiting in for hours. They said you'd get here this afternoon. We was just about to give up and go to bed. We reckoned you'd decided to stay in Wiltshire.'

How did she know I come from Wiltshire?

'It's not on, turning up this time of night,' she said.

I'm still looking around the hall, waiting for it to go back to normal, like it usually does. For a split second, I get a glimpse of Gran's magnolia walls, but then they're gone and the girl has turned away from me. Gathering up the blanket, she reaches up and hangs it over the closed front door.

'I don't know how you got in,' she says over her shoulder. 'But you didn't have to rip the blackout curtain, did you? If the wardens see the light, I'm blaming you.'

'I didn't …' I start to say, but I don't know what I did or didn't do, so I shut up.

Why won't the house go back to normal? Where's Gran? I want to ask the girl, but I daren't. I'm not even sure if she's real. Maybe I'm unconscious? You know, like in that stupid programme Mum liked, with the guy who went into a coma and thought he was a copper in the seventies. I know it sounds completely crazy, but it's all I can think of that makes any sense. I'm really dreaming all this, while Gran and Great-aunt Eleanor are trying to bring me round. They'll have to call an ambulance and I'll wake up in hospital. Gran will be all upset and my parents won't ever let me stay with her again because she made me wear these shoes.

'I'll have to stitch it,' the girl says, pulling the ends of the torn material together. She turns and looks at me. 'Like to make an entrance, don't you?'

'Not really, no,' I say.

She waves a hand. 'Well, I don't care. Just don't break nothing else, all right? We ain't got much, and what we do have we can't afford to replace.'

I nod, my mind spinning. Any minute now, I'm thinking,

any minute now, I'll wake up.

But apparently not yet.

'Leave your case by the stairs,' says the girl, 'and go on down the passage. The kitchen's at the back. My sister's got the kettle on. I'll pin this up for now and sort it out tomorrow.'

I take a deep breath, I still want to ask her where Gran is, but some instinct is telling me to shut up and do as I'm told. I leave her muttering by the front door.

I stop in the doorway of the kitchen, which is exactly where Gran's is. But instead of her fitted oak cupboards and fridge magnets, this room looks like something out of a museum. There's no one around, although it's obvious someone has been here recently. An ancient radio – huge, with a big dial on the front – is playing loudly. Rubbish music. The sort Gran likes. The sink is a big white thing, with a wooden draining board. The window over the sink is covered by another heavy curtain, leaving the room lit by a single light bulb, hanging from the centre of the ceiling. On one wall is an old water-heater, and there's steaming water pouring from it into the sink. The place stinks of fish.

Opposite the sink is the cooker. It's cream enamel, with brass dials on the front. There's a kettle on the hob – a bit like the one my parents use on camping holidays. In the middle of the room is a table covered by a heavy brown cloth. It's a bit bigger than the one Gran has. On it is a salt and pepper set and a newspaper.

I step inside, and nearly have another heart attack when the kettle begins to whistle. I walk over to the stove and try to work out how to turn it off. The dials won't turn, and the shrill whistle gets louder.

'Have you seen her?' the girl in the dressing gown asks me as she comes in. She shoves me out of the way, pushes one of the dials in, and turns it easily to the left. The whistle fades.

I shake my head, but the girl has turned away, running over to the sink and turning off the stream of hot water just before it overflows. 'Blinkin' hell,' she says, 'I swear I'm going to swing for that girl one of these days.' She raises her head. 'MAY!'

Whoa, turn the volume down. Seriously, you need ear

defenders round here. The back door opens and a dark-haired girl comes in and slams it shut behind her. No! I don't believe it! This is getting so weird. It's the other girl from the mirror!

'All right, keep your hair on,' she says. 'I was only on the lav. Where's the fire?'

Dressing-gown girl glares at the dark-haired girl and reaches over to turn off the radio. For a moment there's silence. I start to relax a bit then realise – hang on, what did she call her? May? That's my gran's name. I feel the hairs stand up on the back of my neck. It can't be. In that case, the blonde girl is ...

'You left the Ascot on, and the kettle. This place is like a bloomin' steam bath. We could've had a flood if I hadn't got here on time.' She nods towards me. 'She wasn't much help. Stood there like a lemon, she did.'

'Nelly! You ain't supposed to talk about people like that! What would Dad say?'

'Nelly?' I say, but they ignore me.

'He'd say sort yourself out, May Blake, before you wreck the house. Now, are you making a cuppa, or what?'

''Course I am. I wasn't hiding, you know. I just needed a wee.'

'Well wash your hands before you touch my cup.'

'All right, don't nag.'

'Someone's got to.'

I want to laugh. They sound just like Gran and Great-aunt Eleanor bickering. Except this Nelly isn't posh, just bad-tempered.

What am I thinking? What is going on? Who are these girls, really? Maybe I'm having a breakdown or something. I pull out a chair and sit down, putting elbows on the table and my head in my hands.

'You all right, love?' The dark-haired girl asks me.

'Um ... I think so.' I lift my head and look at her.

'Did you get something to eat on the train? We only had a couple of kippers for our tea. We'd've shared 'em with you if you'd got here earlier. I could do you some bread and dripping if you like?'

'Er, no thanks.' I say, trying not to gag. I've heard about that

23

stuff – dripping – it's like horrible scummy fat that clogs up drains. Why would anyone even consider eating something so disgusting?

'Suit yourself. I'm May, by the way, and she's me sister Nelly. What's your name?'

'Really?' I ask. 'Are you winding me up?'

Both girls are looking at me now.

'Do what?' said Nelly, giving me a very familiar look.

I shake my head, trying to clear it. 'Nothing. I just know a couple of sisters called May and Nelly, that's all.'

'Fancy that,' laughs May. 'D'you hear that, Nell? Two more sisters with our names.'

Nelly doesn't look impressed. 'There's loads of girls with our names.'

God, does she ever cheer up? 'I'm Rosie,' I say.

Nelly tuts. 'That's all we need. Another Rose. We've already got three at the factory.'

'The factory?'

'Cohen's. Down Whitechapel. Where we work,' says May. 'Ain't you coming to work with us tomorrow?'

'I suppose so,' I shrug.

May laughs. 'Well either you are, or you ain't. Don't you know?'

I look at the two girls, wondering what they'd think if I told them the truth – that I'm in the middle of some sort of mad dream; a dream where my Gran and Great-aunt are teenage girls who think I'm going to work with them tomorrow.

'I … er …' What can I say? Out of the corner of my eye I see the kettle on the stove. 'Can I have a cup of tea, please?'

The sisters look at each other, eyebrows raised.

'It's just as well you asked,' Nelly says to me. 'You could die of thirst waiting for someone to make one in this house.'

Oh. My. God. I can't help it and start to giggle. This is hysterical. It's just too amazing. May starts laughing too, even though she has no idea what it's about. Nelly just glares at me, all annoyed.

'Sorry,' I say, trying to calm down. 'I don't mean to be rude. But you sounded just like someone I know.'

'You're all right,' says May. 'I'll put the kettle back on. We want one as well. It's no trouble. Once you settle in, you can take your turn brewing up. I hope you've got your ration book.'

I think about the papers in the suitcase. Gran mentioned a ration book when we looked through it. 'Yes. It's in my case,' I tell her. I hope it's still there.

'Right,' says Nelly. 'We'll need to register you at our shops. You can share what we've got for now, but there ain't much in the pantry, so the quicker we get you sorted out, the better.'

'Did you remember to bring your gas mask?' asks May. 'I'm always forgetting mine. The wardens round here give you a right telling off if they see you without it.'

'There's one in the case,' I say.

'Well it's no good in there, is it? Make sure you get it out and have it somewhere handy,' says Nelly. God, she's so bossy.

'OK,' I say, feeling a bit lost, and tired of all this. 'Whatever.' I really don't care. Any minute now I'll wake up, I'm bound to. This can't go on forever, can it?

'What?' Nelly looks angry again.

Oh crap, now I've annoyed her. Mum says I'm good at sulky and ungrateful. I suppose I must sound pretty rude. It's probably not a good idea to upset anyone while I'm stuck here. Especially not if Nelly's anything like Great-aunt Eleanor.

'Sorry. I meant to say thank you.'

'Ooh,' says May. 'Ain't she posh? I think we should call her Queenie, don't you, Nell?'

'No!' I say. 'I'm Rosie.'

'Yeah, but we've already got Rose Brown, Rosie Jackson, and Rosa Hodgson. So you'll have to be Queenie, or we'll get all mixed up. Anyway, Rose is a boring name, ain't it?'

'I quite like it, actually,' I say.

May giggles again. Nelly smirks, and says: 'Hark at you – "actually"! Well, like May says, no one wants another Rose in our crowd. So like it or not, Miss Fancy Pants, from now on you're Queenie.'

I close my eyes, and take a deep breath. I don't like it at all, but I can hardly explain why to these girls. This is not good.

'I hope you don't want sugar in your tea,' says May. 'We

stopped taking it 'cause we kept running out by the middle of the week. So we save up our rations and make a cake every now and then. We've got a lovely Christmas cake ready. It's been soaked in our Dad's Navy Rum, so it'll be right tasty.'

'Christmas?'

'Are you Jewish, then?' asks Nelly. 'Like the Cohens?'

'No,' I say. What is she on about? 'I'm Church of England.'

May puts a cup of tea on the table. 'Here you go, Queenie. Get that down you. So how come you don't know about Christmas?'

'I do know about Christmas,' I say. 'I was just wondering why you've made your cake so early.'

Nelly frowns. 'Early? What are you talking about? It's only just over a fortnight away.'

'Wh-what's today's date?' I ask.

'It's the 8th of December, of course.'

The familiar sick, dizzy feeling comes back. I take a deep breath, hoping I'm not going to faint or anything. I glance down at the table, and for a moment – just a split-second – I can see Gran's white tablecloth and coffee mugs and biscuit tin.

Then it's gone and I'm looking at the heavy brown cover and an old fashioned cup and saucer in front of me. I pick up the cup with shaking hands and sip the hot tea.

Even that tastes different. I put it down again.

I glance at the paper on the table. It's not like any newspaper I've ever seen.

The pictures are in black and white, and the words are printed really close together. But like all newspapers, the date is printed at the top of the front page.

Sunday, 8th December 1940.

CHAPTER FOUR

I stand up. The chair scrapes on the tiled floor. May and Nelly look at me curiously. I need to get out of here before I completely lose it. 'I have to go.'

'Go where?' asks May.

That stops me in my tracks. Where can I go? I don't know how I got here, so I've no idea how to get back. My instincts are all screaming that the mirror's got something to do with it, but I've walked past it a million times before and this has never happened, so I might be wrong. I can hardly go and stand there, staring at it with these two watching me, can I? I mean, they'll think I'm really, really vain, won't they?

What I *do* know, is that I'm in Gran's house. This is the place I keep seeing out of the corner of my eye, or when I go dizzy. So, that must mean the girls are Gran and Great-aunt Eleanor. I can't believe I didn't realise before.

Should I tell them who I am? *Hi, I'm May's granddaughter, and your creepy house has kidnapped me?* I can see the distrust in Nelly's face. If I said something like that, she'd kick me out for sure. Or get me locked up. Then I'll never get back.

It's got to be safer to stay here with them. Surely I'll have more chance of getting back to my old Gran if I'm not running around London like an idiot. It was dangerous enough in normal circumstances, but now I'm apparently in the middle of a war zone. Can you believe it? How did that happen? Calm. I have to keep calm.

From the expressions on their faces, the girls think I'm a complete nut. 'I … er … need the toilet. I won't be a minute.' I walk out of the kitchen.

'God help us, you really are posh, ain't you?' Nelly shouts after me. 'It won't do you no good looking for the lav in here, Queenie. It's out the back.'

I turn round and walk back into kitchen. Nelly sniggers at my expression. Yeah, she actually sniggers. You know – like giggling but with a condescending smirk?

'Come on,' says May. 'I'll show you. Don't want you getting lost in the dark.' She opens the outside door and holds it for me, bobbing into a curtsey as I walk out into the back garden. This is just so embarrassing.

Gran's flowers and patio furniture are gone. So has all that fancy decking Dad put down for her last year. Instead of the lush green summer garden I'd seen out the kitchen window last time I looked, the moon lights a path across a patch of dirt, bare except for some stalks of Brussels sprouts and some cabbages and overshadowed by the hulk of an Anderson shelter. Beyond them, against the back wall of the garden, is the outside lavatory. I shiver in the cold, tempted to turn around and go back into the warm kitchen, but May is right behind me.

'Hurry up, it's freezing out here,' she says. 'If you leave the door open a bit you'll be able to see what you're doing so long as the moon's out. We've run out of proper paper so Nelly's cut up some old magazines to use. They're hanging from a bit of string on the left-hand side. Will you be all right if I leave you to it?'

I nod, just wanting to be left alone for a minute.

'Right. I'll nip back in then. If the sirens start, don't bother coming back into the house, just go straight in the shelter and we'll see you there.'

Just as I reach the toilet door, May calls out. 'Watch out for spiders in there, Queenie. Oh, and next door's cat likes to sleep on the seat, so make sure you look before you sit down. My friend Elsie got a terrible shock the other night, sitting on Tiddles.' I can hear May's laughter as she goes back inside the house.

I open the door and look inside. Sure enough, a large tabby cat is curled up on the closed toilet seat. I'm tempted to give up and leave it alone, but now I'm out in the cold, I realise I really do need to use the loo.

'OK, Tiddles, time to go home,' I say loudly. The cat shoots outside, yeowling, and disappears over the fence into next door's garden. I can't help laughing. It looked just like a cartoon cat, streaking away like that. If I had my mobile phone with me I could've filmed it and it might've gone viral on YouTube. But I haven't got my phone, worse luck. I wonder if it would work here anyway? The Doctor's friends always seem to manage to get through to him on *Doctor Who*, no matter what time or planet he's on. I will not panic. Deep breath.

I won't stay out here too long: it's seriously freezing and creepy too. But a few minutes alone give me the chance to think more clearly. This is so totally weird, but I'm not completely lost, am I? I mean at least I'm at Gran's house, even if it *is* the wrong time. It is a bit like an episode of *Doctor Who*, isn't it? And I should remember not to tell anyone about the future or it'll cause some sort of crisis in the time-space continuum. 'Spoilers', as River Song was always saying a few years ago.

I've got to stay calm and see what happens. I still reckon I'll wake up soon and find out this is just a freaky dream. Probably. Hopefully.

I wish I could relax and enjoy it. Not many girls get the chance to see their gran and Great-aunt Eleanor as teenagers, do they? It should be a laugh. But right now it doesn't feel the slightest bit funny. I just can't believe this is happening. I can't figure out how it could have happened. What was different this time I passed the mirror? Did it really have anything to do with me getting stuck here, or was it just a coincidence I saw the girls in there before it happened? I mean, I've seen other bits of the house go funny too, like Ne … Great-aunt Eleanor's room did this morning. What was different today? The clothes? Maybe. Think! I've got to work it out so I can figure out how to get back. My head starts throbbing, and I'm shaking with the cold. My nose starts to tingle and I squeeze the end to stop from sneezing. Last time I did that … whoa! The last thing I did before I ended up here was sneeze! I let go of my nose and try to sneeze, but the sensation has passed and it's a pathetic effort, more of a whimper than the real thing. I try again, then realise that if it works, I could end up in Gran's garden with my knickers round my ankles, so I stop and sort myself out. God, that could've been soooo embarrassing, especially if I end up back at the same time – the middle of the flipping afternoon! I can't stop myself from giggling. It must be hysteria.

Once I've calmed down, I go back across the garden, stumbling a bit in the dark. I can't wait to get these bloody shoes off. There's no light at all coming from the house. I suppose it's those blackout curtains.

I hope I'll walk back into Gran's modern kitchen. I always thought it was pretty old-fashioned till I saw the one that May and Nelly are living in. That's like really old. Everything seems so real, but it doesn't make sense. I *can't* be in 1940, can I? It's just not possible. Not in real life. I'm starting to think my theory about being unconscious and dreaming is the most likely explanation. I wiggle my nose a bit, sniffing in the cold air, hoping to make myself sneeze. I feel like a right idiot, but hey if it works …

I'm halfway up the path when a horrible droning sound starts up. I stop and listen. It gets louder, rising in tone. Oh. My. God. A real life air-raid siren. In the dark sky columns of light appear, searching, criss-crossing, like they're dancing.

The back door opens and the girls run out.

'Don't just stand there, get in the shelter,' says Nelly.

But I can't move. The lights are almost hypnotic. I could watch them for hours.

'Come on, get under cover,' Nelly pushes me along the path. 'This ain't a game, you know. Every night we get this. Every bloody night.'

I stumble into the shelter, nearly ending up on my knees as I didn't realise there were a couple of steps down. They follow me in, pull the door shut and drag a curtain across it before May lights a lamp.

It's not very big in here, and it smells like Dad's potting shed. There are benches along the longer walls, and shelves at the back with books and boxed games and various 'odds and sods' as Gran would say, including some blankets. May picks one up and gives it to me.

'Here, put that round you, Queenie. It gets bloody cold down here.' She sits down, wrapping herself up. 'This your first air raid?'

'Yes,' I say, sitting down next to her and snuggling into the blanket. It feels a bit damp, but I expect it's just the cold. I hope so. 'How long will it last?'

May shrugged. 'God knows. Some nights we're here until first light. But if our boys do their job, they'll send Jerry packing before too long. Either way, we have to wait for the all-clear.'

Nelly sits opposite and pulls a book off the shelf and starts to read, ignoring us. I don't know how she can see in this light. The lamp gives the shelter a hazy glow, but it's not exactly bright. May just lays down and curls up. She looks like she's going to doze off. Neither of them seems that bothered. I suppose they're used to it. I pull the blanket round me and sit here, listening.

In the distance I can hear a low rumbling, then it starts – the rat-a-tat-tat of the guns; the howling of the bombs as they fall. Explosions shake the ground, making dirt and dust fall on us from the roof of the shelter.

I won't lie, I'm shit scared. I've never experienced anything like this. I could actually die – right here in this crappy, smelly, rotten shelter – and no one would know what happened to me.

The planes are right overhead now, and even May and Nelly are looking tense. I can feel the vibrations of their engines right through my chest. My mum took me to a Olly Murs gig once at Westonbirt Arboretum and we got right up the front, by the giant speakers. When the music started the sound was so big it flowed right through my chest, just like this is doing now. Only it's nothing like this. Me and Mum were having a great time, and I wasn't in danger of getting blown to bits then.

Thinking of my mum is quite upsetting, you know? I mean, what if I get killed here? We had an awful row before they left. I can't get my head round the idea that I might never see her or Dad again. Didn't Gran and Great-aunt Eleanor say Queenie disappeared? They thought she was dead. Jeez, now I'm totally freaked. Oh my God, oh my God, oh my God!

'You all right, Queenie?' asks May, peeking over the edge of her blanket.

Crash! A bomb explodes somewhere close. I cover my head

with my hands, waiting for the world to fall in on my head. 'I don't want to die!'

'Aw, don't fret, love,' says May, sitting up and putting an arm around me. 'None of us do, do we Nell?'

Nelly shakes her head. ''Course we don't. But if it's our turn, there ain't much we can do about it.'

The smell of burning wood floats under the door. I can hear sirens, guns, and the droning of the airplanes going on and on and on.

'How can you be so calm about it?' I shout. 'This is really serious.'

'All right, keep your hair on. Getting in a state won't make no difference.'

'Are you telling me you're not scared?' I ask her. More bangs, more bombs landing. I try not to flinch.

'Oh, I'm scared all right,' she said. 'Don't let no one tell you they ain't scared, 'cause they'd be lying. But you can't give in to it, can you? If we do that, we might as well just put our hands up and surrender.'

'She's right,' says May. 'I don't know about you, Queenie, but I don't fancy talking German, do you?'

'You can hardly talk proper English,' says Nelly.

'Cheeky mare,' says May, grinning at her sister.

I shake my head. They don't understand. I know they're going to be all right. But what about me?

'Come on, Queenie, don't fuss. You stick with us and we'll see you all right. Your first air raid is always the worst. I don't mind admitting I nearly wet meself the first time. I'm still scared – like Nelly says, everyone is. But you get the hang of it.'

I seriously doubt it. But I'm not going to go on about it. I don't want them thinking I'm a wimp.

'I don't suppose you brought any food with you from the country, did you? It's all farms in Wiltshire, ain't it?' says Nelly.

For a few seconds I don't know what she's on about. *We're being bombed here, in case you hadn't noticed!* Then I realise she's trying to distract me. I try to concentrate.

'Er, no. Sorry. I live in a village, not on a farm.'

'I'll bet you've got a big house though, eh, Queenie?' says May.

'Not really. I'm not as posh as you think.' They look like they don't believe me. 'Honestly, I'm not. Our house isn't any bigger than this one.'

'What does your dad do, then?' Nelly wants to know.

'Ours is at sea,' says May.

I know that already, but I try to look like I don't. But what can I say about my dad? He works with computers, but I can't tell them that – were they even invented in 1940? Wasn't the first computer used to break the German's secret codes? I remember seeing it on the telly on one of those history channel programmes Dad likes to watch. Enigma – that's it! I don't think that was until later in the war, though.

I'd better keep as close to the truth as possible. 'Um … he works on machines,' I say. Woomph! Another explosion rocks the shelter.

'What sort of machines?' asks May, ignoring it. I try to concentrate on her instead of all the chaos going on outside.

'I don't know. He doesn't talk about it.' Or rather, I realise, I never bother to listen. I feel guilty about that now. I might never get the chance to find out.

'And he works on these machines in Wiltshire, does he?' Nelly asks. She doesn't look convinced.

'Most of the time, yes.' I say. 'He works for a big company in Swindon. But he's in France at the moment.'

Nelly and May looked gobsmacked. What's the matter with them?

'But France is in German hands,' says Nelly. 'How can he be there?'

Oh, great! How was I supposed to know? I've never been much interested in history. Hang on, what did we learn about the war at school? I think it started in 1939. So it's being going on for about a year now. The Germans took over most of Europe. They didn't get to us because of the English Channel, so they sent their planes and bombs. Yeah, and I've landed in the middle of it! Just to emphasise the fact there's another almighty bang and the door blows open. In the distance I can see flames and smoke and searchlights. Nelly jumps up and pushes the door shut again.

I know we won the war eventually, of course, but not for years and I can't remember the details. Something to do with beaches in France and atom bombs in Japan. This is getting sooo complicated!

'I shouldn't have said that,' I say. 'Forget I said it.' I feel like Hagrid from the *Harry Potter* films. He always seemed to be saying that when he put his foot in it. And it always led to trouble for someone.

'Ah,' says May, tapping the side of her nose. 'Secret work.'

'You'd better not make a mistake like that at the factory, or someone'll report you,' says Nelly. 'You should know better. "Walls have ears", remember.'

'Yes, sorry,' I say, feeling stupid. I'll never get away with this. I just seem to keep getting things wrong. I wish I was a bit cleverer, like the companions in *Dr Who*. They always seem to know what to do and say. But then again, they've got a bloody script to follow, haven't they!

'What about your mum?' says May while Nelly glares at me, just like Great-aunt Eleanor does. 'She doing war work 'n'all?'

'Er ... yes.' I'd better play it safe. I tap my nose and wink at May. 'I can't talk about it.'

She nods, not even a bit suspicious, bless her. But her sister is.

'How come you've been sent here?' asks Nelly. 'Seems a bit daft to me, you getting a job in London when it's a lot safer in the country.'

God will she ever give up?

'I really don't know,' I say. 'I didn't have any choice.' And that's definitely the truth.

'Done any sewing before?' asked May.

'No.'

'What did you do back home, then?' Nelly frowned.

'I'm still at school. I'm doing GCSEs.'

'G what?' she says.

'Er, you know. Exams.'

'Now, hang on a minute,' Nelly is getting right worked up now. 'You've been sent here to work at Cohen's, but you reckon you're still at school? How old are you?'

I want to slap myself on the head. Why can't I keep my stupid mouth shut?

'I'm fifteen, nearly sixteen.'

'Blimey!' says May. 'I said she was posh, Nell. Still at school and taking exams.'

''Course she ain't,' Nelly snaps at her sister. 'She's one of us workers now. Mr Cohen said she's here for the duration, not just the bleeding school holidays. And I ain't never heard of no GC whatever exams. English people take the School Certificate. So where are you really from, eh?'

I feel sick. Doesn't 'the duration' mean until the war is over? I can't stay here until 1945! 'Look,' I say, raising my voice to drown out the noise of the explosions and crashes and gunfire outside. 'I'm only here because my mum said I had to come. As soon as Dad's job is finished in France, I'm going home to Wiltshire, OK? And I'm going back to school to take my exams because my mum and dad said I have to, and I don't care if you've never heard of them, OK?'

'All right, don't get your knickers in a twist,' says Nelly, backing off a bit. 'We didn't have any choice in this either, you know. You sort it out with Mr Cohen and the Ministry. It's no skin off my nose if you go back where you came from. But I wouldn't count on it, Miss Posh. We've all got to do our bit.'

Another bang. More ack-ack-ack of gun-fire. She really has no idea. Not a clue. I can't count on anything right now. I wonder what she'd think if I told her the truth? Not that I'm going to – seeing as how I don't know what the truth is right now.

'Nell didn't want to leave school, neither,' says May, ignoring the tension between me and Nelly. 'Me, I couldn't wait. I'd rather be working and earning a few bob. It's a good laugh at Cohen's. You'll like it.'

Before I can reply there's an almighty crash. The whole shelter shakes and May squeals and dives under the blanket. Even Nelly ducks, holding her book over her head. I'm so shocked I just sit here with my mouth open. My ears are ringing. I shake my head, trying to clear them. Dust is floating through the gaps around the door curtain, and I have to shut my mouth as it's making me cough.

'Blimey, that was close,' May peeps out from her blanket again.

'Too bloody close,' says Nelly. 'I hope it ain't blown out our windows.'

I can hear bells and whistles outside. 'Should we go and see? They might need some help.' I hope not. It sounds way too scary out there.

'No,' says Nelly. 'The wardens and the firemen will do what they can. They'll shout if they need help. If we go out there gawping we'll only get in the way.'

'Our Dad said we should stay together and keep safe,' says May. 'It's too dangerous to go out before the all-clear. Better stay here. Worrying don't make it no better, Queenie. Try and get some rest.'

Rest? How am I going to rest? It's chaos out there! I know she's only trying to make me calm down, like someone telling me to chillax when I get all stressed about how totally unreasonable my parents are. But there's a bloody war going on and I'm sitting here in the middle of it when I should be out shopping for a new phone charger and some skinny jeans in Oxford Street!

I pull the blanket over my head and put my fingers in my ears and start singing to myself to drown out the noise. 'La la la la la la la la la la la.'

'And you can shut that bloody racket up,' Nelly yells at me.

A couple of hours later I'm trying to stretch the kinks out of my neck when Nelly raises her head, listening. 'I think it's dying down,' she says.

'Thank Christ,' says May. 'Let's hope there ain't no more on the way. I want me bed. I'm bleeding shattered.'

Me too. I'd give anything to be back home in Wiltshire right now.

CHAPTER FIVE

It seems like hours before the all clear siren goes off. We fold up the blankets and turn the lamp out. In the garden we stand and watch the searchlights doing their dance again, only this time the sky's not black but orange and grey from the fires and smoke. In the distance we can hear the sound of fire engines and the hiss of water as it hits the burning buildings.

'They're getting closer every night,' says Nelly.

'I hope our boys got a few of them,' says May.

'It looks like there's a lot of fires.' In a strange way it looks beautiful. Smoke is swirling around the flames, dancing with the searchlights.

'Yeah,' says May. 'People's homes, they are. Jerry don't care what he hits – houses, schools, shops. The bastards.'

'Watch your mouth,' Nelly snaps. 'Just 'cause we think it don't mean we have to say it out loud. Our Mum'd turn in her grave hearing you talk like that.'

'Sorry Nell,' says May, looking guilty. 'I'm just so blinking tired.'

Nelly puts an arm round her sister's shoulder. 'I know. But we've got to keep our standards up, May. We don't want Dad coming home and finding us turned into a pair of savages, do we?'

'I s'pose not,' May sighs, rubbing her eyes. 'Anyway, we've got to get up for work soon. I'm going to use the lav before I go in.'

'Yeah, me too,' I say. No way will I come out here on my own in the middle of the night.

While Nelly and I wait for May to use the loo I close my eyes and try to imagine we're queuing for the loos at Glastonbury. I makes me smile. At least this queue is short and the loo is clean, even if it does have a faint whiff of cat.

I wish I could say something to make them feel better, but this war is going to last for years yet. I know they survive and their Dad comes home safely, but that's all I do know. So what can I say?

Above the noise of the fires I hear the loo flush and May emerges.

'You go next, Queenie,' says Nelly sounding tired. She steps back and lets me go in front of her. I thought she was quite nice to May, even when she was telling her off, and now she's being nice to me. If she keeps this up I could start to like her. 'But don't take all night about it,' she calls after me, spoiling the effect.

The kitchen seems warm and cosy after a few hours in the Anderson Shelter. Nelly boils the kettle and fills three hot-water bottles. I hug mine, glad of its heat.

Nelly glances up at the clock on the wall. 'Better get to bed. Bombs or no bombs, we'll be for it if we're late in the morning. Mr Cohen don't put up with no time-wasters.' She collects up the cups and saucers left over from earlier. 'You show her up, May, and I'll give these a rinse.'

I take the suitcase and follow May up the stairs to the first-floor landing. I know what the bedroom will look like before May opens the door. It was the same room Gran and me cleaned this morning. Only it's the dark, cold version, not the nice cosy one.

'Isn't this Nelly's room?' I ask without thinking. When May turns to look at me, all surprised, I want to slap myself for being so stupid.

'How did you know that?' May asks.

'Er … I'm psychic?'

May giggles. 'Nah, don't be daft. There ain't no such thing, is there? Mind you, Lil over the road reckons she's got the 'fluence on account of her Nan being a Romany who used to live in caravan.' She wiggles her fingers in front of her face and crosses her eyes. 'Mad as a hatter, she is.'

I grin and shrug. 'OK, I'm not psychic. I just guessed.'

May nods. 'Fair enough. It was a good guess. Nelly's moved

into our dad's room while you're here. If he comes home on leave, we'll have to share so he can have his bed.'

'Are you expecting him home soon?'

'Dunno. He's Merchant Navy, not regular. It's more dangerous, you know. The Merchants are trying to keep us supplied, but the bloody U-boats keep going after them.' She's quiet for a bit. Then she looks all serious and says, 'I have nightmares sometimes. I'm scared he won't come home. We've already lost our mum. What will we do if we lose him too?'

I want to hug her. She looks so sad. 'He's going to be all right,' I say. 'I know he will.'

'No you don't,' she says. 'Only God knows, and he ain't letting on. But thanks for trying to cheer me up anyway. Now, there's a bit of space for your bits and bobs. Nelly cleared out the top drawer of that chest, and there's a couple of hangers spare in the wardrobe if you want to hang anything up.'

'OK, thanks.' I wait for her to go, but she sits on the bed.

'What have you got then? Let's see your clothes. I don't suppose you brought an overall for work, did you?'

'I don't know,' I say. I can't remember seeing one. I pick up the case and put it on the bed next to her. She's looking at me a bit funny. 'I – er, my gran packed for me,' I lie. 'I don't know what she put in here.'

May's face clears. 'Well get it open then, let's have a butchers. I love seeing what other people have got. Nelly says I'm right nosy, but I just think it's really interesting. Don't worry, it won't bother me if you've got something I ain't.'

I open the case, bracing myself for the mothballs, but it smells all right, like the clothes have just been washed. It's definitely the same case, but everything is neatly packed, not just stuffed in like it was when I shut it and carried it out of Gran's kitchen. The papers and gas mask box are on the top. I put them on the dressing table, then take out the pretty blue cardigan with the pearl buttons.

'That's nice,' says May. 'Did you make it?'

I laugh. 'God no. I can't knit.'

'You're pulling my leg. Everyone can knit.'

'Not me.'

39

'Didn't your mum teach you?'

'She can't knit either,' I say. 'She tried, but she's useless, which annoys her because some of her friends are really good at it and are always making weird-looking jumpers and throws for their sofas, that sort of thing. I'm glad she can't. I wouldn't want to have to wear some of the rubbish those women produce. They look ridiculous if you ask me.'

'So who made that?' she asks, pointing at the cardigan.

I shrug. 'Dunno.'

I open the drawer May said I could use, and put the folded cardi in. The next thing out of the case is the cotton nightdress.

'Ah, that's lovely,' says May, 'and cosy too. A nice long nightie's just the thing to keep your bum from freezing.'

She said it in my day too, and she's right. It's flipping cold in here. The nightie and the hot-water bottle should keep me warm. I wonder when Gran had central heating installed. Probably not for decades yet.

'Are you two still up?' Nelly is standing in the doorway. 'Come on, it's nearly three o'clock. We've got to be up at six. Get to bed.' She turns and heads for the door of what I know as Gran's bedroom.

''Night, Nelly,' May calls after her. 'Sleep tight.'

Nelly ignored her and shut the door.

'Is she always this rude?' I ask, feeling bad for May.

'She gets a bit grumpy when she's tired, that's all.'

'Have we really got to get up at six?'

'Yeah, so we'd better do like Nelly says and get some sleep.' She stands up, stretching her arms above her head and yawning. 'I'm just next door if you need anything, Queenie.'

I realise that 'next door' is where Gran's bathroom is. I wonder where the bath is in 1940, but I'm too tired to care.

'Thanks,' I say. 'Goodnight.'

'Night, night,' she says as she leaves, shutting the door behind her.

I turn and look at the open case. I start to empty it and put everything away, but then wonder whether I should leave it. After all, I might not be here long. With any luck I'll wake up at Gran's, *when* I should be. I just hope I don't wake up sharing a bed with Great-aunt Eleanor!

I think about sneaking down to the hall mirror to see if I can get it to send me back, but the stairs are creaky and they'll know I'm there and think I'm trying to do a runner – which I am, really. But I'm so tired and it's freezing, so I leave half the stuff in the case, move it onto the floor, turn off the light and crawl into bed with the hot-water bottle.

Even that's a weird experience. There's no big fluffy duvet like I'm used to. Instead, the sheets are freezing and the couple of thin, scratchy blankets don't seem to help at all. I lie there shivering, hugging the hot-water bottle.

When May brought me in here, for a second – just a second – I saw the lemon-painted walls and cream carpet from Gran's. I tried to sneeze, to see if it would get me back there. But I just went dizzy again and here I am, stuck in a freezing bedroom with more of that awful brown lino on the floor. It's funny, I never liked that lemon colour scheme, but I really miss it now.

I roll over and punch the pillow. I'm still not sure how I got here, but I'm beginning to realise this is definitely more than just a dream. But there's nothing I can do about it. All I can do is wait and see, and hope like mad I can get back to real life soon.

I wonder if I'm dead but haven't realised. I know it sounds really stupid, but maybe I really died when I got knocked out, and that's why I woke up in this weird place. I hope not. I don't want to be stuck here for ever and ever.

CHAPTER SIX

I swear Nelly enjoys seeing people suffer. I barely slept anyway, and I'd just dozed off when she was shaking me awake.

This morning has been dead embarrassing actually. I got stroppy with Nelly for waking me up, because I was dreaming I was back at home. So when she woke me up it was like she'd dragged me back to the past again, and I was so upset I told her to 'eff off' – only I used the full word, which I don't usually. But I couldn't help myself.

'Don't you use that language in this house,' she'd said, 'or I'll wash your filthy mouth out with carbolic.'

I could see she meant it, even though I have no idea what carbolic is. It's bound to be something horrible.

'Bloody leave me alone,' I said, turning away from her.

Well, Nelly wasn't having that. She grabbed the bedclothes and pulled them off me. It was so flipping cold, I screamed. Then May came running in, wanting to know what all the fuss was about.

Anyway, it wasn't a good start to the day, so let's leave it at that. I got up in the end because I didn't have any choice. There was a bowl of watery porridge waiting for me downstairs – no sugar of course – and some of that weird-tasting tea. Apparently, it's the 'sterilised milk' that makes it so strange. I think it's like UHT milk, but as we don't use that at home I have no idea whether it tastes the same.

Then, I had to wash at the kitchen sink, using the foulest-smelling soap I've ever encountered. It's called Wright's Coal Tar Soap – honestly. Just don't ask, because I have no idea. The smell is almost as bad as mothballs.

I completely forgot about cleaning my teeth last night. I suppose, when you think you're going to die, it sort of becomes a low priority. This morning I discovered there's no toothpaste, so I had to clean my teeth with some weird powder I found in the suitcase. The toothbrush with it is made of wood and has real bristles. Honestly, it was like putting an old garden broom in my mouth. It was horrible. I'd have given anything for my electric toothbrush and a tube of Aquafresh.

I had to ask May what I should wear for working in a factory. Well, I don't know, do I? I'm just glad that May was around, because Nelly isn't talking to me. I suppose I'll have to apologise to her soon, but she doesn't make it easy. She's just as cross and disapproving now as she will be in the future.

Maybe I should try to get her to lighten up a bit. Or would that amount to messing with the future?

So, now we're on our way to work. It's still dark, and the street lights are off, so I've got to make sure I stay close to the girls or I'll lose them. Thank God I found some flatter shoes in the case, and some nice tailored charcoal wool trousers (high waist though, I'm not used to that), a cream cotton blouse and a dark red jumper. I don't have a big coat, just the suit jacket, but the girls are moving fast, so I'm getting pretty warm almost running to keep up with them. My gas mask box is slung over my shoulder and it's banging against my hip. I'll probably end up with a bruise. I don't suppose they'll have any arnica gel for it. Mum's always got some homeopathic stuff for whatever's wrong with us. Dad calls it mumbo-jumbo, but she swears by it even when he's going on about it having no proven scientific effect.

'Hurry up, Queenie,' says May. 'If you don't get a move on we'll miss the bus.'

'How much further is it?' I ask, trying to hold the box against me so it doesn't keep hitting me.

'Just round the corner.'

I'm almost jogging as we round the corner and – oomph! I run straight into someone, a big someone, banging my nose on hard brass buttons in the middle of his chest. A pair of arms grab me to stop me from bouncing off him and onto my backside.

'Sorry, Miss. Didn't see you there.'

I look up – and it's a long way I can tell you – into the face of a soldier. He's fairly young, I think, although his voice is quite deep and he's very tall. It's still too dark to see all his face clearly, but his smile is quite nice.

'That's all right,' I say, smiling back at him. I don't usually smile at strangers, but there's something about this guy. I suppose it's because he saved me from falling over, and he's so solid. He seems familiar, like I've seen him on telly or something, which is stupid. But I don't have time to think about it because May's beside me.

'Come on, the bus is coming!' she says, grabbing my arm. 'Morning, Jock. Can't stop, we're late.'

'Morning, May. Who's your friend?'

May is dragging me towards the stop where Nelly and a queue of other people are about to get on the bus. 'Her name's Queenie,' she calls over her shoulder. 'New machinist, been billeted with us. See you later.'

'Yeah, all right. You take care. Ta'ra.'

He waved and disappeared round the corner.

'Who's that?' I ask May.'

'Just Jock. His nan lives over the road from us. He's always round our way.'

'He's quite fit.'

May looks at me a bit strange. 'Of course he's fit. He's a blooming soldier.'

'I mean he looks nice.'

'Well why didn't you say that?' May shakes her head. 'You do talk daft, Queenie. But yeah, he is nice, I suppose. Bit boring though. I like my fellas to have a bit of spark about them. Come on, before the clippie rings the bell.'

I get on the bus, May follows right behind me. 'Go on upstairs. We always sit up top.' I climb up and look round for Nelly. I can barely see through the fog of cigarette smoke. Ugh, that is so disgusting. I can't believe nearly everyone is smoking. Don't they know it'll kill them?

Downstairs a bell tinkles and the bus moves off. I nearly lose my balance, but manage to get into the seat next to Nelly without making a complete idiot of myself. May brushes past me, knocking my gas mask box onto my lap as she heads for the seat in front of us.

I look around. Everyone's bundled up in heavy winter coats, mainly black, brown, or grey. The only colour is from the posters glued to inside of the bus – adverts for tooth powder, cod liver oil tablets, cigarettes and snuff (what the hell is snuff?). There are propaganda posters too. "Careless Talk Costs Lives" – I've seen that one in a museum.

'What's the matter with you?' Nelly asks, seeing me craning my neck to look at everything. 'Don't you have buses in the country?'

So she's decided to talk to me. 'Of course we do.'

A waft of cigarette smoke makes me cough. I wave a hand in front of my face.

'Bet you don't get on them though, do you?' she says.

'Yes I do, actually. I get the bus to school, and into town sometimes.' When I can't get a lift off my mum, or Jessica's mum that is. Buses are a pain – we hardly get any through our village, except the school bus, which is full of stupid kids.

'So why are you looking like you've swallowed a lemon? Our buses not good enough for you, Miss Posh?'

'I told you, I'm not posh. It just that you can't smoke on our buses, that's all.'

'Can't smoke on buses? Well I never heard anything like it. Next you'll be telling me they don't let a chap have a puff with his pint at the pub.'

I open my mouth and then shut it again. She wouldn't believe me if I told her.

'Did you hear that, May? Folks can't smoke on the buses in the country.'

'God help us,' said a man sitting across the aisle from us. 'You'd need a good strong tobacco to cover the smell out there. Blooming stink they do, all them cows and pigs.'

'It's not like that,' I start to say, but no one's interested because the ticket collector has arrived. I panic before I remember I found a purse with some money in my suitcase. I pull it out of my jacket pocket and have a look inside. Oh, my,

God. I don't recognise any of the coins in there. And are those bits of paper real money? I peek at Nelly, trying to see what she's getting out of her purse.

'It's thrupence to Whitechapel,' she says.

'Thrupence?' What's that?

Nelly rolls her eyes. 'Three pence. See? Coppers. Pennies.' She holds up three large coins. They are brown and huge, not at all like normal pennies.

'Oh, right.' I rummage round in the purse and find three coins, but they are a bit smaller.

'God help us. Those are ha'pennies, stupid. You need three more of them if you haven't got any pennies, or a thrupenny bit.'

'Like this one,' says May, twisting round in her seat and holding up a funny-looking little coin, about the size of a modern penny, but thicker and with lots of little straight edges.

I look again and find one. A three pence coin. 'How weird is that?' I mutter to myself. But of course, Nelly has to hear me, doesn't she?

'Anyone would think you ain't never seen English money before,' she says.

'You ain't one of them foreign spies we've all been warned about, are you?' It's the man across the aisle again.

'What?' I say. My voice is squeaky. It feels like everyone is looking at me. Oh crap, I must look really guilty – I can feel my face going red. 'No, of course not,' I'm nearly shouting. 'I'm from Wiltshire. It isn't smelly there and I want to go home.'

The man laughs. 'All right, keep your hair on, love. Can't you take a joke?'

I can feel Nelly's disapproval as I give the man an embarrassed smile.

'Sorry,' I say. 'I'm just not used to getting up so early.'

'I thought all you country types got up at the crack of dawn.'

'Only the farmers,' I say. But he's lost interest. The ticket collector reaches us and we all pay our fares.

I subside into my thoughts, ignoring everyone else. I'm really worried about being away from Gran's house. It's too dark to see where we're going, so I have no idea how to get back there. What if I miss my chance to get back to my own time because I'm not at the house? I'm assuming, from my limited experience of watching the odd sci-fi programme like *Stargate* and stuff, that there's a portal at the house and I fell through it when I sneezed and tripped in those bloody awful shoes. To get back, I need to find it again, hopefully in the same place, at the right time. Whatever time that is.

The portal must have closed behind me last night, or I would have been able to go straight back. And this morning, we all walked through the hall to the front door and I tried sneezing. Nothing. Maybe I can't find it when there's someone with me? Perhaps it only works one way? Or it has to be a genuine sneeze? I just don't know. How scary is that? And what if I end up going further back in time? I could be blowing my nose and land in the flipping Middle Ages. Wasn't that when they had plagues and witch-burnings and stuff? Oh. My. God. I could be burned at the stake by some superstitious mob. I'm barely getting away with it here; I'd totally not fit in if I go any further back in time.

Maybe I should tell May and Nelly where I've come from. They'll probably think I'm mad, but who knows? They might believe me. But then again, they might not, and I don't know what will happen then. Actually, I don't know what would happen if they do. I've got to be careful about spoilers. I can't tell people about their future in case they try to change it. If they do things differently, the whole world could be affected. I might start fading from all my photos, like Marty McFly in *Back to the Future*. No, I'll keep my mouth shut.

I'm so tired. I let out a huge yawn. I could easily go back to sleep even if I am choking on cigarette smoke on this smelly bus.

I'm just closing my eyes when Nelly pokes me in the side.

'C'mon, this is our stop.'

How can she tell? It's still dark and the windows are all steamed up. I wouldn't have a clue.

May is already up and on the move. I follow her, nearly going headfirst down the stairs as the bus stops. There's barely time to blink when we get off before May and Nelly are steaming down the road. I run to catch up.

'Do you always walk so fast?' I ask, hoping they'll take the hint and slow down.

'We can't be late, or Mr Cohen'll dock our wages,' says May, power-walking round the corner.

'At this rate I'm going to be worn out before we start,' I complain. But they're not listening. I roll my eyes and speed up, not wanting to lose sight of them. I have no idea where we are now, or how to get back to the house, so without the sisters I'd be in serious trouble.

As I get a bit closer to them I hear May say to Nelly: 'You shouldn't say things like that, not on the bus. Someone might report us and then we'll have the men from the Ministry knocking on the door. She ain't no spy, she's just a country bumpkin. Give her a couple of weeks to settle in and she'll be just like us.'

'Speak for yourself,' said Nelly. 'She ain't nothing like me. And why shouldn't I say it if I'm thinking it? And maybe they should come round. If she don't know the difference between a penny and an ha'penny, she might well be a spy. Better to have someone checking up on her than letting her get away with murder.'

I've had enough of this. 'I'm not a spy,' I shout. That gets their attention. They stop and turn round. 'Look, I know you don't like me, but give me a break. I'm just tired, OK?'

'Don't mind Nell, Queenie, she don't mean it.' Typical Gran – trying to keep the peace. I'm not so sure, and I can see Nelly is definitely not joking about this.

'Bit soft for a country girl, ain't you?' she sneers. 'I'll bet you won't last more than a week round here. The only reason I reckon you ain't a spy is 'cause you're too bleeding daft.'

I open my mouth to tell her to shut up, I'm not soft, I'm a time traveller and I've got more important things to worry about than what she thinks of me. But I don't say anything. What can I say that won't make things worse?

Anyway, she's not interested, she's already turned round and is heading off at full speed again. I can hear May saying: 'Oh Nell, be nice, eh? It'll be right miserable at home if you two don't get on.'

I slow down again, not wanting to hear any more. I'm suddenly scared, more scared than I've ever been, even than when I realised I was in 1940. If they check on me, they might find out I don't exist here in 1940, and think I really am a spy. I'm in the middle of a war. They shot spies in those days, didn't they? What if I can't convince them I'm OK? Should I tell them I'm from the future? What will happen to me if I do?

'Oi! Queenie!' They are standing at another corner, waiting for me. 'Get a move on!'

I want to run in the other direction, but then May giggles and I remember she's my gran, and anyway I don't have anywhere else to go, do I? OK, deep breath, keep calm. That's it. Keep Calm and Carry On.

I walk towards them.

CHAPTER SEVEN

It's barely light when we arrive at the factory. Our breath is coming out in little clouds in the cold air, but I'm pretty warm after having to jog to keep up with the sisters.

Cohen's Outfitters Limited is in an old building down a narrow lane in Whitechapel. The red brickwork is almost black with soot, and the windows are filthy and criss-crossed with tape like just about every other building I've seen so far. I imagine it's going to be like something out of a Dickens adaptation inside – all dark and miserable. I really don't fancy working here, it must be so depressing.

Nelly tells May to take me to the office. She glares at me with her schoolteacher look and says, 'Behave yourself, and watch that mouth of yours,' and then stalks off. I want to poke my tongue out at her, but as she's not looking it would be a bit pointless.

May takes me up some old wooden stairs. I can hear the hum of machinery from somewhere down below, and in the office there's a lady bashing away at a really old typewriter. Weird. She's using all of her fingers to type, like Mum does. She tried to teach me, but I couldn't be bothered. Maybe I should have had a go – this lady is typing really quick, even on the dinosaur machine. It looks impressive.

Everything is old and shabby in here, even the woman at the desk. She's got grey hair done up in a bun and some of those glasses that sit on the end of your nose so it looks like you're not even using them. The only colour in the room is the red lipstick she's wearing on her thin lips.

'Morning, Mrs Blenkinsopp,' says May. 'This is the new girl what's been billeted with us.'

Mrs Blenkinsopp stops typing and looks at us over the top of her glasses. 'Name?'

'Rose Smith,' I say, before May calls me Queenie.

'Papers please.'

'What papers?' I ask.

'I need to check your identity card, and your appointment letter from the Ministry of Works.'

'Oh, right. I left them in my suitcase.'

Mrs Blenkinsopp looks cross. 'You should have your identity card with you at all times. It's the law.'

Oh crap. 'I'm sorry, I forgot. Can I bring them in tomorrow?' With any luck I'll be gone by then.

'I'll make sure she brings them, Mrs Blenkinsopp,' says May. 'It was a bit of a rush this morning, what with being up most of the night with the raid and all.'

Mrs Blenkinsopp sighs. 'Very well. But don't leave the house without your identity card again. Bring it with your letter tomorrow morning without fail.'

'Yes, Mrs Blenkinsopp,' I say. 'I won't forget.'

We clatter down the stairs and May takes me to the cloakroom where we leave our stuff. I put on the overalls that May has lent me. If I stay around I'll probably have to buy some. Luckily May and I are about the same size, except I'm a little bit taller, so these fit fine. In fact, we look more like sisters than May and Nelly do. It's in the genes, I suppose. I can't help smiling, thinking how May would freak out if she knew I was her granddaughter.

My smile slips a bit as I follow her through the door into the workshop. The noise hits me first – an angry buzz like a million gigantic bees. The air smells of machine oil and there's cotton dust everywhere. The room is filled with row after row of sewing machines, with great big spools of cotton spinning away above them, reminding me of surgical drips over patients' beds. There's a woman at each machine, hard at work, their hands guiding khaki cloth through the machines, snipping the threads as they get to the end of the seam, and then throwing their work into a large basket one side of their workstation. Then they pick up the next pieces from an identical basket on the other side and sew the same seams. They work quickly, not stopping to chat. As the baskets fill, a couple of young boys run amongst them, picking the piles of work out of baskets and moving them along to the next row. I spot Nelly towards the back of the room, head down, the cloth shooting through her machine like lightening.

May grabs my arm and drags me over to the desk at the front where the supervisor is sitting. I can't hear what they're saying, but they don't seem to have any trouble communicating. I realise they're probably lip-reading, which I can't do, so I have no idea what's going on. May shouts in my ear. 'Mrs Bloomfield will show you what to do.' She gives me a thumbs up and walks over to a machine half way down the room, waving to a couple of other girls as she goes. I stand there, not sure what to do. Mrs Bloomfield is talking to me but the noise is crazy in here.

'I'm sorry? What did you say?' I ask.

She leans closer. 'I said, you done any sewing before?'

'No. Never.'

She shakes her head and mutters something. She gestures for me to sit at an empty workstation at the front of the room. Mrs Bloomfield leans over and flicks a switch. The motor starts to vibrate, and a light comes on, illuminating the area where the cloth goes under the needle.

'Here, try this.' She gives me a piece of scrap cloth, shouting in my ear. 'Just try and sew a straight line for starters.'

I look around at the others, trying to work out how they do it. The girl sitting next to me gives me a friendly smile before she turns back to her work. As I watch she pushes a lever up to raise the metal foot which holds the material in place, and pulls it down again to secure the next piece.

OK, I can do this. I do exactly what the other girl did. But once I've got the material in place I can't for the life of me figure out how to make the machine work. I look at the girl again, but have no idea how she's doing it.

'Use your foot,' Mrs Bloomfield shouts in my ear, making me jump. She points to the floor.

Oh, I see now. There's a metal plate down there, like an oversized foot pedal for a car. A quick glance to the side and I see how the other girls are operating their machines by pressing down on it. I have a go, but pull back with a scream as my machine roars into life, shooting the material out of my hands. Whoa, that was fast! There's a lull around me as the others lifted their feet, leaving their machines idling as they stop to watch the new girl making a mess of her first attempt at sewing. A couple of the girls, including May, look sympathetic, others giggle. The older women smirk and get back to their work. I'll bet Nelly is having a right laugh at me. But I won't look – I won't give her the satisfaction. I'm embarrassed enough as it is.

'Here, I'll show you. Shift your backside,' says Mrs Bloomfield. I get up and she sits down. 'Watch what I do. Then you can spend half an hour practicing with scraps. Once you get the hang of it, I'll give you your first batch of seams to do.'

I watch carefully as she shows me how to control the material as it goes under the needle while using her foot to control the speed of the machine.

'Got that? Right, work on them scraps in the bin there. Mind you don't get too close to the needle – we're too busy to waste time taking you to the hospital to get a punctured finger sorted out. Give us a shout when you run out of thread, and I'll show you how to put a new reel and bobbin on.'

Left alone, I slowly get the hang of the machine. I reckon if I treat it like a computer game, it'll be easier. I just have to keep my eye on the needle and concentrate on coordinating my hands and feet. That's it, easy. I block out the noise and distractions and soon I'm sewing straight lines of neat stitches.

By the time we stop for a tea break, I'm well into my first batch of seams. I'm not sure where the small pieces of fabric will end up on a soldier's uniform, but I'm quite enjoying myself.

'You getting on all right?' asks May.

'Yeah,' I say. 'No worries.'

'Do what? You always talk funny. Anyway, come and meet the girls.' I follow her to the end of the machine room, where everyone is getting large mugs of tea from a lady with a trolley. I'd rather have a cappuccino, but didn't dare say so. Instead I drink the tea gratefully. The dust from the cloth, plus the smell of the oil used to grease the machines, has made my throat dry and I've got a nasty taste in my mouth. The hot drink, even though it's that horrible sterilized milk again, makes me feel much better.

'Everyone, this is Queenie,' May introduces me.

'It's Rosie actually,' I say.

There's a chorus of groans. 'Not another one.'

'Yeah, that's why we're calling her Queenie,' says Nelly, and everyone nods.

'Good idea.'

I give up. I won't be able to hear anyone call me Queenie at work anyway as it's so flipping noisy most of the time.

I soon lose track of all their names. There's Daisy, the three Roses I'd already been told about, Elsie, Betty, Eileen, Doris, Ivy, Esther and Sadie, and loads more.

'You'll soon get to know everyone,' says May.

They're a nosy lot – they want to know how old I am, where I come from, have I got a boyfriend? I can feel myself blushing as I think about Simon. Not that he's my boyfriend, but I have fancied him forever, and he was finally starting to notice me – until Jess got her claws into him. I can't believe she did that, knowing how much I like him.

In a way, being here in 1940 is what my Gran would call a Blessing in Disguise. I won't have to see them, no one can phone me, and Facebook hasn't even been invented yet so I won't have to face the humiliation of seeing Jess change her status to '*in a relationship*' and post loads of pics of her and Simon snogging. Time travel is a seriously drastic way of escaping all that, but I suppose it's good to have some breathing space until I can come to terms with my best friend's betrayal and my broken heart.

But what if I can never see any of them again? Oh crap, isn't life confusing enough without all this? Someone coughs. They're all looking at me.

'No, I don't have a boyfriend,' I say.

'You can have mine, love,' says one of the girls. 'I've been trying to get rid of him for ages.'

'Christ, you don't want him,' says someone else. 'He's barely house-trained.' Everyone laughs and suggest different potential boyfriends for me.

'My son's house-trained.'

'Yeah, but he's only twelve.'

'Take my brother – soon as he gets married I get his bedroom. I'm sick of sharing with my dozy sister.'

'I expect you've got your eye out for a nice boy in uniform.'

'Thanks, but I'll pass,' I say.

The girl who smiled at me earlier is Esther, and she's the only one apart from me who doesn't have a Cockney accent. She's one of the quieter ones. She seems nice though, and laughs with the rest of us. I think she's foreign, but don't have time to ask before we have to get back to work.

A couple of hours later we stop for lunch – a revolting sandwich made of bread that tastes like cardboard and an unidentifiable filling. I decide not to complain though as Nelly made it for me. When she gives it to me she says, 'I don't suppose it's what you're used to, but it's all you're gonna get while we have to manage on rations.'

I can see she's waiting for me to moan about it so she can have a go at me. Well I won't give her the satisfaction. Instead I smile and say 'Thanks, Nelly. It was kind of you to make it for me.'

Nelly narrows her eyes, still not trusting me. I want to laugh, but just keep on smiling. It feels good to confuse her. I remember how the old Nelly – sorry Eleanor – kept staring at me, making me feel uncomfortable. Well, now it's my turn and even though Nelly has no idea what's going on it makes me feel like I've got the upper hand for a change.

I struggle to finish the sandwich though: it really is nasty. I hope it's not going to be the same every day. I think about the money in the purse. Maybe I can find a shop round here and buy a choccie bar or something? Anything to get rid of the taste of the cardboard.

'How long have we got? Is there time for me to have a walk?'

'What d'you want to go walking for?' asks Nelly. 'It's freezing out there, and anyway, we only get half an hour.'

I shrug. 'I just want to get some fresh air. I've only been

outside in the dark, I'm starting to feel like a vampire.'

She rolls her eyes and looks up at the clock on the wall. 'Well you've got fifteen minutes, so don't go far.'

'OK,' I say. 'I'd better get a move on.' There must be a little shop round here somewhere. I wonder if they had Snickers Bars in 1940? Mmm, my mouth is watering just thinking about it!

'Hang on, Queenie,' says May. 'I'll come with you.'

We grab our coats as a couple of the older women shout after me. 'Had enough, Queenie, love?'

'You can't get rid of me that easy,' I say over my shoulder, giving them my best Terminator impression. 'I'll be back.' Behind me I can hear them asking each other what I'm like, and Nelly saying 'I told you she was daft.' Me and May laugh and keep going. Out on the street, we links arms like we're besties. It feels good – weird but good.

We don't go far. We turn a couple of corners and then stop dead. In front of us are piles and piles of rubble. All the buildings have been destroyed. I can hardly see where the road is. People are milling around, sorting out anything that's useable. Someone is watching over a bonfire of stuff they can't save. An old woman is sitting on a chair in the middle of it all, a blanket wrapped round her legs and another round her shoulders. Next to her is a small pile of stuff – clothes, shoes, pictures in cracked frames, a couple of candlesticks. She's calling out to a younger woman who is searching through the rubble.

'See if you can find a kettle, girl. We need a kettle. And a couple of saucepans.'

'What's the point, Ma? We ain't got a kitchen no more. How we gonna boil a kettle?'

'The Council will rehouse us, don't you worry. You need to dig out our stuff ready for a new place.'

The girl stands up and wipes her face with her sleeve. It leaves a dirty mark on her cheek. 'I told you Ma, everyone round here's in the same boat. The Council ain't got enough places for everyone. We'll have to go to the centre in Bethnal Green, like the neighbours did.'

The old woman crosses her arms and shakes her head. 'I

heard about that place. It ain't no better than the workhouse. You go if you want. I'm staying here.'

'Don't be daft. It's bleeding freezing, and there ain't nothing worth staying here for. Come on, Ma. If we don't hurry up it'll be full.'

They look so upset. I can't imagine what I'd do if our house was wrecked and all my stuff ruined. And I know I'd hate to have to go and stay at some centre with a load of strangers. It must be like a refugee camp or something. I've seen loads of those on telly – mainly around Africa or the Middle East. Thousands of tents and people queuing up for food and water, and flies crawling all over starving children. OK, I know it has to be different here – probably a school hall, and you won't get flies in England at this time of year. But I can still understand why she hates the idea.

The girl looks like she's going to cry. She stands in the rubble looking lost. When she sees us staring at her she gets mad and shouts at us to clear off. 'Who the bloody hell d'you think you are, gawping at us like we're bloody zoo animals? Sod off!'

'Come on, Queenie,' says May.

'Can't we help them?'

'Not much we can do. And anyway, we've got to get back to work.'

'I hope they'll be OK.'

'Yeah. As our old mum used to say, "There but for grace of God go I." It could be us next.'

'My dad says that too.' He must have got that from Gran. He says it every time there's a disaster on the telly. I really wish he was here now.

We turn round and go back the way we came. I don't blame the girl for having a go at us. I didn't mean to be so nosy, but I was just so shocked by the horrible mess the bombs made. This morning it was too dark to see. Or maybe I was so wrapped up in myself that I just didn't notice. God, that makes me sound really selfish.

'Hallo, ladies.'

There's a guy blocking our path who looks like something

out of an old gangster movie. He not much older than us, but I've never seen anything like it in real life – pinstripe suit which looks too big for his skinny body, slicked-back black hair and a really dodgy moustache – like he'd drawn it on with an eyebrow pencil.

I'm trying not to laugh, but May seems impressed.

'Well look who it is. Where'd you spring from? I ain't seen you around lately.'

He shrugs. 'Been busy.'

Yeah, 'course you have, I think. Busy standing in front of the mirror.

'You going down the Palais tomorrow night?' May asks him. 'They got a new dance contest. I fancy having a go, if I can find the right partner.'

Whoa, May's getting all flirty! I can't believe she's batting her eyelids at this guy, he's so unattractive. But she is, and he's lapping it up.

'Reckon you can keep up with me, do ya?' he says.

'I didn't say I'd dance with you, Billy boy. I just said I'm looking for the right partner. Jock's already offered.'

Hang on, what did she call him? No, it can't be.

He laughs. 'You won't win nothing with that dollop. He ain't got no style. No, you want a fella with a bit of flair. You need me if you want to win that prize, girl.'

'Hark at you, Flash Harry. Cocky so and so, ain't you? I'll think about it, that's all I'm saying.'

Phew, thank God. He's called Harry. For a minute there, I thought she said Billy.

He smiles, revealing a row of yellow teeth. 'You do that, darling. But don't take too long. I might ask your friend here.' He nods in my direction and winks at me. 'All right, sweetheart? I ain't never seen you round here. I'd've noticed a lovely girl like you.'

Really? Am I supposed to be impressed?

'What's your name then?'

'I'm Queenie,' I'd rather not to give him my real name. 'And I don't dance, thanks.' Well, not with him anyway. He's definitely not my type. 'May, are our fifteen minutes up yet?'

'Oh blimey, I forgot the time,' she says. 'Come on then, we'll have to run. Might see you later.'

'If you're lucky,' he calls after us.

Unlucky more like. May giggles and waves.

'Great dancer, that feller,' she says, answering my unspoken question. 'A bit flash, but he's all right really.'

Yeah, right. I must have a long talk with May about her taste in boys.

Everyone is back at their machines when we get inside. I sit down and concentrate on not getting my fingers caught under the needle. Apart from another tea break and a quick trip to the (thankfully indoor) loo, I spend the rest of the day sewing seam after seam after seam. I've got to admit, by the end of our shift I'm feeling pretty bored. I mean, it's hardly rocket science, is it? But I don't want to let myself think about it right now. I'd rather go mad with boredom than go seriously insane trying to work out why I'm here and how the hell I can get home. I do think about that girl and her mum for a bit, I can't help it. I hope they find somewhere to go and don't end up at that centre the old woman was so scared of.

That guy Harry was funny. Really fancied himself. But he's not fit like Simon. Now there's a guy I'd dance with any day. For a minute I daydream about what it would feel like. Then I remember that the last time I saw him he was snogging my best friend and I nearly sew my finger to the khaki material. I've got to stop thinking about it. They're not worth it, and anyway, if I don't manage to get home I'll be dead before they do it … or I'll be really old like Gran and Great-aunt Eleanor. How weird would that be, to go and see them when I'm ninety-something. They wouldn't even recognise me. I'd just be some strange old woman freaking them out. I should turn up while they're watching a *Dr Who* episode with those freaky stone angels in. I'd frighten the life out of them. It would serve them right for betraying me like that.

Another near miss with the needle reminds me to concentrate on the job and not on things I can't do anything about at the moment.

Maybe tonight I'll find out how to get back to my old life and this will all seem like a dream.

CHAPTER EIGHT

Bin on right, grab two bits, put them together, needle down, foot down, another seam done. Needle up, cut the thread, chuck-it-in-the-bin-on-the-left. Bin on right, grab –

'Oi, Queenie! You can stop now.' – *two bits* – what? I look up and Nelly is standing next to me.

'It's time to go.'

'Go where?' I ask.

'Home. Our shift's over.'

Home. I wish I could. I really, really want to go home. I'm tired and my whole body aches from sitting in the same position all day. How do these women do it every day? I look around and realise that everyone's stopped work. I was so zoned out I didn't even notice. I'd just got this rhythm going and completely lost track of anything else. I'll probably be dreaming about it tonight.

I put the bits back in the bin and shut off the machine. Standing up is a problem as my knees seem to be locked in the sitting position, with my 'driving' foot stuck at an angle. 'Ow!' Nelly grabs me before I head-butt the over-sized reel of thread on the top of my machine.

'Watch it. Hang onto me. I'll give you this much, Queenie, you're a grafter.' Nelly nods at the pile of finished seams I've done. 'I never thought you'd last the day.'

'Thanks,' I say. I'll accept her compliment, even though it's a bit back-handed. At least now she knows I'm not a wimp. 'Is it normal for your whole body to lock up like this? I feel like I've been set in concrete.'

Nelly laughs, but not in a nasty way. I think I actually might have impressed her. 'You'll be all right in a minute. You're just not used to it. Come on, the walk to the bus will sort you out.'

It's already dark when we leave the factory, and cold too. I do up my jacket, and start walking with Nelly.

Oh my God. Every step is agony. I end up hanging on Nelly's arm, hobbling along like an old lady.

'Where's May?' I ask.

'Probably at the bus stop already. If we don't get a move on we'll miss her.'

I'm a bit hurt she didn't wait for me, but Nelly doesn't seem bothered. Obviously, the sisters don't do everything together. They'd probably drive each other mad if they did. I noticed on our tea breaks they were talking to different girls. Still, I thought she'd wait for me on my first day. Anyway, she's there at the bus-stop – I can see her now we've turned the corner. And so is that guy Harry.

Nelly tuts. 'What's she doing, talking to that useless so and so?'

'We saw him at lunchtime,' I say.

She narrows her eyes and her lips go all thin. Looks like May's in trouble. I hope she's ready for it. Nelly doesn't say anything, but speeds up to reach them as the bus comes down the road. 'Come on. I ain't leaving him alone with her.'

'Ow! Hang on,' I say, nearly falling over when my stiff knees refuse to go any faster.

Nelly shows no mercy. 'Stop whining and hurry up.' She drags me along, my gas mask box banging against my hip. I will definitely have a bruise there. We make it to the bus stop just in time.

'All right, Nell?' says Harry, 'Hallo, Queenie darlin''

Nelly ignores him, and I just nod. He steps back to let us get on the bus first, then follows us up the stairs. I can feel his beady eyes on my bum. If he touches me I'm going to kick him.

'What you doing, slumming it round here?' says Nelly.

'Just a bit of business.'

'Monkey business, I expect. Ain't it about time you acted like a man and signed up?'

Harry's smile slipped. 'I got a medical dispensation. On account of me bad lungs.' He coughs. Totally fake. What a loser.

I look in disbelief at the cigarette in his hand. Nelly sneers.

'You're having a laugh,' she says. 'There ain't nothing wrong with your lungs. It must've cost you a pretty penny to buy that bit of paper.'

'Nelly, leave him alone,' says May.

Nelly shrugs and shuts up. I'm too tired to make conversation, so I sit here waiting for my body to seize up again now that I'm sitting down. But Nelly was right – the walk to the bus stop seems to have loosened me up and I feel OK. A bit achy, but I reckon I'll live.

May and Harry are sitting together. May's flirting like mad, ignoring the black looks Nelly is sending her. Harry is lapping it up, looking really cocky. I can't believe May fancies him. Does she really like that slicked-back hair and ridiculous-looking moustache? He takes a puff on his cigarette and I notice the yellow stains on his fingers. Ewww! That is soooo disgusting.

The ride back doesn't seem to take as long as the journey to work this morning. Harry follows us off the bus, his hand on May's shoulder.

'So, we going to win this dance competition next week darlin'?' he asks May. But before she answers, Harry has to let go of her when his way is blocked by a tall soldier.

'Watch where you're going, mate,' he snaps.

'I know where I'm going. Not sure about you though.'

Harry looks annoyed, but gets out of the taller guy's way. Nelly smiles up at the soldier.

'Hallo, Jock ,' she says. 'How's your nan?'

'Fine thanks, Nell. All right, May? Queenie?'

I stare at the soldier as he gets on the bus. It's not till he smiles and waves as the bus pulls off that I realise it's the guy I bumped into this morning. I smile back. He really is quite fit.

'I don't know who he thinks he is,' says Harry, straightening his tie. 'Just 'cause he's got a flipping stripe on his arm he reckons he's got some balls now.'

'Watch your mouth,' says Nell. 'At least he's got the nerve to fight.'

'He ain't doing no fighting,' he sneered. 'He's having his tea round his nan's every night.'

Nelly looks like she's going to slap Harry, but May steps in. 'Come on, leave it, all right?'

'Just for you, doll. I'll see you tomorrow yeah?'

'Yeah,' she smiles. 'Eight o'clock at the Palais. Bring your dancing shoes.'

Nelly rolls her eyes and walks off. I follow, and May catches up with us a couple of seconds later, coming in between us and linking arms so we take up the whole of the pavement and people have to walk into the road to get round us. No one seems to mind though as May is smiling and they can't help but smile back.

'I hope you know what you're doing, hanging around with that shifty little toe-rag, May Blake,' says Nelly.

'Don't fret, Nell.' says May. 'Harry's all right. He's the best dancer round here, and I've got me eye on that prize money.'

'You watch your step, that's all I'm saying.'

May laughs. 'What else am I going to be doing when we're dancing, eh?'

Nelly tuts. 'Just you keep an eye on what Flash Harry is doing. He's a bit too free with his hands, if you ask me. People see you with him and you'll be getting a reputation.'

May rolls her eyes. 'Oh Nelly, stop fussing. It's only a dance competition.'

Nelly sighs and gives up. 'Where's your ration book, Queenie?' she asks me. 'We need to get you registered at the shops. If we don't hurry up they'll be shut.'

I pat my pocket. 'It's right here.'

'Good. May, you run on and get the tea started. Spam fritters tonight.'

May pulls a face. 'I hate those things. They taste bloody awful.'

'It's all we've got in the house,' says Nelly. 'So unless you've got a better idea, stop moaning and get them in the pan. We won't be long.'

May lets go of our arms and hurries away. Nelly and me cross the road and head for the shops.

'Can't we buy something else if you don't like what we've got?' I ask. 'I've got some money.' I'm not sure how much it's worth, but there's some paper stuff in the purse, so it should be enough for some food shopping. I refuse to think about how long this money is supposed to last me. Or who it really belongs to.

Nelly shakes her head. 'It's not a matter of money, it's what rations we get. If you're thinking about using your cash to bring black market stuff into our house, you can think again, my girl. Those thieving beggars are making money by taking the food out of our boys' mouths you know, nicking supplies when all the decent menfolk are fighting for King and country.'

'Whatever. I only asked.' Why does she always have to go on? Can't she chillax? She should have my problems. 'I'm too tired to care what I eat anyway. Let's just get it over with.'

'Well, you should care. Our dad's out there, God knows where, risking his life for the likes of you.' Nelly turns her head away, wiping at her eyes.

Oh my God, I've made her cry! I feel awful. I realise this isn't just her dad Nelly's talking about. It's my dad's grandpa – my great-grandpa. I can't tell her that though. She'll think I'm nuts. I start to hear Gnarls Barkley singing *Crazy* in my head and like he says, I probably am.

'I'm sorry, Nelly. He'll be all right. Trust me. I know he will.'

She sniffs, acting like she isn't upset. 'What do you know? Got the ear of the Admiralty, have you? Know who's gonna live and who's gonna be blown to kingdom come, do you?'

'Not exactly,' I say slowly. 'But my gran always says you have to carry on as though it's all going to work out all right in the end, otherwise you'll go mad.' I'm glad I remembered that. That's exactly what I need to be doing right now as well. 'I'm trusting that your dad will come home safe after the war. Just like I'm sure you and May will be all right, and I'll find my way home in the end.'

'You make it sound like you're lost, or something.'

'That's exactly how I do feel at the moment,' I say.

'Why didn't your mum and dad send you to live with your gran while they're away?' she asks.

I nearly say 'they did', but stop myself just in time. I shrug.

'It wasn't convenient,' I say. 'So, are you going to show me these shops?' I hook my arm through Nelly's, like May did with me, and just like I do with my bestie – or rather ex-bestie Jess. Why did I have to go and think about that now? Isn't it weird how I can somehow go back over seventy years into ancient history, but can still remember what's happened in my own time, even though technically it hasn't happened yet?

Nelly looks surprised for a moment, and I think she's going to push me away, but she doesn't. 'Come on then, Queenie Posh. Let's see if we can get something for the larder. Truth be told, I'm sick of spam n'all.'

CHAPTER NINE

Registering at the shops was scary. I had no idea what to do. I kept waiting for someone to realise I shouldn't be here. Thank God Nelly knew what she was doing. I felt like an idiot, and I'm sure the old guys in the grocery and the butcher's shop looked at me like I was a criminal or something. If only they knew the truth, I'll bet they'd have had heart attacks.

Anyway, I let Nelly do the talking – she seemed to know everyone anyway – and I just stood there grinning like a right fool. I got my ration book sorted and came home with some food, so now I don't feel like I'm sponging off Nelly and May anymore. With any luck I won't be here for very long, so they might end up with a little bit more food, sort of like compensation for putting up with me. If I can just figure out how to get home …

The rations I got for the week were pathetic – honestly, I could eat that much in one meal, and that doesn't mean I'm a pig or anything. Not that I fancy eating any of it, because it all looks absolutely minging. I'm not sure about the nutritional value of the fatty bacon, or the lump of butter they gave me, and I'm not sure what I'm supposed to do with the loose tea leaves. Apparently teabags haven't been invented yet. And I don't use sugar. Oh well, I can give that to the girls for their cakes.

May served the spam fritters with a tin of really nasty peas – I think they're called 'marrowfat'. They were just as revolting as Nelly said they'd be. But I was so hungry I ate everything on my plate. I felt a bit sick afterwards, but that might have been because of the air raid …

The sirens start just as we finish washing up. I nearly drop the plate I'm drying. Nell catches it and puts it away in the cupboard in one smooth move.

'Wow! Awesome reflexes!'

'For Chrissakes, I wouldn't need them if you weren't so flipping clumsy. I told you we can't afford no breakages, so watch what you're doing.'

'Sorry,' I say, trying not to get annoyed with her. Doesn't she ever chill? We could've had a laugh about it, but she has to complain instead.

May grabs the tea-towel out of my hands and dries hers. 'There ain't no time for rowing, Nell. I'm sure she didn't do it on purpose.'

'No, I didn't.'

'There you go. Now, we'd better get shifted before Jerry gets here.' She turns to Nelly. 'They said on the radio it's going to be freezing tonight. We'd better get the old coats. Those blankets ain't going to keep us warm.'

'All right. Get down there and get the lamp on. It might help warm the place a bit.'

'Will you bring my coat?'

'Yeah, now get going, before we're blown to kingdom come.'

I follow Nelly into the hall to grab my jacket. As I reach for it on the hallstand I look in the mirror and catch a glimpse of Great-aunt Eleanor behind me. At last! I spin round, expecting to be back in Gran's hall, but Nelly is standing there, glaring at me. I nearly burst into tears.

'Is that all you've got?' Nell tuts at my jacket. 'That won't keep the cold out.' She pushes me out of the way and then almost dives into the mass of coats hanging on the stand. I move so that I can look in the mirror again, but it's just my own miserable face staring back at me.

Nell is muttering something but I can't hear what she's saying as her head's still buried in the coats. I step back just as she does. She's got her arms full of coats. She hands me one. 'Here, our nan's old coat. It'll keep the chill out.'

'Is that real fur?' I don't think I've ever touched real fur before. It feels gorgeous, but I don't think I should be liking it.

'Too right. Lovely bit of rabbit, that is. May's got our other nan's fox fur. I prefer grandad's old army coat meself. Here, hold that a minute.' She dumps the other fur coat, a lovely golden brown colour, in my arms and pulls the heavy woollen coat on. It comes down to her ankles. 'He was a big man,' she grins, pulling it round her and tying the belt and picking up her sister's coat. 'This old coat kept him warm in the trenches in the last war. I'll be snug as a bug in this.'

'I don't know if I should wear fur,' I say.

'Why? You allergic or something?'

'I don't think so, but aren't they illegal or something?'

That wipes the smile off Nelly's face. 'For gawd's sake, what you on about now? That's a good coat, that is, not some mangy old rag from down the market. And what do you mean, "illegal"? That was our nan's best coat, and since she died it's ours. There ain't nothing illegal in this house, so don't you go saying there is, right? What's the matter with you? You only wear mink, is that it, Miss Posh?'

Now what have I said? 'I told you, I'm not posh. I don't have any fur, nor does my mum. It's just ...' I stop, realising that my views on fur products are probably a modern thing, so Nelly's not likely to understand what I'm on about. Maybe I *should* pretend to be allergic, but I don't fancy having to sit out in the shelter in just this jacket.

'Well, we ain't got time to argue about it now,' Nelly pushes past me. 'You can wear it or freeze, I don't care. Make sure you shut the back door behind you. We don't want to come back and find Tiddles eating our rations.' And then she's gone.

There's a huge boom and the whole house shudders. I don't hang around. With the fur coats in my arms I sprint down the hall and through the kitchen, slamming the back door behind me. The sirens are still wailing, and now there's the distinct sound of aircraft flying over. I can hear the ack-ack-ack of the anti-aircraft guns, and as I run down the garden to the shelter I can see the lights searching the sky. Nelly is just in front of me, pushing aside the thick curtain inside the doorway. We pile inside and the curtain swishes back to block out the light from the lamp.

'There you are,' says May. 'You took your time.'

May takes her coat and puts it on. 'Thanks, love. Ooh, I do

love this old coat. When the war's over I'm gonna remodel it so's I can wear it up town.' She sits down next to her sister and looks at me. 'Don't you want to get that on, Queenie? It's blooming cold out here. If this goes on for long you'll be freezing your bits off.'

I look at the coat in my arms, torn between wanting to put it on and taking a stand against animal cruelty. I see Nelly glaring at me from the corner of my eye and decide I'd better go with the flow and worry about political correctness another time – or *in* another time. Ha! Get it? Oh crap, now I'm being stupid. It's bloody cold and the coat looks really cosy. I slip it on, feeling its heavy weight on my shoulders. The lining is silky as the coat settles around me.

'Your nan must have been a big woman too,' I say to Nelly as sit down opposite her and snuggle into the coat. Mmm, it feels so glamourous. I'm like a little kid dressing up in her mum's clothes.

'Yeah, Dad says she was a substantial woman,' says May. 'I'm glad we take after the other side of the family.'

'Queenie ain't never had a fur coat,' says Nell. 'Thought we'd nicked it, she did.'

May looks furious. 'Bloody cheek!'

'I did not!' I snap. 'Don't put words in my mouth, OK? Where I come from we've got animal rights and people who would freak if you wore this in public. I saw a picture once of some catwalk models who had blood thrown at them for wearing fur. It was gross.'

The sisters look at me as though I've gone mad. I glare back at them. I can feel my cheeks flushing, and I wish I've never said anything about this.

An almighty explosion shakes the whole shelter. It happens so quickly I don't have time to react.

'Jesus, that was close,' says Nelly. 'Wait for it …'

Before I can ask what we have to wait for, there's a load of clattering as debris rains down on the shelter roof, and I duck, holding my hands over my head, expecting the whole lot to fall in on us. Puffs of dust seep in under the door, making us cough. The whole ground is shaking, we're choking on the dust and the

72

noise is terrific.

What will Mum and Dad think if I just disappear forever? They might blame Gran. There'll be a police search – people will think I've been kidnapped or murdered or something. *Oh my God! This is getting serious. I've got to find a way home.* I curl up on the bench and covered my ears, trying to work out how on earth I can get back to my own time when I had no idea how I ended up in 1940 in the first place.

As the raid goes on and on, I wish I was at home, with Mum and Dad. I miss them so much. I'd hate it if I never saw them again. But then again, if I'm dead I won't know the difference, will I?

After what seems like ages, the noise is coming from further away.

'Sounds like Jerry's hitting the City now,' says Nell.

'Good,' says May. 'I'm busting for a pee. I'm going to nip out.'

'Is it safe?' I ask.

'Gawd knows. But if I don't go now, I'm going to wet meself.' She pulls aside the curtain and pushes open the door. I get a glimpse of lightbeams shining through the darkness, searching for planes. The buildings are black silhouettes, outlined by the orange glow of fires. The little patch of garden lit by the glow of the paraffin lamp is covered in dust, broken bricks and pieces of charred wood.

'Be careful!' I shout, as May trips on something and only just manages to keep her footing.

'I'm all right. Just shut that door before Jerry spots the light.'

Nell stands up and closes the door. 'She'll be all right. It's only a couple of yards to the lavvie.'

'I know,' I mutter under my breath, trying to stop my heart from racing right out of my body. 'I know.' I sit up. 'If it's all right to go out, can we go back in the house now?' I shift from one butt cheek to the other, trying to ease the ache from sitting on a hard wooden bench for hours.

'Not yet. We have to wait for the all-clear to sound. The planes could turn around any time, and if they've got any bombs left, the beggers will drop 'em anywhere. You might as

73

well get comfortable. We'll probably be here all night now.'

'I don't think I can sleep.' I draw my knees up to my chest, pulling the coat over my feet. Ah, that's warmer at least.

'You'd better try. We've still got to go to work in the morning – unless the factory gets hit. If you don't get no sleep, you'll be good for nothing. That's when girls get machine needles through their fingers.'

'Eww, that sounds gross.'

Nelly frowns. 'You keep saying that. What does it mean?'

'What?'

'Gross.'

I shrug. 'You know, horrible, nasty?'

'Then why don't you say so? I ain't never heard anyone say "gross" when they mean "horrible" before. Round here a "gross" is twelve dozen.'

'Really? I didn't know that. But I'm pretty useless as Maths. So, if a gross is twelve dozen, does that mean twelve times twelve? '

Nell shakes her head. 'You really are daft, ain't you?'

I can't help giggling at her face. Now I know where Great-aunt Eleanor got her collection of disapproving looks from.

The door opens and May comes back in. 'That's better,' she sighs. 'I thought I was going to burst.'

'You could always use the pot under the bunk,' says Nelly. 'You don't have to go out there.'

May wrinkles her nose. 'No thanks. That's the last resort, that is.'

I look under the bench where Nelly pointed. On the floor is a large china potty. For a moment it doesn't click, then I recognise it. The last time I saw it was on the windowsill at the top of the stairs in Gran's house. There, it's full of cactus plants. I remember when Gran first told me what it was, I laughed so hard I nearly wet myself, imagining Gran squatting over it and getting prickled by the sharp cactus needles. Mum told me off for being rude, but Gran thought it was hilarious too.

'That's your "gazunder"!' I say. That's what Gran calls it, because it 'goes under' the bed, ready to be used if someone needed to go in the night and didn't want to go outside to the toilet.

'That's right,' said May. 'And I ain't using it in front of you two. It ain't dignified.'

I don't think I could either. 'I know what you mean. My gran keeps spiky cactus in hers. You definitely don't want to be using that!'

May shrieks with laughter, just like Gran does. 'Oh my God,' she says (only it sounds more like 'gawd' with her accent). 'Prickly plants in a gazunder! Oh, don't! Ha ha ha!'

Nell tuts. 'You're as daft as each other, you two.' We just look at her, grinning like Cheshire cats.

The long, uninterrupted wail of the all clear starts up at last. 'Thank God,' says Nell. 'We can sleep in our own beds tonight. Let's get out of here before Jerry changes his mind again.'

We pile back into the kitchen and take off our big coats. The clock on the wall says ten thirty. I offer to put the coats back on the hall stand. Who knows? Maybe I'll just fall through it into the future. I approach it a bit nervously. I mean, what if it grabs me flings me to another time? I could end up anywhere. No, that's daft, as Nelly would say. I saw Great-aunt Eleanor in there earlier, so it must still be connected to my time somehow. I just need to figure it out. I hang the coats up, staring into the mirror, willing it to take me home. Nothing. Damn.

I'm exhausted and totally fed up, but go back to help the others finish tidying the kitchen before we go to bed. Nelly is as fussy about getting things done now as she is in the future, and I reckon it's a good idea to keep on her good side. When the kitchen is spick and span, we say goodnight and go to our rooms.

As I lie shivering in bed, I think about the day, and how different it's been from the way I spend my time in the twenty-first century. Working in the factory is sort of fun at the moment, but I can see that it could become really boring if I had to do it day after day, week after week. I've never particularly liked school, but I don't like the idea of having to leave to go to work, like Nelly and May did when they were only fourteen.

I yawn and turn over, snuggling under the covers. I really must start to work out how to get back to my time. But right now, I'm just sooo tired. Maybe when I wake up, I'll be home again …

CHAPTER TEN

It's still dark when I wake up. I know straight away I'm still in 1940, because May is shaking me awake.

'Come on, lazybones. Time to get up. Shift yourself, Queenie, or we'll miss the bus.'

I groan and turn over, pulling the covers over my head. 'Go away. It's the middle of the night.' How can she be so bloody cheerful this time of the morning, when it's freezing cold and miserable?

May laughs. 'Don't you country bumpkins get up at the crack of dawn to milk the cows?'

Not again. 'That joke is getting old, May. I told you, I don't live on a farm. Seriously this is not even dawn. It's still dark.'

'Come on, it's nearly Christmas. It's always dark this time of year. We still got to get to work, though, so shift your bum.' She tries to pull the covers off me, but I grab them back and roll myself up so she can't get them. I'm not getting out of here till I really have to. May gives up. 'Suit yourself, Lazybones. There's a nice warm cuppa downstairs, but if you don't get a move on, you won't have time to drink it. Nell says we ain't waiting for you today, so I hope you remember how to get to work on your own.'

Pants! I suppose I'd better get up then. I throw back the covers as May clatters down the stairs. Brrrrr! It's sooo cold! How do they stand it? How did I ever not notice central heating before?

I just about manage to drink half a lukewarm cup of tea and eat a slice of bread with a thin scraping of my precious butter ration before following the girls to the bus stop. I take a bit more notice of where we're going today, just in case I have to find my own way anytime. Not that I want to wander around in the dark on my own, but you never know. I'm scared that if I let May and Nelly out of my sight I'll get lost, and if I can't find my way back to the house I'll never find my way back to Gran. It makes me feel sick, just thinking about it.

We're at the bus-stop early in the end. I stand here shivering, thinking that I could have had a few more minutes in bed. But I don't say anything because Nelly will only have something sarcastic to say about it, and I'm not in the mood for another row with her. So I stamp my feet, trying to get warm and pull my collar up so that I can keep the icy wind off my neck. It was so bright and warm when I got to Gran's last week, it's even harder to accept this awful weather. Like walking from the sunshine into a giant fridge. Brrrrrr! I stuff my hands in my pockets and wish the bus would hurry up.

Just along the street is a newsagents. A bell tinkles as someone opens the door. I look round just as a tall soldier comes out with a newspaper tucked under his arm. He's lighting a cigarette, cupping hands to shelter the flame from his lighter. Ugh! Filthy habit! I've never understood why anyone would want to take up smoking. Some of the kids at school have, and they stink.

I'm just about to turn away when the soldier straightens up, taking a long drag from his cigarette. For a moment I think it's my dad and I nearly call out. But then I realise it can't be. Dad's safe in the twenty-first century, somewhere in France, fixing a computer system. Anyway, this guy is much younger than my dad. I feel even more miserable now. I wish it was Dad, come to rescue me. But he can't, can he? He probably doesn't even know I'm missing yet.

'Hello there.' I look up to see the soldier smiling at me. He definitely looks familiar.

'All right, Jock?' says May. Ah, of course. Now I remember him. Disappointment coils tight in my stomach. Just a friend of the girls, that's all. He still looks fit.

'Yeah, May. How about you?'

'Not bad. You going to the Palais tonight, or are you on duty?'

He grins at her. 'Got a couple of nights off, so I reckon I'll see you there.'

'Good,' says Nelly. 'You can stop her making a fool of herself. She's only trying to get Flash Harry to be her partner for the dance competition.'

Jock frowns. 'Bloody hell, May. You don't want to be seen with him. You'll get yourself a bad name.'

'Oh, don't you start n'all,' says May. 'I only want to dance with him. We'd be a shoe-in to win that prize, and it's well worth having.'

Jock shakes his head. 'You better watch yourself with him. I reckon your dad won't be none too happy about you stepping out with the likes of that toe-rag.'

May sticks her nose in the air. 'Well he ain't here and he didn't make you me uncle, so if you want to stay mates with me you'd better mind your own business, thanks very much.'

'He's only saying what we're all thinking, May,' says Nelly. 'That fella's bad news.'

'Oh, shut up, for Christ's sake! I'm sick of hearing it. It's only a dance. I can look after myself.'

Whoa! I've never seen May so bad-tempered. Even Nelly looks a bit shocked.

'Well, see you do,' she says.

Jock looks like he wants to say something else, but Nell shakes her head and he gives up. I shift my feet, cold and fed up. The movement catches his attention and he looks at me surprised, like he's forgotten I'm here. Nice. Make me feel better, why don't you?

Nelly sees him looking. 'This is Queenie,' she says. 'We didn't have time to introduce you yesterday.'

'Oh yeah, you're billeted with the girls, ain't you?' I nod. 'Nice to meet you.'

He holds out a hand and I reluctantly take mine out my warm pocket. Even though he's not wearing gloves, his large grip is warm as we shake hands. I get the weirdest feeling – like electricity has flowed between us, or does that sound too Mills and Boon? It's true though. I feel a tingling all the way up my arm and my heart starts to pump like I'm running, but I just stand there like an idiot. He must feel it too, because he drops my hand really quickly and steps back. Oh no, this isn't good. This sort of thing shouldn't be happening. I can't fancy a guy who was born decades before me. That's just not right. I take a deep breath, trying to think of something intelligent to say, but my mind is blank. I open my mouth and shut it again, and look at Nelly. She's got a smirk on her face.

'Well, it was nice to meet you, Queenie,' says Jock. 'I'll maybe see you girls at the Palais tonight then?' He's looking at May as he says it, but she ignores him, so Nelly says 'Yeah, all right, Jock. We'll see you later. Say hello to your nan for us.'

'Will do, Nell.' He takes another puff of his cigarette, then drops it. He grounds it out under his boot, then with a last quick nod he's marching off down the road just as the bus pulls up.

I can't tell you how many times in my life Gran has gone on about 'the good old days'. I stopped listening when I was about five. How was I to know that one day I'd actually end up here? I really wish I'd listened to her now. I definitely didn't believe all those stories about how great the dances were. I'm still not completely convinced. I mean, how can you have a good time in the middle of a war?

But here I am at the Palais, standing on the edge of a dance floor, wearing a borrowed dress from May, my hair pinned up, feeling really sophisticated, and at last I can see what Gran meant. The place is full of people – loads of them in uniform, and the rest are in gorgeous dresses and sharp suits. There's a fog of cigarette smoke in the air, giving the effect like a dry ice machine at a rave, only smellier. Not that I've been to any raves.

A big band is playing on the stage and couples are doing some amazing dancing, just like on *Strictly*. They're jitterbugging and jiving, and oh my God, May is out there with some guy and she is absolutely awesome!

I always thought that dancers on the telly all exaggerate the moves for effect, but now I know, the real thing is fantastic. The guys are picking the girls up and swinging them over their heads. The girls land on their feet and carry on dancing without missing a beat. Everyone's having a great laugh, even Nelly. I can't believe how much she's laughed since we got here, and she's not a bad dancer either. But May – well, all I can say is my gran didn't exaggerate and she is amazing.

At the end of the song some of the couples take a break, including Nell and the soldier she's been dancing with. He goes off towards the bar and she comes over to check on me. She's seen guys ask me to dance and I've turned them all down. Well, I don't how to do this stuff, do I? I'd look a right idiot. So I'm staying off the dance floor and just enjoying watching it all. The trouble is I'd really like to have a go. I love dancing. Maybe I'll get May to show me some of the moves at home.

'This is sick,' I say to Nell.

'You ain't one of them Bible bashers who don't hold with dancing, are you?'

'Of course not! I'd love to have a go, but I'd probably land on my backside.'

'Well, why did you call it sick, then?'

'Because it's fantastic,' I laugh, realising that 'sick' doesn't mean the same thing here. 'Sick is good.' That's another one for my list of words that mean different things in 1940. Like 'gay' – here it means happy, nothing to do with sexual orientation. I found that out when Daisy at work was talking about her son being gay and I asked if there were a lot of gays around. It took me ages to realise she was talking about something else completely.

Nell shakes her head. 'We might both be talking English, Queenie, but you make it sound like another language sometimes. If it weren't such a daft idea, I'd think you must be a Nazi spy, 'cause you don't talk like no Englishwoman I ever met.'

'I am not a spy,' I say. I wish she'd stop this. I could end up getting arrested if someone hears her. 'Don't you dare say things like that about me. I'm British, and proud of it!' I'm not sure where that came from, but surprisingly, I mean it. Before I came here, I hadn't been bothered. But after everything I've seen over the last couple of days, how much everyone is suffering to beat Hitler, I really am very glad I'm British.

'All right, keep your hair on. I suppose it's just the funny way you talk in the country.'

Yeah, like she really believes that. With a sigh, I turn back to the dancers. Another song comes to an end and the crowd claps and whistles. I join in, 'Woohoo!' feeling the excitement and sheer happiness of the crowd. It's infectious, I can't help laughing out loud. 'This is amazing. Do you do this every week?'

'When there ain't a raid on,' Nell nods.

'What happens if the sirens go now? We won't be able to hear them.'

'Someone'll come in and make an announcement and we all pile into the nearest shelters or down the underground. A couple of weeks ago we ended up in the same shelter as most of the band, and they kept on playing. We had quite a party.'

'Well, I hope there isn't a raid tonight.'

'Too bloody right. Here, hold my drink. I've just spotted a fella who promised me a dance last week.' She hands over her glass of shandy and waves at someone on the other side of the dance floor. A man in the grey-blue uniform of the Air Force sees her and waves back. Nell dodges through the dancers and he meets her in the middle of the floor. They chat for a few seconds, oblivious to the people dancing around them. Nell's eyes are sparkling as the guy takes her in his arms and they start jiving. Wow! She looks so different, laughing and dancing like she doesn't have a care in the world. Nell takes everything so seriously: it's good to see her having a good time.

'Hallo, darlin'. You all on your own?'

I jump as someone speaks in my ear, his hot breath far too close. I nearly drop Nell's drink, but manage to keep it upright – just.

'Sorry, love. I didn't mean to scare you. I just thought you looked a bit lonely all on your own. It's Queenie, ain't it? How about a dance?' Harry, his black hair slicked back, his suit shiny, puts his clammy hand on my shoulder.

I twist a bit, pretending to be turning round so I can talk to him, but really I just want to get his paws off me. Hasn't he ever heard of personal space? Apparently not, because he doesn't take the hint. He moves closer. I might just have to pour

Nell's drink over him.

'No thanks. We only do Morris dancing where I come from.'

That was completely lost on him. He gives me a slimy smile. His teeth are yellow, just like his fingertips. God, he really doesn't realise how repulsive I find him. 'Come on, Queenie, it'll be a laugh.'

I shake my head; I'm not going to argue with him.

'Queenie, eh? You look like a princess to me.'

Ewww! This is sooo embarrassing. I hope no one I know can see me. Oh, hang on, all my friends haven't been born yet.

'So, your majesty, are we going to have a dance?'

'No, seriously, I'm looking after my friend's drink.'

'Aw, come on, darlin'. It'll be all right on the table there.' He takes the glass from me and puts it on a table. 'There you go,' he says. 'Now we can dance.'

'But I can't,' I say, pulling back when he takes my hand and leads me into the crowd. 'Honestly, I've never done this before. You're going to regret it, trust me.'

The music changed to a slower beat just as Harry spins round and pulls me close. I lose my balance and land against him. 'Umph! Sorry.' I try to step back, but he holds me tighter. The wiry little twit is stronger than he looks. And I think he must have had a bath in his aftershave. I try not to gag. Mind you, if I throw up all over him it will make my point, won't it? I hold my head away from him, trying to find some fresh air. I don't want to get any of his greasy hair product on me either. I wriggle, trying to get loose.

'That's it, darlin', shake it for Harry boy,' he says. Can he really be so thick? 'You're lovely, you are.'

I don't feel lovely. I feel stupid. And he is starting to really annoy me now. 'I can't dance,' I say. 'And I don't want to, so bloody let me go.'

'Don't worry, darling, no need to be shy. I'll lead, you follow. It's easy,' he says, smirking and letting his hand wander down my back towards my bottom.

That does it, I'm going to kick him in the –

'Excuse me, mate, I think May wants a dance.' A soldier taps him on the shoulder. Next to him is May, who winks at me.

'Come on, Harry, you keep telling me what a twinkle-toes you are. Well, now you can show me. Queenie, Jock'll look after you.'

At first, I think Harry is going to argue, but May isn't having any of that. She grabs his hand and peels him off me.

'Those hands of yours are going to get you into trouble one of these days, Harry, me lad.' says May, taking my place. 'Now keep 'em to yourself, or you'll be explaining a black eye to your mum.'

They dance off, looking very impressive. The two of them are obviously good at that sort of thing, they make it look so effortless, though I'm definitely going to have a talk to May if she thinks Harry's all right. I give Jock an apologetic smile, but he didn't notice because he's watching them. Mmm. Looks like he doesn't trust Harry either. Good. After a bit he remembers I'm here. He looks a bit sheepish and offers me his hand.

Tempted as I am to take it – he's a lot fitter than Harry after all – I hold up my hands and step back. 'You really don't have to dance with me, Jock,' I say. 'I'm a terrible dancer. I'll probably step on your toes.'

'That's all right,' he says. 'We all have to start somewhere. May used to be diabolical. I had to give her lessons.'

'Really?' I'm so surprised I let him take me in his arms. Ooh, nice! Before I know it he's leading me round the dance floor in what I think is a waltz. It's not exactly *Strictly*, but it's not as hard as I thought, and it feels nice being close to Jock like this. 'So, you and May, eh? What hasn't she been telling me?'

Jock laughs, a rich, warm sound. Couples around us turn to look, smiling at his amusement. 'Nah. Me and May go back a long way – my nan lives over the road from her place. I think I'm the brother she never had.' The slight twist of his mouth as he smiles tells me how he feels about that. Ahh, so that's how it is. Poor Jock. I know what that's like.

I think about Simon, and how I was always pretending not to care, especially when he was with other girls. I feel really sorry for Jock. I wish I could make him feel better, but what can I say, it's hopeless. Gran married a guy called Billy, not Jock. I don't know when she met him or anything. At least it won't be Harry; I'd hate to think of that slimeball being my Grandpa.

I look up at Jock and smile. He's very tall, making me feel tiny, even in these high heels (I'm getting the hang of them – haven't fallen over yet). He's got a nice face, with lovely brown eyes. There's something about him that looks familiar. Who does he remind me of?

'Why the frown?' he asks.

I feel myself blushing. 'Sorry, Jock, I just … you remind me of someone, and I can't figure out who.'

He shrugs. 'I reckon I've got one of them faces. Ordinary. Look like everyone, me.'

'No, you're not ordinary. It … you've got a nice face, Jock.'

He grins. 'Nice? Not handsome?'

I swat at his shoulder. 'Don't push your luck, mister,' I laugh. 'I was just saying you look like someone I know. But I can't for the life of me think who it is.'

'I've got loads of cousins round here. Maybe you're thinking of one of them.'

'I haven't been here long enough to know many people, so I don't think it's that.'

He raises an eyebrow – and suddenly I realise who he reminds me of.

'Jock?'

'Yea?'

'You haven't got a cousin called Bill, have you?'

He stops, right there in the middle of the dance floor. 'You're joking, right?'

'Er, no.'

'Did May put you up to this?'

'No, why would she? I don't understand.'

'It must have been May, or Nell. They both know.'

'Know what?' Couples are starting to bump into us now. 'Look, why don't we get out of everyone's way?'

He nods and with a warm hand on my back guides me off the dance floor. 'Want a drink?' he asks.

'I'd really prefer some fresh air,' I say. My eyes are stinging from the cigarette smoke and I suddenly go dizzy. For a minute

I think I'm going back to the future, everything's going all wavy and weird. I panic. I mean, what if I end up in the same place? Is this building going to be there in the twenty-first century? Or will I find myself in a strange house, or office, or shop? Or the middle of a bloody great traffic junction?

'You all right, love?' Jock asks, peering at my face. 'You're as white as a sheet.'

Everything comes back into focus. I don't know whether to be pleased or cry my eyes out. 'Uh, yeah. Thought I was going to get sucked into a wormhole there. Just need some air.' I leave Jock standing there and head for the door. I can't believe I just said that. How stupid did that sound?

Outside on the dark street, I take deep breaths of the frosty air, blowing out clouds of vapour as I try to calm down.

Jock has followed me out. 'Do you want me to get the girls?'

'No, honestly, I'm all right. I just went a bit dizzy, that's all. I'm OK now.' I smile at him. 'But thanks anyway.'

'If you're sure,' he looks doubtful.

'It's cool.'

He takes his jacket off. 'Yeah, bleeding freezing,' he says. 'You'll catch your death. Here, put this round you.'

'No, I meant …' I start to giggle. 'I didn't mean it literally.' His jacket is warm from his body. It's so sweet of him. He'll get cold now, standing there in his shirt.

'I don't know what you're on about, Queenie. You're a funny girl, ain't you?'

'Rosie,' I say.

'Eh?'

'My name's Rosie. May and Nelly call me Queenie because they know loads of Roses already.'

'So how did they come up with Queenie?'

I smile. 'On account of me being so posh, innit?'

Jock laughs. 'Yeah, you're a right Queenie. So, nice to meet you, Rosie. I'm Bill.'

'Sorry?'

'You didn't think Jock was me real name, did you? You're not the only one who has to put up with a nickname.'

'Bill? Really? But …'

'Yeah, just like me old dad and granddad, God rest 'em. All Bill McAllisters. They decided I needed a nickname, so as not to get me confused with the old fellas. I thought Nell or May had told you, and you were teasing me.'

Whoa, hold on! 'Did you say Bill McAllister?'

'Yeah,' he nods. 'That's why they call me Jock – on account of me having a Scotch name. Mind you, as far as I know all my family come from London. Always have done.'

I put a hand to my forehead. It can't be!

'Hey, are you sure you're all right?' he asks. 'I reckon I'd better get the girls for you.'

'No. No don't. It's just …' I can't stop staring at him.

Bill McAllister … Oh. My. God. I've just been dancing with my grandfather!

I don't remember my Grandpa Bill, he died when I was a baby. But I've seen pictures, and everyone says Dad is the spitting image of him. It was that eyebrow-raising thing that reminded me so much of Dad. He does it exactly like that. And his eyes are the same, except Dad has some wrinkles and lines round them these days. But hey, Dad is *old* – at least fifty-five. Bill's not much older than me.

'You wouldn't believe me if I told you,' I say. 'I don't believe it myself. This is seriously awesome.' I hug myself, the itchy wool of his soldier's jacket making my skin tingle. Bill looks at me as if I'm mad and I start to laugh, really laugh, so hard that I have to clutch my belly and tears are streaming down my face.

Bill stands there watching me. The poor guy doesn't know what to do. People are coming in and out of the Palais, some of them calling out to Bill, most of them thinking I'm drunk or something. I can't help it. If only they knew. *I'm standing here with my grandpa.* No one else in the whole wide world knows. He definitely reminds me of my dad, so I suppose that's what dad looked like when he was younger. I never realised he was quite fanciable, I always wondered what Mum saw in him. Now here I am, trying not to fancy my own grandpa! What am I like?

'What the hell's wrong with her?' It's Nelly, looking all disapproving, like Great-aunt Eleanor. If only she knew.

'God knows. She just went off on one,' says Bill, smiling despite himself. 'She ain't drunk, but something's tickled her funny bone.'

Nelly tuts. 'I swear she's a bleeding nutcase, that one.'

'She's all right, Nell. At least she's happy.'

Before she can reply the air-raid siren goes off. Everyone stops and looks up. Straight away the searchlights are beaming into the darkness. I take a deep breath, trying to calm down. This is serious stuff now, so I'd better sort myself out. Bill hands me a clean white hankie and I wipe my face and blow my nose.

'Feeling better?' he asks.

'Yes, thanks.' I go to give it back to him, but realise he won't want my snot in his pocket. 'I'll, er, wash it and let you have it back.'

'Fair enough. Now, we'd better get down the shelter. You coming, Nell?'

People are pouring out of the Palais, and heading off in different directions.

'I'll find May. You all right with her?' She points at me. 'She's still ain't used to raids. I can hang on to her if you like.'

'Na, don't worry. I'll look after her. You get May, and we'll see you later.'

'Thanks, Jock.' She glares at me. 'You behave yourself. This ain't no time for hysterics, my girl.'

I try to look serious, but the effect is spoiled by a hiccup. Bill laughs as Nelly rolls her eyes and turns back into the Palais to find May.

'Shouldn't we wait for them?' I ask.

'Don't worry. They'll be all right. Come on, or the nearest shelters will be full up.' He grabs my hand and pulls me along the street just as we hear the heavy drone of the bombers overhead.

CHAPTER ELEVEN

The first shelter we get to is full, so we keep walking. The anti-aircraft guns have started up now, and somewhere in the distance I can hear bombs landing with a *whoomph*. Bill quickens his pace, almost dragging me along. I do my best to keep up with him. The only lights are the beams searching the sky and the traces of the bullets aimed at the bombers.

A woman trips over a kerb and cries out as she falls. A couple step over her, they're not stopping for anyone. I pull on Bill's hand and he turns round. Between us we help her to her feet.

'Are you all right?' I ask. 'I can't believe how rude that couple were.' The woman leans on me, still a bit shaken. Her knees are bloody.

'Oh my goodness, look at the state of my nylons,' she cries.

I can't believe she's more bothered by the holes in her stockings than the horrible grazes she's got, but there is a war on, I suppose. Nylons are like gold-dust according to May.

'Move along now!' A guy in a tin hat with ARP painted on it is yelling through a megaphone. 'Into the shelters with you. Don't hang about.'

'Doris, where are you?'

The woman looks up. 'Over here, Alf.'

An older man hurries over. 'Oh thank goodness. Are you all right, old girl?'

We step back and leave them to it. Bill takes my hand again as the woman calls out her thanks. I smile at her and follow Bill.

We run through the streets, the noise of the guns and bombs getting louder. I start to wonder if we'll find a shelter. It's not exactly safe out here, and these shoes are definitely not made for running!

Just when I think I'm going to run out of breath completely, we arrive at a shelter – a great big, brick-built thing in the middle of a road. We duck inside. It's almost full of families and couples, and even more are coming in behind us. Bill and I settle down next to a woman with a baby in her arms and a toddler standing by her on the bench clinging to her shoulder. The little one is fast asleep, but the toddler is crying.

'It's all right, Tommy. You be a brave boy now and sit down here. Try and get some sleep, darling.'

'Come here, love, I'll give you a cuddle.' An older woman tries to take little Tommy onto her lap, but he's having none of that. He clings to his mum and cries louder.

'Will you shut that kid up?' yells an old guy in the corner. 'It's bleeding bad enough having to put up with Jerry, without your snotty kid whining all night.'

'Well he ain't going to shut up with you shouting like that and frightening the poor little mite,' says the older woman. 'Leave him alone.' There's a general murmur of agreement and the old man gives up. Tommy is getting tired and his crying subsides to a soft grizzle as he wipes his nose on his poor mum's shoulder. She doesn't take any notice. I think she's as tired as he is.

I haven't been in one of these big shelters before, and the first thing I notice is the smell – stale sweat, cigarettes, and a sort of damp tar. It's pretty gloomy in here, with just a couple of lanterns hanging from nails along the walls. There must be about thirty people in here, and we're all squeezed up against each other along benches on each side. Little Tommy is literally being held upright between me and his mum. I can feel him get heavier as he falls asleep. I'm also noticing a weight across my shoulders and realise that Bill has his arm around me.

I'm not sure how I feel about that. Is he trying it on, or is he being protective? If I didn't know he's my grandpa, I'd probably want it to be more than just looking out for me. But I do know, and he doesn't, so it's really weird.

I look up at him, not sure what I'll do if he's looking all google-eyed at me. No worries on that score though, he's got his head back and eyes closed. Everyone is quiet now, some of them asleep, their heads on their chests or resting on the nearest shoulder. A few people are looking tense, flinching at every bang and pop outside. A couple more are using torches to read by. There's a huge crash, not far away, and everyone jumps. I would've fallen off the bench if Bill hadn't been holding onto me. Little Tommy starts to slip and I grab him. Bless him, he sleeps through it all. I slide him onto my lap and he snuggles in. His mum looks grateful for the break.

'Blimey, that was close,' someone says as we all settle back against the wall.

'Not 'alf. I reckon that was Percy Street.'

'Christ, I hope not. My old dad lives down there. He won't come to the shelter – says he won't give Hitler the satisfaction.' She stands up. 'I'd better get round there, make sure he's all right.'

'Don't be daft, woman. You can't go out there.'

She hesitates. The noise out there is horrible. The drone of the planes, the high-pitched whine of the bombs dropping, the ack-ack-ack of the anti-aircraft guns, all combined with shouts and hisses and pops. It sounds like total chaos. The woman looks miserable, and sits down again, bowing her head as though she's praying. Someone pats her knee. 'Don't worry, love. I'm sure he'll be all right. It probably weren't anywhere near Percy Street. You stay here where it's safe.'

Good call. I wouldn't go out there, I can tell you. At least I don't think so. How would I feel if it was a relative of mine?

'I hope May and Nelly are all right,' I whisper to Bill. Maybe I should be praying for them too?

'They'll be fine, don't worry,' he says softly. 'They know what they're doing. And I'll see you right n'all 'cause I promised Nell, didn't I? If anything happens to you, she'll have my knackers in a bag.'

'Eww! Nice picture you're painting there, Bill! But I doubt it. Nell hates me.'

'Don't talk daft. Nell's all right. She's got a good head on her shoulders, my nan says. Mind you, she frightens the life out of me,' he smiles, and I feel a bit better. It's not just me then.

'She's like a strict teacher, isn't she?' I can't resist it.

'Yeah, now you come to mention it. I can imagine her giving someone a right caning.'

I giggle. 'Stalking down the corridors in her mortar board and gown while everyone gets out of the way.'

'Yeah. I've got a sergeant like that. When he's on the prowl, lads will dive through open windows to get away from him.'

'Do you like being a soldier?'

He shrugs. 'It's all right. Better than doing nothing. I suppose I could've got work down the docks, but I didn't fancy it. It's sod's law I ended up defending the bloody place. I was hoping the army would get me out of here.'

'Don't you like living in London?'

'It's all right. I wanted to see other places, though, just to check it was the best place for me. And I do like being a soldier. I feel like I'm doing something important, you know?'

'Don't you get scared?'

'Christ, yeah. Everyone gets scared, Rosie. You'd be daft not to. But at least if Jerry comes up the Thames I know how to use me gun and can do me best to send him back where he came from. We all feel like that. It's a rotten job, but me and the lads would rather be ready than sitting on our backsides learning bloody German.'

'It won't come to that.'

'Well, we hope not. But who can tell?'

He looks up, and we both listen to the sound of the battle raging outside. I want to tell him it won't last for ever, but who's going to believe me when we're sitting here in the middle of it all?

Another big bang, followed by the sound of debris crashing on the roof of the shelter. Dust showers down on us. I cover Tommy's head to protect him. He looks so sweet, except for the twin lines of snot running out of his nose.

'Hey, where did I put that hanky?'

'In the pocket I think,' Bill fumbles round near my hip and pulls it out for me.

'Thanks,' I say, a bit embarrassed. Have I just been groped? I don't think he meant anything by it. Now if it had been that slimy Harry I'd have been sure and definitely have smacked him one. Bill moves his hand back to my shoulder, and I give him the benefit of the doubt. I'm quite pleased actually, to think my grandpa isn't taking advantage of the situation.

I wipe Tommy's nose as best I can without disturbing him.

'Nice little tyke, ain't he?' says Bill.

'Aren't they all when they're asleep?'

'I suppose. They're a handful at that age, I can tell you.'

'How do you know?'

'I've got half a dozen brothers and sisters. I don't half miss them.'

'Where are they?'

'Me older sister is married and lives over Clapham way. Mum got evacuated with the littl'uns 'cause the youngest is about this one's age.'

Tommy's mother stirs. 'I'm going next week,' she says. 'My husband didn't want me to go, but I got a telegram yesterday. His ship has gone down with all hands. I ain't risking losing my babies now.' Her eyes fill up with tears, and so do mine.

'I'm so sorry,' I say.

She sniffs. 'Don't be. He was a sod. I don't reckon being in a war would've made him any better. Now I know he's not coming back I can make the best of it for the kiddies. I'm just scared we'll be blown to kingdom come before I get out of London. I'll never forgive myself for staying here, putting them through all this.'

Well, that was unexpected. I glance at Bill and he raises his eyebrows. I don't know what to say, but the baby in her arms is stirring, and the woman turns her attention to it.

'So, where's your mum and the kids?'

'Some place out in the middle of nowhere in Wales.'

'That's nice,' I say.

'That's not what Mum says. She says it's a pokey little place and the locals all talk funny. She can't understand a word they say. It's miles to the nearest town, and there's nothing but mud and trees everywhere.'

'Well, I suppose it might seem a bit different from London. But, hey, at least they're safe.'

'Yeah, I suppose so. Where are you from, Rosie? You ain't

from London, that's for sure.'

'Wiltshire. And no, I don't live on a farm.'

'But why come here? I mean, you'd've been better off becoming a land girl, wouldn't you? London ain't no place for a young girl who ain't used to it.'

'Tell me about it,' I sigh. 'But sometimes we just don't have any choice. I was only going to buy a charger, but I fell into a space-time vortex or something in Gran's hall and ended up ...' Oh God. Did I really just say that? Bill is staring at me like I'm an alien, so I must have done. I feel my stomach knotting up. The people around us are either sleeping or chatting softly with their neighbours, so I don't think anyone else heard me. But Bill did, and it's clear he doesn't know what to say.

'Bill?'

He sighs and shakes his head. 'I'm starting to see what Mum means. You country folk talk right funny sometimes, don't you?'

Phew, maybe I got away with it.

'There's nothing wrong with being different. Life would be dead boring if we were all the same.'

'But there probably wouldn't be no wars though, eh? If we was all the same there wouldn't be nothing to fight about, would there?'

'Good point.'

We sit here, me cradling little Tommy, Bill's arm round me, lost in our own thoughts. The old man in the corner is snoring loudly. Someone near him laughs. 'Bleeding hell, he's making more noise than that poor kid did. Silly old sod. Give him a poke.'

'Oh leave him. At least while he's snoring he ain't moaning.'

I don't know if I'm just getting used to it, but the noise outside seems to be lessening. Finally, the all-clear sounds. A collective sigh of relief runs round the shelter and people stand and collect their things. I stay where I am, not wanting to disturb Tommy, but he senses something's happening and starts to wake up. He takes one look at me and wails for his mum.

'It's all right, Tommy. Your mum's here, see?' I point, and

he wriggles off my lap and attaches himself to her leg.

'Do you need any help?' I ask her.

She shakes her head. 'No thanks, love. Ta very much for holding him for me, but we'll be all right now. Our place is just round the corner. I'll get them home and start packing. Please God, we'll be down at my sister's in Kent by tomorrow night.'

'Well, good luck. Bye, Tommy.'

The little boy gives me shy wave as they leave the shelter. I stand up and stretch, and shiver. Holding Tommy had kept me nice and warm. Now he's gone I can really feel the cold. Bill stands up and nods his head towards to door. I follow him out, feeling guilty because I've still got his jacket on.

'Here, you'd better have this back,' I start to take it off, but he stops me.

'It's all right. You keep it. It won't take long to get you back home. If we walk fast I'll soon warm up.'

'Are you sure?'

'Well, I wouldn't say no if you wanted to cuddle up a bit while we walk,' he grinned.

I laugh. 'So long as you don't get any ideas Billy-boy.'

'In this weather? Not a chance,' he says. He puts his arm round my shoulders and I put my arm round his waist. He's really tall, so I barely come up to his chin. 'Come on, it ain't far. You know the drill.'

'What drill?'

'Don't hang about. Watch your step. Keep your eyes peeled for incendiaries and unexplodeds, and don't trip over the hoses.'

'Oh right. *That* drill.' Around us the sky is glowing orange from the building fires.

Bill looks grim. 'Looks like the docks got it again.'

The air is heavy with smoke. I hang on to his solid presence as we make our way along the crowded street. As we turn a corner, there's chaos in front of us.

The road ahead is in ruins. A man is pulling up bricks and wood and flinging them aside. Others join him and soon everyone is scrabbling in the rubble.

'Oi! Give us an 'and! Someone's stuck down 'ere!'

Bill immediately starts organising a line to pass stuff from hand to hand. I stand here, watching, not knowing what to do.

'Don't just stand around gawping, girl! Get over here and help out,' a woman shouts at me from the middle of the line.

'Sorry,' I run over and join in. Someone immediately shoves a lump of concrete into my hand and I pass it on. 'Do you know who's down there?'

'It don't matter. Whoever it is needs help, don't they? The quicker we get 'em out the better. Let's just hope they're still in one piece.'

We carry on passing bricks and bits of wood and metal from hand to hand. I don't know how long we're there, it could be a few minutes or a few hours. Every now and then someone shouts for quiet and we stop and listen. I hold my breath, willing them to hear something. My arms are aching and my hands are scratched and sore, but no way will I give up until everyone else does. I remember the news reports from earthquake zones, and I realise now how awful it is to be searching for signs of life in the rubble. Even worse to be stuck underneath it all. I start to pray. 'Please find them. Please let them be all right.' Sweat runs down my forehead into my eyes, and when I wipe my face with the sleeve of Bill's jacket I realised it's filthy with dust and ash. I hope he doesn't get into trouble with his sergeant.

'How much longer can this go on?' I ask the man next to me in the line.

'As long as it takes, my girl. There're people down there. If it takes all night, we'll get 'em out.'

'I wasn't complaining,' I say. 'I just wish they'd find them.'

We carry on, moving rubble from hand to hand. In the streets around us other teams are fighting fires and the searchlights carry on seeking out stray bombers in the night sky. There's an occasional crash as a building collapses. The air is thick with dust and soot and the smell of wood-smoke.

A lorry races past the end of the road, followed by a fire engine.

'What's all that about?' someone asks an Air Raid Warden as he jogs past, heading in the same direction.

'UXB near the gasworks,' he shouts, not stopping.

'Oh Christ.'

I'm just about to ask what a UXB is when there's a bright, blinding flash. I drop the chunk of wood I've just been passed.

A huge explosion rips through the air, sucking the air out of my lungs. I'm flung across the rubble on the hot blast.

I land in a heap and curl up in a ball with my hands over my head, waiting for the world to collapse on me.

'Rosie!' Bill is there, picking me up like I'm a little kid. 'Jesus Christ! Are you all right.'

'I ... I think so,' I mutter into his shirt. 'What was that?' I look up, and behind Bill's worried face I can see an even brighter glow.

'The gas works. We'd have been walking by it by now if we hadn't stopped here.'

There's a shout behind us. In the area where we had been clearing rubble a man is calling us over. 'I heard her! She's down there all right. Come on, everyone. We've got to get this lot moved so we can get her out.'

We start clearing again. Even though we're all tired (and I'm covered in bruises from my unscheduled trip across the bombsite), we work quicker, knowing there's a good chance of getting someone out of there alive. After a few minutes they call for quiet again. A couple of men, Bill included, are hanging down into the hole we've created. We all crowd round.

Bill pulls himself out, grimacing in frustration. 'I'm too big. There's not much room down there. We need someone smaller to get in and clear the way.'

CHAPTER TWELVE

I look around. It's obvious who's the smallest. My hand goes up before I have time to think. 'Can I help?'

'Don't be daft, girl.'

'No, Rosie, it's too dangerous.'

'Let her have a go.'

'She's just a kid.'

Now if there's one thing I hate is being told I can't do something because I'm a girl or because I'm too young.

'Look, I've been potholing with my dad, and I've done a first-aid course.' The caving trip was ages ago, but I loved it, and I got my Brownie first-aider badge when I was ten. But seriously, even that must count for something. I reckon I can remember how to do a leg splint if I need to.

No one else comes forward, so in the end I'm the only option. I take off Bill's jacket and kick off my shoes. May's dress isn't the most practical gear to be wearing, but there's not much I can do about that.

'Here, love, you don't want to ruin those stockings,' says the woman who'd yelled at me earlier. She and another woman use their coats to shield me as I take them off. Bill is actually blushing as he takes them and puts them in his pocket.

Someone ties a rope round my waist and gives me a torch. 'There's a woman down there in the cellar, a few feet to the right, I reckon. See if you can get to her. If you can get in, we should be able to get her out.'

'Take this.' Someone gives me a canvas bag. I have a quick look inside. First aid stuff. A flask and a pack of sandwiches. I loop the bag over my head and shove the torch inside.

'Can you shine some light in while I'm going down?' I ask. 'I want to keep my hands free until I get to the bottom.'

'Good idea. Ready?'

Bill's looking like he wants to stop me. I stand on tiptoes and kiss his cheek. 'It'll be a doddle.' I say. 'Don't worry.' He can't see that I've got my fingers crossed. What the hell am I doing? 'I've got to do this, Bill. It might be the reason I'm here.'

'What you on about, girl?' he says, starting to get angry.

'Nothing,' I say. 'It's just that someone's got to do it, and it looks like I'm the only one who can. Maybe it's my destiny.'

'Bleeding hell, Rosie. I swear you're a strange one. Are you sure you're up to this?'

'Definitely,' I say, nodding. I'm trying to convince myself as well as Bill. 'Let's do this.'

Reluctantly he steps back.

'You go careful, now, or the girls will blame me.'

I smile at the thought of this tall soldier being frightened of two teenaged girls.

They lower me gently down through the hole until my bare feet touch damp earth. I take out the torch and switch it on.

'Hello? Can you hear me?' I call. I hear a soft groan in answer. I shine it in the direction of the noise. There's a great heap of debris. I start shoving it out of the way, but as I move a big bit of wood I've just moved shifts towards me. I scream, and scramble out of the way. When it settles I've even less room.

'Rosie!'

'I'm all right,' I call up. 'Can you lower some buckets down on ropes to take some of this rubble away?'

Within seconds I'm loading buckets and they're pulling them out. I work steadily, clearing some space. I leave the bigger pieces in place. They look like they're holding a ton of other stuff up, and I'm worried if I try to move them the whole lot will come down on us.

All the time I'm talking to the woman on the other side of the blockage. 'Don't worry. I'm coming. We'll get you out. It won't be long now. You'll be all right, I promise.'

She's crying softly now, and it's breaking my heart. Oh God, please let me get her out.

I pull on something and it shoots out and whacks me on the

head. I fall back, dropping the torch and knocking over an empty bucket which clatters really loudly in the small space. The woman screams and above my head people are shouting down, wanting to know what's happened.

Oh, my head! I put up a hand and feel something warm and sticky in my hair. 'I'm all right,' I call out.

At least, I think I am. I sit up slowly and everything starts spinning. I'm feeling really sick. I take a deep breath and blow it out. I've got to do this. I can't give up now. I pick up the torch and point it towards where I've been working and immediately drop it again. It goes out as it lands on the floor, leaving me blinking in the darkness. I scramble around on my hands and knees until I find it, telling myself I didn't see what I just saw. When I finally find it I switch it on. My hands are shaking.

The beam of light shines on a gleaming red car. This isn't a bombed out basement, and that's definitely not an old-fashioned car. I'm in an underground car park. I move the light and it picks up other cars. On the wall is a sign saying 'Have you paid and displayed?'

Am I dead? Did that bang on my head kill me? No, I can't be. You don't die and go to a car park, do you? If I was dead there'd be a light at the end of a tunnel or something, right? If I'm not dead, I must be back in the future. *Woohoo!* I start to grin, so relieved I've got back, wherever I am. But just as I stand up and start to walk towards the exit I hear her again – the woman who's trapped in the basement. I look round and behind me I see the hole I've been working in, shimmering.

I tell myself she'll be alright. They know she's there. Someone will dig her out. She groans again. I feel a huge knot in my stomach as I stand there, half way between the past and my own time. This might be my only chance to get home. I *have to* go, don't I?

The knot in my stomach tightens, my head starts to throb. What if I go, and they can't find someone else small enough to help rescue that poor woman? I could be her only chance.

I can't do it. I can't just walk away and leave her. The hole is shrinking. I step back into it, not letting myself think about how close I've been to getting home; not letting myself wonder if I'll ever get another chance to leave.

'It's OK,' I call out. 'I'm going to get you out.' I start digging again and don't stop until I've created a tunnel through the debris.

At last I push through and my hand grasps thin air. 'I'm through!' I shout. Behind me I can hear a muffled cheer from above. In front of me the woman grabs my hand.

'Oh thank God! Help me, please. It's so dark down here.'

'Hang on,' I pull my hand back and get the torch. 'Here.' She takes it, crying with relief at the light. I carry on in the dark, pulling stuff out of the way, trying to make the hole bigger. Now I really am in a tunnel, and heading for the light!

Something warm touches my leg and I jump, hitting the back of my head this time. 'Ow!'

'It's all right, Miss. I'm here to help.' Someone is in the dark behind me.

'Well you might have warned me you were coming. I thought you were a rat. Now I've got another bloody bruise on my head. You frightened the life out of me.'

'Sorry about that. Be careful now, and I'll try to clear some more while you see to the patient. You're a first-aider, right?'

'Sort of.'

'What do you mean by that?'

'It was a long time ago, OK? Look, I was the only one small enough to come down here, so instead of criticizing me, just help me get to the lady and then find someone who can tell me what to do.'

'All right, girly. No need to shout.'

'Sorry,' I mumble.

It's quicker work with this guy behind me, taking the stuff away, and after a few minutes I can squeeze through into the cellar. The woman is sitting on the floor, cradling her pregnant belly. Oh my God, I hope she isn't in labour or anything. I can't put a splint on that!

As I scramble in, she grabs me and pulls and I land in a heap next to her. She's crying and hugging me. 'Oh you're an angel. You've saved us. God bless you.'

I hug her back, nearly crying myself. 'It's not just me. There's a load of people out there. We'll get you out. I told you we would.'

A face appears in the hole. That must be the phantom leg-grabber. 'Any injuries?' he asks.

'No, I'm all right,' says the woman. 'But I can't get out through that little hole.' She points to her huge baby bump.

'Bloody hell. You look ready to pop.'

'Don't say that,' I say. 'She can't have a baby down here. We've got to get her out.'

'Is there anyone else?'

'No, I was on my own in the house. I didn't fancy walking to the shelter. I thought I'd be safe in the cellar.' She starts to cry again.

'Don't you fret, love. I'll get some more help down here.' He turns to me. 'You make her comfortable.' I nod. 'It might take a bit longer, but we'll get you out, missus, don't you worry.' He disappears back down the hole and reappears with the canvas bag. 'Here. I'll get some blankets sent down for you.'

We settle down with our backs against the wall opposite the hole. It feels like being in a little den – the floor from above has crashed down at an angle, leaving a triangular space. Thank God the wall behind us didn't collapse. I pour out some hot, sweet tea from the flask and offer her a sandwich. 'Sorry, it's not exactly a banquet.' I have a sniff. 'Fish paste, I think.'

'Anything'll do,' she says, taking the tea and half a sandwich, still a bit tearful. 'I never thought I'd get the chance to eat again. You've saved my life.'

I haven't really. I mean, she's still stuck in the cellar, isn't she? I just hope they hurry up and widen the hole. It's pretty grim down here. I shiver and rub my arms. When a couple of blankets are pushed through to us I wrap one round the lady's shoulders, then snuggle into mine. Ah, that's better. A sip of the tea, even with that revolting milk, helps warm me up a bit. We share the sandwich, listening to the noise of the rescue operation.

'When's your baby due?' I ask, trying to distract her. Or

maybe I'm trying to distract myself. Every now and then there's another collapse and a lot of swearing on the other side of the blockage. I'm trying not to think about the whole lot shifting and trapping us both on this side of it. The other thing I don't want to think about is that car park. What if that was my only chance to get home?

'Middle of January I think. I don't know what we're going to do now the house has been blown up. I suppose I'll have to evacuate somewhere.'

'What about your husband? Is he around?'

She shakes her head. 'He's in the army. I haven't got a clue where he is. He can't tell me. I don't know when he's going to see the baby after it's born. How's he going to find us now the house has gone?' She starts to cry again. I try to get her to drink some more tea. I don't know how to deal with her tears. It must be pretty awful, no home, your husband away fighting, and having to cope with a baby.

'Please don't cry, it can't be good for the baby.' Oh crap. Wrong thing to say – she cries even harder. I pat her arm, wishing I'd just shut up. I am such a total loser. Now I want to cry too.

Eventually she calms down. 'I'm sorry. I shouldn't be so silly. You've been so kind, coming in here to save me. For a while back there I was thinking I was a goner for sure. And my poor baby.' She fills up again, but sniffs and shakes her head. 'But I reckon I'm the luckiest woman in London tonight.'

Seriously, if she carries on like that I'm going to the one bawling my eyes out.

'Do you know if it's a boy or a girl?' I ask.

She laughs. 'Of course not! No one knows 'till it's born, do they?'

'Oh, right.' No ultrasound scans in the 1940s. 'But don't some people reckon they can tell?'

'Well, my friend Kitty swears it's a boy, seeing as how I'm carrying it all at the front. But my Aunt Dolly did the needle test and says it's a girl.'

'Needle test?'

'You know, they thread a needle on some cotton and hold it

over your belly. If it swings round it's a girl, if it goes from side to side it's a boy. Or is it the other way round? Oh, I don't know. All I care about is having a healthy baby. A boy would be nice for my Fred. He'd be proud as punch to have a son. But I'd quite like a little girl.' She sighs and strokes her bump.

Our rescuers are getting closer. I can hear swearing and what sounds like a pickaxe popping away at the brick and concrete barrier.

'Not long now. Have you thought of any names?'

'Definitely Fred if it's a boy. I don't want to lumber a little girl with a name like Shirley though.'

'Is that your name?'

'God love us, we ain't even introduced ourselves have we?' she says. 'You saved my life and I didn't even tell you my name. What am I like? Yes, I'm Shirley.'

'And I'm Rosie,' I grin. 'Nice to meet you.'

'Rosie,' she smiles. 'Now that's a nice name for a girl.'

'Well, I like it.'

'And if a little Rosie of mine grows up to be half as brave and kind as you, I'll be well pleased.'

I can't believe how chuffed I feel. That's the nicest thing anyone has ever said to me.

Another crash makes us both jump. A load of rubbish and dust shoots through the hole, making us cough. When the dust clears, there's Bill pushing his shoulders through the bigger hole, all filthy and sweaty and the most beautiful sight I've ever seen.

CHAPTER THIRTEEN

It didn't take them long to get us out after that, and everyone cheered as we emerged. They all seemed to want to pat me on the head or shoulder, which didn't do my cuts and bruises much good. But they were all so pleased with me that I didn't have the heart to complain.

Shirley was taken off to the hospital to be checked over. As she left she shouted over to me 'If it's a girl, I'm calling her Rosie.' I waited until she was out of sight, then burst into tears.

Now I'm sitting in the back of an ambulance while a first-aider is sorting me out. I don't know what he's using to clean the cuts, but it really, really stings. I try not to be a wimp, but can't help hissing through my teeth when he gets to the cut on my head.

'All right, Miss, nearly finished. You're lucky, none of these cuts are too bad. You won't need any stitches.' He finishes up and starts putting his kit away.

Bill appears, looking through the window in the back door (that's how tall he is – I'd never reach it). The first-aider sees him and opens the door.

'All done. She'll be fine. Just needs a cuppa and a bun and she'll be right as rain.'

'Thank you,' I say, getting up. I sway a bit, but I'm fine, really.

'You're welcome. And well done. It was a brave thing you did.'

'I didn't feel very brave,' I grin, trying not to cry again.

'None of us do, love. It's the ones what do it even when they're scared that mean Hitler will never win. You mark my words. Now, I'll leave you to put your bits back on, then your young man can get you home safe.'

Bill hands me my shoes and stockings as the first-aider gets out the ambulance. They shut the door to give me some privacy. I can hear them talking outside while I struggle to put the stockings on. My nails are completely wrecked and my fingers are covered in cuts, my legs have got grazes and bruises all over them. I can't remember getting any of them, I was so focussed on getting to Shirley. I've a feeling it's all going to start really hurting soon.

Oh no, May's dress is absolutely wrecked. I brush some of the dust and muck off, but can't do much about the rips and stains. I hope she's not going to be angry with me. I'll have to look and see if the money I've got is enough to buy her a new one.

When I'm done I take a deep breath and open the ambulance door. Bill catches me round the waist and lifts me down.

'You all right, old girl?'

I laugh. 'Oh, right. I look so awful you're calling me old now?'

He shakes his head. 'Not true. You look l–'

I put a hand up. 'Don't even think of saying I look lovely, because I know you'd be lying.'

He tuts and says 'What are you like? I was going to say you look like you've been digging in an hole.'

'Right.' Now it's my turn to blush. 'You know how to make a girl feel good, Bill, don't you?'

He shakes his head, his eyes smiling. 'Ah, Rosie, you are priceless. Of course you look lovely. A bit bashed up, but that just makes it better, don't it?' He brushes a strand of hair off my face. His touch is so gentle it makes me want to cry again. 'You're a very special girl, you know?'

'That's so sweet. Will you give me a hug?'

He frowns at me, searching my face for something. I don't know if he finds it, but he opens his arms and I fall against his chest. Ah, that's better. With his arms around me, and the steady beat of his heart against my ear I feel a bit better. But not much. I put my arms around his waist and hang on. I'm shaking. There's so much stuff swirling round my head. I can't believe I had the chance to get back home and I didn't take it. But I couldn't leave Shirley down there, could I? But what if I was *meant* to leave her there? I might have just changed history, and because Shirley and her baby survive, things will be so different in the future. Maybe I won't even exist? How will I know? Will I just start fading from photos and collapse into nothing? If I just could figure out how I got here, I might be able to work out how to get back – *if* I can get back. I just want to go home. To see Gran and Great-aunt Eleanor, and Mum and Dad, and even Jess. None of them will believe where I've been. I doubt if anyone will.

I feel a soft kiss on the top of my head. 'Come on then, I'd better get you home. Can you walk, or do you want me to carry you?'

'I can walk,' I say. 'I'm too heavy to carry.'

'Nah, you're as light as a feather, you. It'll be like carrying a baby.'

Suddenly I remember a photo that Gran keeps on her sideboard. It's of me and my grandpa when I was a few months old. The old man is laughing at me, and I'm giving him a big gummy grin, like we're sharing a great joke. My Grandpa Bill. I look up at the younger version of him and see those same eyes smiling at me.

I've got to tell him. If I don't tell someone I'll go mad.

'Look, while we walk I need to explain something to you. Promise me you'll listen, and even if it sounds totally mad, you have to listen to it all. It's so weird you won't know what to think, but I really need you to hear it, OK?'

'You don't need to tell me anything now, Rosie. You've had a rotten time of it tonight, and you've been a real trouper. Let's get you home to bed and worry about it tomorrow, eh?'

If he pats me on the head I'm going to smack him.

'Don't patronise me, Bill. I need to tell you this now. Trust me. It's now or never. I'm not likely to have the nerve to say anything in the cold light of day, and if I don't tell someone soon I'll go completely out of my mind.'

He does that eyebrow thing. 'All right. Tell me.'

CHAPTER FOURTEEN

We walk slowly away from the bombsite, our way lit by the fires that continue to burn, and I tell Bill everything. From catching Jess snogging with Simon, to being with Gran and Great-aunt Eleanor and falling into May and Nelly's lives. Occasionally he opens his mouth to say something, then shuts it again, keeping his promise to hear me out.

'So you're not from the country?' he asks when I eventually stop talking.

'Yes, I am from the country. But not from this time. You know, 1940. I was born after the millennium. May is my gran. When I left my time she was in her nineties.

'Bloody hell! Are you sure that bang on your head ain't brought all this on? I've heard stories about people being changed by a knock on the bonce.'

'Bill, I promise you, it has nothing to do with my head wound. Think about it – Nelly's been suspicious of me since the minute I arrived. And I arrived in their hall when the door was locked. How else could I have got there except to fall through a hole in time? I haven't got a clue about what I'm doing here, I was supposed to spending my summer holiday in Italy. Well, till I fell out with my friend Jess.'

'Don't be daft. Everyone knows we're at war with Italy.'

I shake my head. 'Not in the 21st century we're not. And you saw me try to dance tonight. I haven't got a clue.' I pull away from him, desperate to make him understand. 'Nelly wants to report me as a spy.'

'She wouldn't do that. Would she?'

'Who knows? I probably would if I was her. I talk different from everyone too – even you've noticed that, haven't you?'

'I thought that was just how everyone talks in the country.'

'It's not the same – and I'm seriously not getting most things round here. I mean, I can't even figure out pounds, shillings, and pence. I'd never seen a ha'penny before Monday morning because we've got a decimal system and different money where I come from. I really am from the future, Bill.'

He frowns and we walk on in silence for a bit. I can almost see his brain working, trying to sort this out.

'So, if you know the future, what happens?'

I laugh. 'Loads of stuff. I can't tell you everything that's going to happen over the next seventy-odd years. I wasn't born for most of it.'

'But what about the war? Who wins?'

'We do. But not for a while.'

'How long?'

'1945.'

'Blimey. That's longer than the Great War.'

'I know.'

'So, will the Yanks join in anytime soon?'

'Yeah, but I can't remember exactly when. I think they came in after Pearl Harbour in 1941. I'm not very good with history, sorry.'

'What's Pearl Harbour?'

'A naval base in Hawaii. The Japanese attacked it. We went there a few years ago on holiday; that's how I remember why the Americans joined the war.'

'Where the blooming heck is Hawaii?' he asks, but I don't get the chance to answer before he goes on. 'Hang on, did you say the Japs attacked it?'

'Yes,' I sigh. 'This war is going to be fought all over the world, Bill, not just Europe, but Asia, and Africa too.'

'And London? Will Jerry invade? Will we be fighting them here?'

'No. They'll keep on bombing, but they won't land here.'

'Thank Christ for that!'

We carry on walking. Bill must be thinking about everything I've said, but doesn't ask any more questions for a while. Down one street our way is blocked by another bombsite, so we find a different route round. I'm starting to feel so tired. I trip over a bit of drainpipe on the path and Bill catches me before I fall flat on my face.

'Thanks,' I say, giving him a tired smile. It's obvious he doesn't believe me. I feel so alone. I'm welling up when Bill notices.

'Ah, come here, you daft 'apporth,' he says, pulling me back into his arms.

With a sigh I snuggle up and carry on walking, glad that he's looking after me, even if he does think I'm crazy.

There's damage everywhere – glass from blown out windows, rubble and bits of household goods from people's houses. In some places buildings are still on fire and the roads are criss-crossed with water hoses as teams fight the blazes. As we get nearer to the house the way gets clearer. It looks like our street got off lightly last night. We pass a church. The clock on the tower shows a quarter past six. It's still dark, but it's almost time to leave for work.

'I hope the girls are all right,' I say.

'Don't you know?'

'I think I do, but what if my being here has changed things?'

'How?'

'Well, I don't know what I'm doing here, right? What if I change something, and that changes history, and everything ends up different? I mean, I know May and Nelly are supposed to survive, but ... if they don't for some reason, then I won't exist at all, will I?'

'Bloody hell, I can't take all this in.'

'Tell me about it. How do you think I feel? It's totally doing my head in.'

'But hang on. If you've come from the future, why haven't loads of other people?'

'I don't know, do I? There could be thousands of us wandering round like idiots, or I could just be some random freak of nature, one of a kind, some cosmic joke! I could've gone back tonight, you know. It was right there in front of me. I could see an underground car park with modern cars – there was one just like my dad's, so I'm pretty sure it was the right time. All I had to do was step through that hole and I've have been back where I belong. I'd have disappeared into thin air, and someone else would've had to try and rescue Shirley. But I couldn't do it, could I? I could hear her, she was so scared. I had to stay and help her, and the hole just disappeared. I missed my chance, and now I'm scared to death I'm stuck here and I've messed everything up by saving someone who wasn't meant to be saved.'

Bill shakes his head and pulls me into a bear hug. 'Calm down, don't be daft, you ain't changed nothing. If you hadn't saved her, someone else would've. We weren't going to leave her down there. I'm just glad you didn't disappear, or I'd have had to face May and Nelly and tell 'em I'd lost you. They'd have had my guts for garters.'

I laugh. 'Probably.'

'So don't you fret. I reckon if this mysterious hole has appeared once, I bet it'll happen again, you'll see.'

I take a deep breath and blow it out, clinging onto him for dear life. 'You do believe me, don't you, Bill? You're not just humouring me?'

'To be honest, I don't know what to believe. I know you believe it. And there's definitely something very funny about you, missus.'

I punch him in the stomach. Not that I make a dent, because he's solid muscle. We stand there for a bit, just holding each other.

'You were great tonight,' I say. 'You got everyone organised.'

'Least I could do,' he says. 'You do what you can, and hope someone'll do the same for you if you're in trouble.'

'And you're a soldier. That must be scary.'

I feel him shrug.

'Everyone's scared, Rosie. At least joining up means I'm doing my bit. I couldn't sit back and let Jerry win, could I?'

'So you chose to be a soldier. You didn't wait to be called up?'

'Nah. Better to get on with it, I say.'

I'm almost dozing off when he moves back and looks down at me.

'I don't' suppose you know what happens to me? I mean, you've seen May and Nelly in the future, but ... well, it'd be nice to know whether get through this n'all.'

I don't know what to say. I haven't said anything to him about him being my grandpa. Should I say anything? He and May seem like good friends, but what if they need a nudge in the right direction? Or what if that horrible Harry messes it all up?

Bill takes my silence the wrong way. He drops his hands and looks away.

'Bill, I ...'

'Nah, it's all right, Rosie. Maybe it's best if I don't know.'

'It's not that. It's ...'

'I mean it, you don't have to tell me.'

'Oh for God's sake, you are not going to die in the war, Billy McAllister!'

He looks at me again. 'Really? You're not just saying it? Don't say it if it ain't true.'

'Just tell me something,' I say. 'How much do you fancy May?'

He blushes. He actually blushes! In the soft light of the dawn, Billy McAllister goes bright red. 'Who says I fancy May?'

'No one. But your reaction is telling me loads, so don't deny it.'

'All right I won't. But what difference does it make? It ain't never going to happen. I'm the brother she never had.'

'Well you'd better make it happen, Billy boy, because my life depends on it.'

'What are you talking about?'

'My name isn't Rose Smith. I don't have a clue who she is or why I've ended up with her suitcase. My name is Rosie McAllister, and you're my Grandpa.'

He looks completely stunned.

'I'm your grandpa?'

I nod. 'And May is my gran. Go figure.'

He's shaking his head and smiling at the same time. 'Nah, you're having a laugh.'

'No way. You're going to marry May, and have my dad, who's going to meet my mum, and I'm going to be the happy result.'

'But May don't see me like that.' He looks miserable again. 'It don't matter how much I want her to, she'll never take me serious.'

I roll my eyes. 'It's got to happen. Or I won't be born. But as I have been born, that means it has happened. You've just got to work out what you're going to do about it.'

'I can't take all this in. You're not kidding me, are you, Rosie. You really think you're from the future, and all that stuff's going to happen?'

'I am seriously not kidding, Bill.'

He takes a deep breath and nods. 'Right. Let me think about it for a bit.'

'OK. I know it's a lot to take it, but I'm really not joking about all this. The thing is, I haven't told anyone else. I mean, Nelly already thinks I'm a spy or something. If I try to tell her the truth she'll have me locked up for sure, and then I'll never get home.'

'Right. Mum's the word. To be honest, I don't reckon anyone would believe me if I told them, so I'll keep schtum.' He looks at me with narrowed eyes. 'You really need to meet my nan while you're here.' He gives his head a little shake. 'Now, let's get you back to the girls at least. They'll be heading off to work soon.'

'Oh God! I'll have to go to work too. I'll never make it in time.'

'Well, after the night you've had, I reckon you should be staying at home anyway. You never know with head injuries. If the girls are working, I'll get me nan to pop over and see you're all right.'

'OK. It'll be nice to meet her. After all, she is my, what – my great-grandmother? No, it must be great-great. Wow.'

'Oh Christ, don't go telling her nothing about this, girl. She's as mad as a hatter anyway, without you making things worse.'

'Fair enough. Now, let's get a move on. My feet are killing me.'

'Well why didn't you say so?' He swoops and hooks an arm

under my knees and swings me up into his arms. 'I said I'd carry you, didn't I?'

We're both laughing as we turn into the street and come face to face with Nelly and May on their way to work.

'Where the hell have you been?' Nelly shouts, hands on hips.

'Oh my God, look at the state of you!' May runs forward and touches my face. 'Are you all right?'

'I'm fine, May.'

'Then why is he carrying you?' asks Nelly. 'You were supposed to keep her safe, Jock. What were you thinking?'

'It's not his fault,' I say, as Bill lowers me to my feet. 'There was a bomb and a woman called Shirley was trapped in her basement –'

'And Rosie here's a heroine,' he interrupts. 'She went down there and dug with her bare hands. She got to the woman and stayed with her till we could dig them both out.'

'Bloody hell! Well done, Queenie!' May hugs me, but backs off a bit quick when she realises just how filthy I am. 'Is that my dress?'

'Yeah, what's left of it. Sorry.'

I wait for her to shout at me for ruining her lovely dress, but she shrugs. 'It wasn't my favourite, thank God. I might be able to salvage something from it – make a new blouse maybe. What's more important is sorting you out before we're late for work.'

'You go ahead. No point in us all having our wages docked. To be honest, I've been up all night and I'm aching in places I didn't know existed, so I'm going to bed. Can you tell them for me?'

'We can't leave you like this.'

'Honestly, May. I'm fine. I just need to clean up and have a lie down.'

'I'll look after her,' says Bill.

'Oh no you won't,' says Nelly, so fiercely that he takes a step back. 'It's bad enough you've been out all night, I'm not leaving her alone with you in our house. What will people say?'

'She'll be safe with me, Nell, I promise.'

Nelly looks torn. She looks at her watch and then at me. 'You ain't in no fit state for work, that's for sure. We'd better take you home and sort you out.'

'No, it's all right, really,' I say. 'You can't miss work. I don't want you to get into trouble because of me. I'll be OK. It looks a lot worse than it is,' I grin.

'How you going to get the bath out and fill it when you're all cut and bruised?'

'I'll do that, then go and get me nan to help her,' says Bill. 'I swear I won't hang about like some peeping Tom. What d'you take me for?'

'He ain't wrong, Nell,' says May. 'Old Lil will make sure she's all right.'

'Well, see you knock on her door and get her over to ours straight away,' says Nelly, digging in her handbag. She hands me a key. 'Here, you look after that. I don't want to be locked out of me own house when I get back.'

'Don't worry, I'll be fine. Bill and his nan will look after me.'

'Bill? Oh, you mean Jock. No one calls him Bill.'

'Well I do,' I smile at their confused faces. 'I'll see you later.'

'Are you sure?' says Nelly. May's looking at Bill like she's never seen him before.

'Absolutely. Go on, and see if you can make sure I keep my job.' I might need it for longer than I thought.

'Right,' says Nell. 'Come on, May. See you later.' They clatter off down the road.

'OK,' I say turning back to Bill. 'I'll go and put the kettle on, and you'd better see if your nan's up. I'm looking forward to meeting my great-great-grandmother.'

'Bloody hell, please don't tell her that, whatever you do, or we'll all end up in the loony bin!' With a groan and a shake of his head, Bill crosses the road to knock on his nan's door while I let myself into the house and kick off my shoes.

CHAPTER FIFTEEN

Meeting Lil McAllister was amazing. She didn't come over to the house, but instead sent Bill over to get me.

'She's got the boiler on for washing, so she says you can have a bath over there without having to wait for the water to heat up. I've already got the bath out and she's filling it up.'

As I walked into her kitchen, Bill's nan was tipping a bucketful of hot water into the tin bath. She wasn't what I expected. Lil McAllister was a little round woman with laughing brown eyes and red cheeks – but that might have been caused by the steam in the air. Her silver-streaked dark hair was tied up in a bun, but little wispy curls were escaping, and softening the edges of her face. 'Hallo, love. My, don't you look a sight! Not to worry. A nice hot bath'll see you right. Here Billy, you get another bucketful while I pour the girl a nice cup of tea.'

He took the bucket and ducked into a little room off the kitchen. Through the doorway I saw a huge steaming copper vat and an old mangle.

'Sit down, dear. You look done in. What a night you've had! I hope our Billy looked after you.'

'Oh he did, Mrs McAllister. He's been great.'

She tutted and fussed just like gran as I sat at the kitchen table. 'He's a good boy,' she said putting a cup of strong tea in front of me. 'And the name's Lil, love. Mrs McAllister sounds like me mother-in-law, God rest her.'

Bill brought through two buckets and topped up the bath water.

'Thanks so much for this, M – er, Lil. I'm sorry to interrupt your washing.'

'I'm not,' she laughed. 'I bleeding hate wash days. You've done me a favour.'

'Any danger of a cuppa, Nan?' asked Billy.

'It's on the side, darling. Nice and strong, just how you like it.'

'Ooh, ta.'

He stood by the sink sipping his tea while Lil tested the water and pulled a screen round the bath.

'Right, that's ready. Come on, dear, and we'll soon get you sorted. Billy, you pop over the road and bring her back some clean clothes. Then you can light the fire in the front parlour. When we're done, your friend can go in there and you can have a soak as well. I love you dearly, boy, but you don't half need a bath this morning!'

Bill burst out laughing and put his tea down. 'Thanks, Nan. I love you too. I'll nip round and be back in a minute. Chuck us the key, Rose.'

I told him where he could find my stuff. A couple of seconds later he slammed the front door behind him and I turned to Lil with a smile. That's when I realised something was wrong. She was staring at me, white as a sheet, her damp hands clutched at her chest.

'Are you all right? Shall I get Bill?'

She shook her head. 'No, love. What did he call you?'

'Rose.'

'I thought you were called Queenie.'

'May and Nelly call me that. But my real name is Rosie.'

'Come here,' she beckoned me over urgently. I walked over to her and she took my face in her damp, shaking hands. 'I never recognised you with all that dirt on your face. Is it really you? Oh my God, oh my God, I never thought I'd see the day. After all these years.'

'I'm sorry?'

'Don't you remember?'

'Remember what?'

'You and me have met before. Years ago. By rights, you should be as old as me now, but you ain't.' She shakes her head. 'You told me this would happen again, but I didn't believe you.'

'I'm sorry, Mrs McAllister – er, Lil, I don't know what

you're talking about.'

'That's right. Let me think. You said you wouldn't know about it because everything was out of order. How old are you, Rosie?'

'I'm fifteen.'

'Well I never ... You came here first, didn't you? First time I saw you, you was about sixteen, and I was a nipper.''

'That's not possible.'

'Nor is you being here, eh? But you are,' she said, patting my cheeks and letting me go. 'It's all right. I won't tell no one. It'll be our secret, just like it was back then. Now our Billy will be back in a minute, so you get yourself in that bath and soak off that mud and dust. I'll help you with your hair. And I've got some nice lavender soap you can use. You don't want to use the usual stuff on that lovely skin. You ain't used to roughing it, are you?'

So here I am, sitting in a tin bath in Lil's kitchen, in total shock. It's not possible. Is it? But it shouldn't be possible for me to be here now. I mean, what if she *did* meet me years ago? Does that mean I'm not going to get home, but will be stumbling around in time for the rest of my life? Oh God, I can't cope with this!

'How you getting on, dear?' asks Lil from the other side of the screen. 'You ain't fallen asleep?'

I nearly jump out of my skin, and some water slops over the side of the bath. 'Er, no. I'm all right.' I splash water over my face, wishing I could relax and enjoy the hot water after days of cold washes. But I'm so wound up I feel like I'm going to have a complete breakdown or something. *Why is this happening to me?*

'Ready to do your hair?'

'I can probably do it.'

'Don't be daft.' She appears round the edge of the screen. 'I've got a couple of jugs of clean water ready for rinsing. Now,' she puffs as she kneels down next to the bath. I hope she hasn't knelt on the wet patch. I should be dead embarrassed, but I'm too tired and confused to care. 'You haven't even taken out your hairpins. Here, let me.' She does it quickly and I feel the relief as my hair floats around my face and shoulders. 'That's better, now dunk yourself in and get it wet, dear.' I do as I'm told and she starts to massage soap into my hair with strong, sure fingers. Oooh, it feels lovely, until some soap gets into the cut on my forehead and I hiss with pain. 'Sorry, dear. Here, let's rinse that with the fresh water.' It feels better straight away, and I sigh with pleasure again. 'Right, now lean your head back, that's it.'

Lil finishes cleaning my hair, taking care not to go near my forehead again. She works in silence and I begin to relax. The front door slams again. Bill's back. I hear him come into the kitchen.

'You stay right there, Billy,' calls Lil.

'I ain't coming in,' he says. 'I'm just putting her clothes on the chair. I'll get that fire going and wait in the front room.'

'Good boy. There should be some tea left in the pot.'

'Righto.' He pours himself a cup. I can hear the teaspoon tinkle against the china as he stirs the milk in. 'I'm off into the front room then.'

He closes the door behind him as Lil starts to rinse my hair. 'There you go. I'll bet that feels better, don't it? Now, what about the rest of you?' She picks up my hand. There's loads of little cuts and dirt, and my nails are wrecked. What I wouldn't give for a proper manicure right now. Jess does them for me sometimes; she wants to be a beautician when we leave school. Lil tuts and gently washes my hands and arms, then my feet and lower legs, which are beyond filthy from crawling through the rubble in that basement. 'Blimey, you have been in the wars, haven't you?'

'I was the only one small enough to get through.' I say, feeling a bit tearful.

'Well, you're a brave one, that's for sure. I suppose it comes from being a time traveller.'

I stare at her, and she looks back at me, calm as anything. 'What makes you say that?' I ask, hoping I'm so zoned out that I've misunderstood what she's saying.

'Because you told me. It was a long time ago, and I never believed you back then. But you are, ain't you, seeing as how you're here, and now you're cleaned up I can see you look just the same.' She frowns and picks up my right hand and traces along the back of my thumb. 'Only you ain't got a scar here. Not yet.'

'What?' I pull my hand back.

She frowns. 'Oh cripes, I shouldn't have said nothing. I'd better not say any more.'

'Why not?'

'Well, you can't go round telling people what's going to happen, can you? Spoilers, you called it. Said it wasn't a good idea.'

Oh. My. God. That's something I *would* say. But if I did, that means ...

'When did we meet, Lil?'

'Let's see, I'm sixty-three now, and I was just a girl when I first met you.'

'First?' I ask, not sure if I heard her right.

'That's right. You was the teacher at the Board School while old Miss Pritchard was ill.''

I sit up, sploshing water everywhere. 'You're kidding me, right? Tell me this is a joke.'

'No. Us kiddies loved you.' You was a lot more fun than that old battle-axe. A really good teacher.'

'At sixteen?'

'Well, you told everyone you was older. We didn't know no different, what with you having such a good education.'

This is crazy. I just want to get back to my own time, where I'm just an ordinary schoolgirl. Why is this happening to me?

I cover my face, trying not to cry. Will I ever get home? I don't want to be Lil's teacher. I just want to get back to Gran and Great-aunt Eleanor!

'You weren't there for long, mind,' she went on. 'Only a couple of weeks. I never knew the truth then of course. I didn't see you again for ever such a long time.'

I take my hands away and look up. 'Again?'

Lil is staring into space. Is she crazy or am I?

'That's right. I was married then and had the kids. My Ethel was in an accident and you brought her home. Gave me a terrible shock, I can tell you. You had to let me in on it then, to shut me up.'

'An accident?' I ask.

'Oh it weren't nothing serious. You was both all right.'

'When was this?'

'1910. I nearly fainted dead away when you appeared. You'd gone up in the world.' She looks at me again. 'Mind you, you looked a bit older then. Not an old married woman like me, mind. You was brave then, n'all. I couldn't believe it when you got arrested.'

I feel the breath leave my body. Did she just say –?

'Ooh, I shouldn't have said that, should I? Now don't you worry, dear. You weren't in jail for long, your young man saw to that, then you were gone again.'

'Gone?'

She nods and laughs. 'Ooh, you led 'em a right dance.'

They said you escaped and the coppers spent ages looking for you. Decided you'd left the country in the end, they did.' She tapped her nose. 'But I knew better.'

'But where did I go?' I ask, but I'm not sure I want to know.

'Why, you went home, dear. Back to the future. Mr Lucas told me you had it all sorted.'

'I don't know a Mr Lucas.'

Lil raises her eyebrows. 'Oh, I'd better keep schtum then, hadn't I?' She taps the side of her nose with her finger.

'No! I mean, I need to know. Who is he?'

Lil looks doubtful. 'What about spoilers?'

'Please, Lil. I need to know if I can get home. If this Mr Lucas has anything to do with it, I need to find him.

'Don't you fret none, darling. You told me you always find your way back home. You don't need to find him. You'll be right.'

Home? 'I definitely told you I was going home?' I focus on that.

'Yes. Oh, and now I think about it, you gave me a message for when I saw you again. Only I can't remember everything after all these years. I know you said to say that you got home to your gran all right, but to be ready for it to happen again one day. Now, what else? Oh yes, that's it, you said not to worry, 'cause you was getting used to it and if you use your head you'll work out how to get back.'

'Use my head?' Oh no! I touch the cut on my head. I nearly got back last night after that plank hit me, didn't I? And it must have been hitting my head when I tripped in Gran's hall that got me here. I can't go around bashing myself on my head trying to get home – I'll end up with brain damage or something. 'Are you sure?'

Lil laughs. 'Oh bless your heart! You said you'd worry about being bashed on the bonce. But you didn't mean it like that.'

I sigh. This is not helping. Use my head? How the hell can I do that when it's full of so much stuff? I can't take this in.

Lil grabs the side of the bath and nearly tips me out as she struggles to her feet. 'Oh Christ, my old bones. Come on, young Rosie, let's get you out of there before you go all wrinkly.'

'But what else did I say? How am I supposed to use my head? What does it mean?'

'I don't rightly know, dear. I did write it down, but I can't for the life of me think what I did with the paper. I'l have to have a look, but it's probably long gone now. Or maybe Ethel's got it. I'll have to ask her next time I see her. If I think of anything else I'l tell you, I promise. Now come on, out you get before you catch your death.'

I want to argue, to get her to remember. I've got so many questions, but she shakes her head.

'Sorry dear. My old brain ain't what it used to be, and you took so blooming long to come back. I just can't remember.'

She holds out a thin towel and with a sigh I get up and wrap it round me. Another one goes round my head, and yet another round my shoulders. I step out onto the rug as Lil rummages through a drawer full of clutter in the dresser by the cooker. She brings out a hairbrush, pulls some stray hairs from it, and gives it to me. 'Now, I'll leave you to get dressed. Go on through to the front room when you're ready, dear, then Billy can have his turn.'

I look at the grimy water. 'I don't think he'll get very clean in that.'

'Don't you worry. There's plenty more water in the copper. He'll dump this lot in the yard and have a nice fresh one.'

She shuffles out and I dry myself. The warm water has helped, but I'm still quite stiff and sore. But that's the least of my worries at the moment. Can I believe what Lil has said, or did that knock on my head do more damage than I thought? When I'm dressed I leave the towel wrapped round my hair, and go and find Bill on his own in the front room. It's lovely and warm.

'All right?' he smiles, 'You look better.'

'Yeah, well, anything would've been an improvement, right?'

'I s'pose.'

'Where's your nan?'

'She's upstairs somewhere,' he said.

I shut the door behind me. 'Bill, who's Ethel?'

'My aunt. Why?'

'Where is she?'

'She lives down Canvey Island.' I must be looking blank because he goes on: 'It's in Essex. Why?'

I'm not likely to meet her, then. So I've got no way of checking Lil's story.

Lil could be telling me the truth, or she could be as mad as everyone says she is. I'm sort of hoping she's completely off her trolley. But then again, how on earth would she know about me being from another time? It could be one huge coincidence I suppose, and she really is completely mad, but that's pretty unlikely, isn't it?

'What's this all about, Rosie?' asks Bill.

'You're not going to believe this, but –'

'Come on, Billy,' Lil calls out. 'Get your filthy carcass in the bath, boy. I want me kitchen back!'

'You'd better go,' I say. 'I'll tell you later.' I need some time to think about this. I sink into an armchair by the now-blazing coal fire as he gets up and goes to have his bath. I take the towel off my hair and start to brush it out. It soon begins to dry in the warmth of the fire. I don't even care that it's going frizzy.

I try to get everything straight in my mind, but so much is spinning round my head, and I'm getting sooo tired. In the end I give up and lean back in the chair and close my eyes.

CHAPTER SIXTEEN

I slept for most of the day, finally waking up because my stomach was cramping with hunger. Lil had a pot of some kind of stew simmering on the hob and insisted I had some before I went back over the road. I'm not sure what it was, but I was past caring and it tasted great. Bill had gone home to bed, so I didn't see him.

I wanted to talk to Lil about what she'd told me, but she was determined to avoid the subject.

'Take no notice of an old woman,' she said. 'I don't know what I'm talking about half the time. Me mind ain't what it used to be, dear. I can't remember what's up or down these days.'

'But Lil, you knew about ...' Spoilers. Of course. I'd told her about spoilers, and now she was acting like she hadn't told me anything. But, for God's sake, she could help me get home! But no matter how I phrased it, she refused to answer any questions.

'Don't you fret none, love. You'll be all right,' she said, patting me on the shoulder. 'Now, it's been lovely having you, but why don't you pop back over the road and get the house nice and warm for the girls? They'll be home soon.'

It was already dark outside and it was clear I wouldn't get anything else out of her, so I gave up and left. 'Thanks for looking after me,' I said. 'And thank Bill for me, will you?'

'Course I will. Ta-ra then.'

So here I am, alone in the house for the first time. It's dark and cold. I turn on lights as I walk down the hall and into the kitchen. While the kettle boils I go back and stand in front of the coat stand and stare into the mirror.

I look bloody awful. My hair is all frizzy and there's a bruise on my forehead. The cut is right on the edge of my hairline, so it's not too obvious. I play about with my hair a bit and manage to cover the bruise too. But that doesn't take away my puffy, bloodshot eyes and the dark shadows under them. I pinch my cheeks to get a bit of colour into my pale face. I remember the last time I properly looked in this mirror, and how I thought I looked dead grown-up and sophisticated. Gran and Great-aunt Eleanor had been there, right behind me, so pleased with my French pleat and all that dressing up.

My eyes are filling up. I miss them so much. I wish I could see them now. I've had enough of all this.

For a split second there's something there in the mirror. Is it Gran? But when I blink it's gone. There's a scraping sound as a key turns in the lock and May and Nelly come in through the front door.

'Hallo, Queenie. You feeling better, love?' asks May.

I shrug. I haven't a clue.

'What are you doing, standing out here in the hall?' asks Nelly.

'Nothing,' I say.

In the kitchen, the kettle starts to whistle.

'Ah, now there's the best sound in the world to come home to,' smiles May. She links arms with me. 'Come on, let's have a nice cuppa and you can tell us all about your adventures. The girls at work all send their love. They're dying to know what you got up to with Jock McAllister all night.'

Over tea I get the third degree from both of them. I have to tell them everything, from leaving the dance to getting back here. The only things I don't mention are the portal in the basement, what Lil told me, and what I've told Bill.

When Nelly starts cooking dinner I tell her I'm going to bed.

'You've got to eat,' she says.

'Lil fed me. I slept all day and only woke up about an hour ago. She gave me some stew. Honestly, I'm still full.'

I clean my teeth at the sink while she peels some potatoes, then I leave them to it.

The next day I miss seeing Bill at the bus stop, but then remember he had a couple of days off. I never got a chance to tell him what Lil said to me. I hope I see him later. I really need to talk to him. I have no idea what 'using my head' is supposed to mean. I'm feeling really fed up, and to make things worse May doesn't shut up about Harry.

'I've had my eye on that one for a while,' she says as we finish our dinner this evening. Corned beef hash. Better than spam, I suppose, but still pretty revolting. 'He always dresses so smart, and he's a handy dancer. Did you see him swing me about?' she giggles.

Me and Nelly both roll our eyes. For once we're in total agreement.

'Bill's a good dancer too,' I say. 'And he looks well hot in uniform.'

'Hot? 'Course he gets hot when he's dancing. We all do,' says Nell.

I shake my head. 'No, I didn't mean warm. I meant, you know, hot, sexy. I'm really surprised he hasn't got a girlfriend.'

May looks shocked. 'Sexy? Our Jock? We talking about the same bloke here, Queenie?'

'Yes,' I say. 'And he prefers his real name. Don't you think he's good-looking?'

May frowns. 'Dunno. I never thought about it. He's just Jock. He's a mate.'

I grit my teeth in frustration. May has to change her mind about Bill. If not, the future could be very different. It might not even happen. 'Well I think he's lovely.'

'He's not bad-looking I suppose,' said Nell. 'And he does look quite smart in uniform.'

'Not as smart-looking as Harry, though,' May insists.

'Harry should be in uniform too,' says Nell. 'Not swanning about in sharp suits like a spiv.'

'What's a spiv?' I ask.

Nell looks at me like I'm a total idiot. 'A flash geezer who earns his money on the black market,' she says. 'Dodgy characters. They ought to be in jail, the lot of 'em.'

'He is not a spiv,' says May, hands on hips. 'He's a businessman. He told me.'

'Funny business if you ask me,' says Nell. 'A young fella

131

like that don't have no business on civvy street when so many of our boys are fighting for king and country. And fellas round here can't afford suits like that if they're doing an honest day's work.'

'Don't you go saying things like that, Nelly,' says May. 'You don't know nothing about him.'

'And neither do you, May. That's what worries me. You take care, my girl, or he'll lead you into trouble.'

May laughs. 'Don't be daft. I'm not stupid. Me and Harry are going to win that dance competition, you'll see. Do me a favour and find yourself a fella, Nell. Then you'd be having a good time too, and wouldn't have no need to go poking your nose into my business.' She dances out of the kitchen, humming a tune.

As we listen to her running up the stairs, Nell sighs and puts her head in her hands.

'I don't like him either,' I say. 'He's what my mum would call "a smarmy git".' Actually, that's exactly what she called Simon once.

'Yeah. That sounds about right. But now I've gone and made it worse, haven't I?'

'Probably. Now she knows you don't like him, it'll make him more attractive.' I put the kettle on for a cup of tea and get the milk out of the larder. I don't think I'm ever going to get used to sterilised milk. I would die for a skinny latte right now. 'You know what it's like. As soon as someone disapproves, we convince ourselves we're crazy about them, even if they really are a right minger.' Is that what I've been doing?

Nell looks up. 'A right what?'

Oops, not again. 'Um, minger. You know – horrible, unsuitable, looks like he should crawl back under a stone?'

Nell bursts out laughing. 'Oh my gawd, you don't half come up with them, Queenie. Minger. I've never heard that one before. But you're right. It describes Harry to a tee.'

'The question is, how do we get May to see it? I mean, she'd be much better off with Bill.'

'Bill? Oh, you mean Jock. Hang on, I thought you had your eye on him.'

'Um, I would … he's lovely, right, but I'm pretty sure he fancies May, and I've just got a feeling that they'd be really good together.'

Nelly stares at me, and I have to force myself not to squirm.

'Mmm, you might be right. I never thought about it before, but they do get on well. But what if they start courting and end up hating each other? He's a family friend, and his nan's ever so good to us, even if she does have her mad moments. If they fell out, his family'd never talk to us again.'

'Yeah, but if I'm right and they do get married, we – I mean you'd all be related.'

'Married! She too young for that sort of thing. Don't you go putting ideas like that in her head.'

'I'm not talking about straight away,' I say. 'But maybe in the future.'

'If we have a future.' She puts her elbows on the table and rests her chin in her hands. 'We could all be blown to kingdom come one of these nights. Not much point in talking about the future.'

'Come on Nelly, you can't just give up.'

Nelly sighs and rubs her eyes. 'I suppose. I'm just so bloody tired. I'm sick of the raids, night after night. Every morning the bus has to take a different route 'cause Jerry's blown up another street.'

'I thought it took longer yesterday morning,' I say. 'I didn't realise. I still don't know my way around here.'

'There ain't much point. It changes every time a bomb drops. Soon there won't be nothing but rubble between here and the docks.'

'But that's miles away.'

'I know.'

'Oh, come on, Nell, don't let it get you down. We can't let Jerry win.' Oh God, I can't believe I just said that. 'Anyway, about Bill. It took me a nanosecond to see he's mad for May. They'd make a great couple. Trust me. He's perfect for her.'

Nell frowns. 'He always runs off when he sees me coming. I reckon he's a bit of a girl, meself.'

'No, he's not. You just make him nervous.'

'Why? I've never done nothing to him. Why would I make him nervous?'

I shrug, trying to keep it light. 'Well, you're obviously brainy. And you don't suffer fools. I think he's quite shy, and feels a bit intimidated when you're around.'

Nell looks thoughtful. 'Who says I'm brainy?'

'Come on, it's obvious. You're always reading; and you're clever at numbers, because I saw you doing the house accounts earlier and you can work it all out in your head. I'm useless at maths without a calculator.'

'A calculator?'

Oh crap. Pocket calculators aren't invented for ages yet. 'Um, er, an adding machine.'

'Don't tell me you've got an adding machine at home, Queenie. They only have them in offices and banks, not houses.'

'No, of course not. I, er, used one at my dad's office. Look, what I'm saying is you're clever, and some boys are scared of clever girls. They're probably frightened you're going to win all the arguments and make them look stupid.'

Nell nodded. 'Yeah. I usually do. Maybe that's why I don't have a fella.'

Oh God, why do I always say the wrong thing? I'm trying to cheer her up, and now she's getting seriously depressed.

'You were dancing with loads of them the other night,' I point out.

'I know, but as soon as we stop dancing and start chatting, well, I get so impatient. I don't like silly beggers who think a uniform is a ticket into your knickers, and I don't hold with daft compliments. I want a *conversation* with someone. If I ask them what they think about the new prime minister, Mr Churchill's latest speech, they tell me not to "worry my little head about it", 'cause they're so cocky they reckon they're going to sort out Jerry single-handed. Bloody idiots!'

'I'm sure they're not all like that. There must be some decent guys around,' I say, then I remember what a prat Simon really is. She might just be right. How depressing is that?

'Maybe,' said Nell, but she didn't seem convinced either.

For a moment she looks really fed up about it, but then she straightens her shoulders. 'But I haven't got time for courting, and if our May starts carrying on with that flash Harry I'll have my work cut out for me, keeping her on the straight and narrow until Dad comes home. You're right though, Queenie. We've got to think about the future. Once this war is over – and please God we all live to see it – I want to do something with my life. I ain't staying round here. Not if I can help it.'

'You won't,' I smile, knowing just how far Nell is going to go.

'Don't you mock me, Miss High and Mighty. Just 'cause I left school at fourteen don't mean I can't work hard and make something of meself.'

'Of course you can. I didn't mean ... Look, I *know* you're going to go far, Nell. Further than you've ever imagined.'

'Oh, yeah? Well what would you know about what I imagine, eh? Read minds, do you?'

Spoilers, Rosie, spoilers! I ignore the voice in my head. Nell looks so miserable, I've got to do something to cheer her up. 'No. So tell me what you imagine.'

'It don't matter,' she sighs, getting up from the table and starting to clear up the dishes.

'Yes, it does,' I say, standing up to help. 'Everyone needs dreams, and isn't this war supposed to make a better world for us all?'

For a moment, I think she's going to ignore me. She fills the sink up with soapy water and starts to wash up. I grab a tea-towel and dry. But in the end she says: 'I wanted to be a teacher.'

I want to punch the air, but I keep it cool and smile. 'I can definitely see you as a teacher. You'd be good at it. Maybe one day you'll be a headmistress.'

Nell laughs. 'Now you're talking daft. It's a pipe-dream, that's all it is. I'll be lucky to make it to the school gates. I ain't got no qualifications.'

'So get them.'

'I can't go back to school now. I'm too old.'

'You'll find a way. After the war, I bet loads of people will

135

want to change their lives. Technology is developing much quicker in war-time. Everyone will be learning new stuff.'

'But we'll all be working,' she says. 'God knows, there'll be plenty to do, rebuilding everything Jerry's smashed.'

'You can take evening classes,' I say, seriously pleased with myself. I'm not spoiling anything. Nell is determined to do something, and she is going to be a very good teacher. A bit scary, maybe. But hey, a lot of teachers are scary. They get you through your exams, though, so really they're quite cool.

But Nelly isn't so sure. 'Yeah, and I'm a monkey's uncle,' she says. 'I've never heard of anything so daft in all my life.'

I shrug. 'Suit yourself. But lots of people will be doing it. If you really want to teach, you can do it.' She might not believe me now, but I'm feeling just a bit smug, because I know something that know-it-all Nelly doesn't for a change. I can't resist adding: 'My Great-aunt Eleanor reckons you can do anything you set your mind to. It might take some people longer than others, but if you're prepared to work at it you'll get there in the end.'

'Eleanor, eh? That's my name. I never get called it though. I'm just plain old Nelly.'

'Really?' I say, trying not to smile. 'Eleanor's a lovely name. You should use it.'

She shrugs. 'It's a bit posh for round here.'

We're still halfway through the washing up when the sirens start up.

'Here we go again,' sighs Nelly, drying her hands on the tea-towel I'm holding. 'Leave it and get down the shelter. I'll get May.'

CHAPTER SEVENTEEN

I can't believe I've been here nearly a week, *and* I've nearly finished my first week at work. OK, so I know I missed a day at the factory, but hey, that was because I had a night of bloody hard work helping dig Shirley out, didn't I?

It's about four o'clock, and someone from the office comes into the workshop carrying a bundle of small brown envelopes. Everyone cheers and stops what they're doing.

'What's going on?' I ask Esther, the girl next to me.

She smiles. 'It's pay day.'

'Do you think I'll get anything? Don't I have to work a month first?'

'What you on about, Queenie?' says one of the older women. 'You rich enough to wait a month to get paid? Us peasants get our money every Friday, thanks very much.'

I feel a right idiot as everyone laughs. The cashier from the office ignores them, and sits down at the supervisor's table. The machinists all get up and form a queue in front of her. I don't know what to do until Esther calls me over. As each worker reaches the table, they give their name. They're handed an envelope and have to sign the list the cashier has on a clipboard in front of her. When I get to the table, there's one envelope left.

'Smith?'

'Er, yes. Rose Smith. That's me.'

She gives me the envelope. I can feel the weight of coins inside. 'Sign here.' I scribbled something illegible, and go back to my seat. The others are opening their paypackets, counting out their wages. I notice that Esther just tucks her unopened envelope into her pocket.

'Aren't you going to open it?' I ask.

Esther shakes her head. 'I give it to my uncle. He takes care of us.'

'Don't you live with your parents?'

'No. They are still in Amsterdam. My little brother Rudi and I came here two years ago.'

'They sent you on your own?'

'We were very lucky. My uncle sponsored us, and he'll take care of us until our parents come to England.' She sighs. 'But I worry that they will not be able to get here until after the war. There are so many restrictions on travel, even in our home town. And with a yellow star on their coats, it's not easy to move around without being noticed.'

'So you're a Jew, right?'

'Yes.' She looks a bit miffed. 'Does that bother you?'

'No, of course not,' I say. 'It doesn't matter what religion you are. My friend Saffi is Muslim, and she's cool. I ... I just didn't realise ...' But I'm suddenly thinking about reading *Anne Frank's Diary* at school last year, and studying the Holocaust. I remember all those pictures of bodies piled up in the concentration camps, the gas chambers, the starving survivors with their heads shaved. I thought they were awful before, but suddenly I'm talking to someone whose family could be in one of those camps. It's horrible to realise Esther's mum and dad could be caught up in that. Oh my God, they could die and she has no idea what's going on! This isn't some boring history lesson, this is real life.

'Er ... are in you touch with your parents, Esther?'

'Not for a while now,' she says, looking sad. 'My uncle says we must pray for them, and try not to worry. He has some contacts and they say my parents are well. But it's hard to get news – the war, you know?'

I want to give Esther a hug, but Mrs Bloomfield is yelling at us. 'Oi, you two. Just 'cause you've been paid, don't mean it's time to stop. You're still on the clock, so get on with it.' So we get back to work.

But I can't stop thinking about Esther's parents, trapped in Amsterdam. I'm probably the only person in Britain who knows what is going to happen to the Jews in Europe. It's making me feel sick, and I don't know what to do.

Esther might even know Anne Frank; they're about the same age. That would be really weird. Maybe I should ask her? Oh God, what am I thinking! I am seriously freaked right now.

Spoilers, spoilers, spoilers ... it's like a chant in my head. I desperately want to tell Esther about the Holocaust – maybe she could do something to get her mum and dad out of danger –

Spoilers, spoilers, spoilers ... my mind is going to explode. What if I did manage to get someone to believe me – there's a bloody war on, so what could they do? If I tell Esther, what could she do? She's just a kid like me. And if it all happens anyway, that would be seriously horrible. At least now she thinks her mum and dad are OK.

But what if I *could* stop it? That would be really awesome. Maybe that's why I'm here, stuck in 1940. To change the world. I should at least try. You know, use my head like Lil told me. But how am I going to explain how I know about this? Who's going to believe me? Nelly already thinks I'm a spy.

Arghh! I've got a splitting headache. My hand slips on the material I'm working on and I nearly puncture my finger on the needle. Seriously, I can't cope with this. I start to cry.

'What's the matter now?' Mrs Bloomfield looms over me.

'Nothing,' I sniff, wiping my eyes. 'I'm all right.'

'Yeah, you look it. Can't say the same for your seams,' she says. 'You'll have to unpick that lot.'

'Sorry,' I grab my unpicker, but I'm shaking so much I drop it.

'Give it here, before you stab yourself,' she picks up the tool and plucks the material out of my hand. 'Go on. I heard you helped dig someone out Wednesday night. That must've been rough. It's nearly five. Go and wash your face. Then go home and sort yourself out. But I want you back to speed on Monday, young lady. We can't afford no slackers round here. There's a war on, you know.'

'Thanks,' I say. 'I'm sorry.' I glance at Esther, who smiles in sympathy. It's too much, this is so awful. I run from the room, and when I finally lock the door to the loo, I break down and cry my eyes out.

I don't know how long I've been hiding in here. After crying so much I think I'm going to throw up, I start to calm down a bit. Eventually, someone bangs on the door.

'Come on, hurry up. There's a queue out here. Some of us are bursting!'

'All right, I won't be a minute,' I say, wiping my wet face on my sleeve. I take a deep breath, hoping no one will say anything about my puffy face and bloodshot eyes, and unlock the door. I keep my head down and wash my hands quickly, not looking at anyone. In the corridor I see Esther going out the main door. I wonder if I should go after her, but I don't know what to say. In the end I just stand here, doing nothing, hating myself.

'There you are, Queenie,' May frowns when she sees my face. 'You all right, love?' She looks so worried I nearly start crying again.

'Yes, I'm fine. I … I just got some dust in my eyes.'

'Blimey. Made a right mess of your face.' May puts her coat on and picks up her bag. 'Ne'er mind. It's Friday.' She grins. 'No work 'till Monday. We'll go out and paint the town red tonight.'

'I don't think I'll go, if you don't mind,' I say, grabbing my things. 'I'm … I'm not feeling great.'

'Oh, don't be daft. You'll be fine by the time we've got our glad rags on. I'll do your hair for you, if you like. I reckon you'd look dead sophisticated with one of them French pleats.'

I remember Gran doing my hair like that, and feel a wave of homesickness. I take a deep breath, determined not to cry again. Can I really go out dancing again after everything that's happened this week?

'I don't know. I feel like just going home to bed.' Home home, not this one. I just want to crawl under the duvet at Gran's and forget it all. I feel so bloody useless.

'Aw, come on Queenie, love. I know you've had a rough week, but it ain't all been bad has it? I mean, you saved that woman, and you've got your first paypacket. That's got to be worth celebrating, ain't it?'

'I suppose,' I say, feeling bad about letting May down. 'But

140

do we have to do it tonight? I really am tired.'

Nelly joins us and we head for the bus stop.

'You coming down the Palais tonight, Nelly?' asks May.

She shrugs. 'I might leave it till tomorrow.'

'Oh bloody hell, you two are like a pair of old women. Queenie's taking to her bed. It's Friday night, for Christ's sake! Well, I'm going. I need to get some practice in if I'm going to win that competition.'

'So Harry will be there, will he?'

'He might be. But there's plenty of other fellas I can dance with if he ain't. Oh come on, Nell, it'll be a laugh.'

Nelly doesn't look convinced. She looks at me and shrugs. I know she doesn't want to let May go on her own, not if there's a chance that Harry will be hanging around.

'Don't worry about me,' I say. 'I'm going to have an early night.'

'What if there's a raid?'

I roll my eyes. 'There's always a raid, isn't there? The sirens will wake me up and I'll go down to the shelter.'

'On your own?'

I shrug.

'You could always pop over to Lil. She's got a shelter n'all.'

'OK, if there's a raid, I'll go to Lil's.'

'All right,' she says to May. 'I'll go with you.'

May lets out a whoop and dances down the street.

CHAPTER EIGHTEEN

I don't know how I feel about being here in the house on my own. I thought it would be all right, but now I'm not so sure. It's creepy.

I remember what it was like at Gran's, when this older house would show itself to me. Now it's the other way round. I swear I can hear Gran and Great-aunt Eleanor talking in the front room. But when I go in there it's still the cold, drab room in 1940, and echoes of Gran's laughter swirl around the walls.

I stand in front of the hall mirror for ages, trying to use my head and figure out how the hell I'm going to get back. But all I can see is my pale face staring back at me – no Gran and her sister, young or old, in sight.

I decide to give up for now and go to bed. I'm so tired I can't think straight. But once I'm there I lie shivering in the dark, going over everything that's happened to me over the past week. It doesn't feel like a few days, it feels like I've been here for ages. I'm cold, battered and hungry. I never knew how hard it would be to live on rations and face bombing raids every single night. God, I miss Mum and Dad! I took everything for granted, didn't I? I'd give anything for a taste of Mum's fish pie right now; I've never told her it's my favourite. I'll even laugh at Dad's silly jokes if I can just get home. I'll never roll my eyes and get embarrassed by him again.

And I was so disrespectful to Gran, acting like she was stupid and sulking like a little kid because I had to go and stay with her. That's not right. It wasn't her fault that Simon preferred Jess, or that Jess would rather snog him than be my best friend.

Look at what the May and Nelly are living through! May has been really cool, and so kind to me. Even though Nelly has been a pain, they've both looked out for me. Look at how Nelly

143

yelled at Billy about keeping me out all night. I smile. She needn't have worried. I'm not going to anything naughty with my own grandpa, am I?

'*Use your head*.' Seriously, what does that mean? I've tried and tried to figure it out, but I just don't know what I'm supposed to do. I don't know why I'm here, or what I have to do to get home. I think about what Lil said about me being in other times, and this man she mentioned, who is he? What if I don't find my way back, but have to spend the rest of my life travelling through time? I know she said I got home, but what does she know, really? Maybe she's just totally mad and I shouldn't take any notice of what she says.

Now wide awake, I get up and turn the light on and rummage through the suitcase, which I still haven't unpacked. I mean, I'm not staying, am I? I find the notebook and crawl back into bed to try and keep warm while I write down everything that's happened to me since I arrived at Gran's. I write in text speak because I don't want May, or even worse Nelly, finding this and reading it.

Everything's coming out in a rush when those bloody sirens go off again. I'm tempted to stay here, but then realise that's a stupid thing to do. I drag on some trousers and a jumper and head down to the shelter. I have to stop on the way to collect a coat and shoes, then to make sure the gas is turned off like Nelly told me to. I'm out the back door and in the shelter before I remember I promised to go over the Lil's. But the planes are overhead now and the guns are going off. There's no way I'm going outside now, so I light the lamp and make myself comfortable and carry on writing.

I must have fallen asleep, because I'm waking up as the girls come bursting into the shelter. My cheek is plastered to the notebook. It's lucky I've been writing in pencil otherwise I'd have ink all over my face.

'What you doing here? Why didn't you go over to Lil?'

'I forgot,' I say, yawning and tucking the notebook into my coat pocket. 'What time is it?'

'About half eleven. Didn't you hear the all-clear?'

'No, I must have slept through it.'

'We got home and you weren't in,' says May. 'So I popped over to Lil's, but she said she ain't seen you. The old girl's in a bit of a state, I can tell you. She's having one of her turns. It's just a well you never went over there.'

'Is she all right?'

'Oh yeah,' Nelly waves my concern away. 'She's well known round here for her turns. She's goes off on one for a bit then she'll be right as rain tomorrow.'

'What do you mean she "goes off on one"?'

'Oh, Queenie, you should hear her, it's so funny,' says May. Nelly glares at her. 'Well, it does make you laugh, Nell, you know it does.' She turns to me. 'Anyway, she reckons she's got special powers, sort of like the 'fluence.' She wiggles her fingers and rolls her eyes. 'Old Lil sees ghosts and the like. Just now she was ranting on about time, and how something's happening again and she never thought she'd live to see the day and we'd better mind ourselves 'cause strange things are going on round here. She reckons she's packing up and going off to Ethel's tomorrow. Said she'd done her bit and was getting out before she gets blown to kingdom come.'

'It's a bloody wonder Jock's such a sensible fella, with a nan like that,' says Nelly. 'Anyway, Lil will be all right down Ethel's, but I won't if we stay out here much longer. It's blinking cold. Come on, let's get to bed while it's quiet.'

'Maybe it's just the war getting to Lil,' I say as we walk up the garden path. 'You know, when she says it's happening again – she's probably remembering the last war.'

'Yeah, I expect so.'

'And let's face it,' I go on, for some reason not wanting them to think that Lil is crazy, even though I'd been thinking it myself. 'There's definitely a lot of strange things happening round here with bombing raids everything night. You could hardly call it all normal, could you?'

'Yeah, all right, Queenie, we know what it's like. That's why we ain't too worried about the old girl. We all go off on one now and again, eh Nell?'

'Not me,' she says. 'You won't catch me acting like a

bleeding mad woman. I ain't got no time for nonsense like that. There's a war on, ain't there?'

'That's the whole point,' I say. 'This war is enough to do anyone's head in.'

'Well, I ain't going to argue with you,' says Nelly. 'I'm off to me bed, and I suggest you to do the same.'

CHAPTER NINETEEN

The next morning I wake and can't understand why Nelly and May don't seem to be moving around making a noise like they usually do. Its freezing but I throw off the bedclothes, determined not to be late again. As my feet touch the cold lino I realise its Saturday and we don't have to go to work. I nearly cry with relief and snuggle back down under the covers to enjoy a lie-in.

I didn't surface again until I heard the girls moving about at around eight o'clock. I'm glad I did, because once breakfast was over there wasn't much chance to relax. Nelly announced there were jobs to be done, and started ordering us around like an army sergeant. Between us we cleaned the house from top to bottom – and with no vacuum cleaner or modern cleaning products it was hard work, I can tell you. Floors had to be swept and rugs hung over the washing line in the back garden and bashed with a carpet beater shaped like a tennis racket to get all the dust out. The furniture had to be polished with wax out of a tin – no Pledge spray here. We changed the bed sheets, none of which are fitted, so now I know why my bedding keeps going all lumpy when I toss and turn in my sleep.

After a quick sandwich for lunch, May announces she's going up town to meet Harry.

'What about the washing?' asks Nelly.

'I've only got a few bits, I'll do them later. Anyway, with Queenie here, there's no point me hanging around is there? The three of us will get under each other's feet. Harry's promised to take me to the Lyon's Tea House. I ain't missing that treat just to wash me smalls.'

Nelly sighs. 'All right. But don't be late back.'

'Yes, Mum,' says May, laughing and running upstairs.

'If I was your mum you'd be better behaved,' Nelly shouts after her. 'She wouldn't have put up with the likes of Harry.'

So, we get on with the washing. It all has to be done by hand in the kitchen sink. We don't have a big washing copper like Lil has over the road.

I've got to say, I was shocked by how hard it is to get everything clean without a washing machine. First, it all has to be washed in hot soapy water, using an old-fashioned washboard to scrub the dirt out. I've seen this thing before – Gran still has it, and ages ago she explained how it works. She still uses it sometimes, even though she's got a state-of-the-art automatic washing machine. I thought it looked like a doddle, but it's really hard work. Seriously, I had no idea how hot and sweaty you get using a washboard. It doesn't help that, apparently, I've used too much soap.

'Oi, what you doing, using all that?' Nell yells at me. 'You don't need that much, and we can't afford to waste soap.'

'Sorry,' I say, wiping my forehead with my arm. 'I didn't know how much to use.'

Nell tuts. 'I suppose your mum does the washing at home? She's doing you no favours, waiting on you hand and foot. You'll be no use to man nor beast in the end.'

I want to point out I do know how to use the washing machine at home, and sometimes put a load on for Mum, but to be fair I don't do it very often. 'I suppose you're right,' I sigh.

'Well, get on with it now, and mind you rinse that lot properly. When you're ready to do the next lot, I'll show you how much soap to use.'

'OK, thanks.'

Eventually, I have a pile of soggy, but well-scrubbed clothes. Nell helps me put them through the mangle, feeding the material through rollers to squeeze out the water. Next we lower the wooden racks which were hanging by ropes from the ceiling, and hang the clothes up because it's far too cold to put them out on the line in the back yard. The racks are pulled back up and secured, and Nell lights the fire so that the heat in the kitchen will dry the wet washing. Watching the fire in the grate, I suddenly realise why Gran's kitchen seems bigger than this one – she's had the chimney breast taken out.

The kitchen is damp and steamy, and there's water all over the floor by now. I mop up the puddles, while Nelly gets on with her own washing. She's much quicker at it than me, and makes a lot less mess.

'Shall I make us a cup of tea?' I ask, arching my back, hands on hips. I really want to just lie down somewhere, I'm so tired. No wonder Gran always said women have it easy in the future.

'If you like.'

I make a pot of tea, all the time dreaming about chocolate chip cookies. It's so hard, doing so much manual work whilst living on rations. There's never enough to eat, and I'm getting totally sick of the stodgy, flavourless meals we've had. What I wouldn't give for a pizza, or a curry! Even some herbs or garlic would make a huge difference, but the only flavourings we have are salt, pepper or vinegar. Even pepper isn't the same as at home – it's ground into a grey powder and isn't anything like the fancy peppercorns my mum uses.

I've never been fat, but I'm noticing that my clothes are getting looser. At this rate, I'll end up looking like an anorexic if I don't get home soon.

I'm just pouring the tea when there's a knock at the door. Nelly is up to her armpits in washing, so I go to answer it. It's Bill.

'Hiya,' I smile. 'Come in. I've just made some tea. Do you want a cup?'

'Er, hallo,' he said. 'I've just taken Nan to the station. She thought you girls might like some of this veg. We had a good year on the allotment, so there's plenty of spuds and onions left over. There's a few carrots in there n'all, and sprouts, and some turnips. But what with all this cold, she don't think they'll last much longer. We thought it was better to share it with the neighbours than let it go rotten in the frost.'

He holds out a sack, bulging with vegetables. I feel tears well up. Extra food! Oh, bliss! My mouth waters as I step back.

'Bill, that's so kind. Come in, come in. Wait till Nelly sees this lot. She'll be made up.'

He looks at me a bit odd, then shakes his head and comes in.

He wipes his feet on the mat and steps into the hall. He looks at the coat stand. 'It don't look like magic to me,' he says quietly. 'You sure it had something to do with – you know?'

'I haven't a clue. If I did I'd have gone back the way I came.' I pull a face in the mirror. 'It doesn't explain the portal in that basement, does it? I just don't know anymore, Bill.' I shrug. 'Anyway, don't mention it around Nelly, OK?'

He nods. 'Is May not around, then?'

'No, she's out. But if you stay for a cuppa, she might be home soon.'

'Oh. All right. Just a quick one.'

Nelly greets him politely and thanks him for the food. Then she pulls me to one side and hisses, 'Take him in the parlour, for God's sake. I don't want him watching while I wash me smalls!'

'Oh, right. Sorry,' I say, trying not to laugh. 'Come on, Bill, we'll take ours in the parlour.'

'Put the paraffin heater on in there, it'll be quicker than lighting the fire to warm it up, or you'll catch your deaths,' Nelly calls after us.

It's easier said than done. I've never lit one before, and in the end Bill takes pity on me – either that or he's fed up with standing there shivering – and shows me how to do it.

Bill sits in an armchair and I take the sofa. I hope the heater warms us up soon.

'Thanks,' I smile. 'I'm pretty useless around here. I think I just used about a month's worth of soap flakes on my washing, and I nearly singed my eyebrows off the other day, trying to light the grill on the cooker.'

Bill laughs. 'I'll bet Nell's been putting you right.'

I roll my eyes. 'She's worse than my mum sometimes.' I suddenly feel really homesick. All things considered, Mum's not so bad. I wonder if I'll ever get the chance to tell her.

We sip our tea. The only sounds in the room are the hiss of the heater and the tick-tock of the clock on the mantelpiece. Bill looks at the clock and frowns. When he sees me looking me gives me an awkward grin.

'What's the matter?'

'I ain't got long. I'm on duty later on.'

'You're a private, aren't you?'

'Yeah, I've just heard I'm getting me corporal's stripes next week.'

'Cool. We'll have to salute you from now on, Corporal Bill!'

'Too right,' he grins.

'Will you be sent overseas?' I ask.

He does that eyebrow thing. 'Don't you know?'

'I don't know everything, Bill. And if I did, I don't think I should tell you.'

'Yeah, I know. Spoilers. Nan told me. You talked to her about all this, didn't you?'

'Er, not exactly. She talked to me.'

'How come?'

'Seriously, I've no idea. She said loads of strange things about me being younger, and I'd been a teacher and got locked up and all sorts of stuff. To be honest, Bill, she scared me. From what she said it looks like I might be time-travelling for ever. But she said I told her she had to tell me it's going to be all right. I've just got to use my head, if that makes any sense? But I don't understand. I mean, how does she know? I just want to go home –'

'Hang on a minute, Rosie. Calm down, love.' Bill gets up and comes across and kneels in front of me. 'You're getting yourself in a state.' I take a deep breath, trying to calm down. 'Now, I've got no idea what you're talking about half the time, but if Nan says it will be all right, and if she heard it from you another time, then I reckon you'd better listen.'

'The girls think Lil's mad.'

'Yeah, well, there's a lot of folks who say that. I've thought it meself a time or two. But you know what? I believe what you told me – about you coming from the future – and if Nan says she's seen you in the past, well, that sort of makes sense n'all in the circumstances, don't it?'

'I suppose so, but she's gone away now, hasn't she? I can't ask her any more about it. What if –'

He puts a finger to my lips, shutting me up. 'Ain't no point in what if, Rosie. It's like this war. There ain't no point in wanting it to be different. It's here and we've got to sort it out, 'cause if we don't, we'll all be talking German soon. Now, I thought about what you said about spoilers and the like, and I agree with you. It's best not to know, 'cause then you do what you can and don't take nothing for granted.'

My throat is tight and my eyes fill up with tears. 'But what if you do know something – something really, really terrible. Shouldn't you try to change that?'

Bill looks at me. He has no idea what I'm talking about. He hasn't seen the pictures of the Holocaust survivors, so thin and afraid; or the ovens and the piles of shoes and – Oh God! I rub my eyes, trying to clear my tears and the images in my brain at the same time. Bill sits on the sofa next to me and pulls me into his arms.

'Hey, it's all right. Don't fret, come on. You'll make yourself ill.'

'Oh God, I don't know what to do.'

'Maybe you'd better leave it to God, then. I don't reckon there's much else you can do.'

'Do you believe in God?'

'I thought I did. But these days? Who knows? I like to think he's out there somewhere and he's on our side. 'Cause if he ain't, what's the point?'

'I can't help wondering if God is having a huge joke at my expense, sending me here to teach me a lesson. I know I've been horrible to Mum and Dad sometimes, and I've been disrespectful to Gran, but I'm not nearly as bad as some of my friends. I'm quite a good girl really. I mean, I don't smoke or do drugs and I haven't done more than snog a couple of boys. Why would God do this to me? Maybe he does want me to change things. Maybe I have to tell everyone so that it doesn't happen. But if I do, what will happen to the future? I might be like Marty McFly and end up going back to a different future, and I'll have a horrible step-dad and everything will be terrible and -'

'Rosie, stop it. I don't have a clue who this Marty bloke is, but you've got to calm down.'

I squeeze my eyes shut and take a deep breath. 'You're right.

'I'm being stupid.' Tears well up again. 'It's just really, really hard, and it's so cold and I'm always hungry and frightened, and I just want to go home.'

'Hush now.' He holds me tight and lets me cry for a bit more, then he starts to talk softly. 'You know, I ain't never met a girl like you. I don't know anyone who would have climbed down that hole in your pretty dress to get that woman out. Not even Nelly or May.'

I hiccup and can't help a little giggle. 'Nelly would have stood there and shouted to the woman to sort herself out. I'm not sure about May. She's really kind. I think she'd have tried. Actually, I think Nelly would have too. When something has to be done, she gets on with it, even if she doesn't like it. Look how she's put up with me. I'm useless, but she won't let me give up till I've got it right.' I hold up my hands, which are red and dried out from the washing. 'Look at the state of my hands – I don't think I've ever worked so hard in my life. My Mum would have given up and done it for me.'

'What's she like, your Mum?' He asks. I hesitate. 'I ain't asking for spoilers, Rosie. I'm just curious. From what you say, she's going to be my daughter-in-law. It'll be nice to have a bit of advance knowledge when my boy starts bringing home girlfriends.' He laughs. 'Hark at me! I ain't even got a girlfriend meself yet, and I'm talking about me son's sweethearts.'

I smile. 'I'm glad you believe me.'

'Well, why not? I've always had a soft spot for May. If you reckon we're going to get hitched, that's all right by me. It'd be nice to get some sign that May's interested, mind. She always treats me like a mate. I don't think she fancies me at all.'

I shrug. 'Well, she will, I'm sure. Gran always –' I stop talking. I was going to say that she always talks about how much she loved him and he loved her. But if I say that, he'll realise that in my time he's dead. I look up at his young face, he's waiting for me to go on, but there's a great big lump in my throat. I wish he hadn't died so I could have known him then. I shake my head. 'Spoilers,' I say, feeling like a fraud.

He nods and sighs. 'Yeah, I know. But can't you give me a clue as to how I'm going to get May to go out with me?'

'Have you asked her?'

'Ain't much point. I've seen her flirting with fellas she fancies. She ain't never done that with me.'

Mmm. I remember May's reaction when I said Bill was fit. She was really surprised. 'Let me think about it,' I say. But I really don't have any idea. I rest my head on his shoulder and we sit in the quiet, cuddling up on the sofa. It's not like I'm an expert on dating – I've been hanging around waiting for Simon to notice me, and it's been completely pointless because he's a muppet who doesn't know a good thing when it's right there under his nose. Not that I want him to notice me now, not after he snogged Jess. And as for Jess – no, I won't think about that now. But ... maybe there is something ... 'Has she ever seen you with another girl?' I ask.

'Only girls I've danced with at the Palais. She's never taken no notice.'

'But she's never thought you were serious about any of them?'

'No, 'cause I haven't been. We just dance and chat, that's all. I don't play around. I ain't bleeding Harry.'

I wave a hand. 'Seriously, I don't know what she sees in him.'

'Too right.' Bill looks at the clock on the mantelpiece. 'I'd better go.'

I'm really reluctant to let him go. I feel so safe and warm. I sit up, untangling my arms and he stands up. He holds out a hand and pulls me up. We're standing close together and Bill is kissing me on the cheek when May walks into the parlour.

'Oh! Sorry, Nell said ...' May looks embarrassed.

'Hello, May. We didn't hear the front door,' says Bill, going a bit pink.

She stares at Bill like she's never seen him before. Interesting! I slip my arm around his waist and he automatically puts his arm round my shoulder. Her eyes follow my movement and she frowns slightly before pasting a smile on her face. 'No, I don't suppose you did. Nell's put the kettle on. Do you want another cuppa?'

'Not for me thanks, I'm off.'

'Oh. All right. See you around, Jock.'

'It's Bill,' I say. Bill squeezes my shoulder.

'But he's always been Jock.'

'It doesn't mean he likes it,' I say.

May looks confused. I don't think it's ever occurred to her that people don't like nicknames.

'It's all right, May. You ain't the only one, everyone does it. But if you could see your way to calling me Bill, well, I'd appreciate it.'

'Well, I'll try to remember,' she says. 'But it'll be hard after all these years.'

I have an idea. 'Why don't you imagine you've never met him before? Here,' I grab his hand and pull him towards May. 'May, let me introduce my friend Bill. May, Bill, Bill, May.' They both look at me like I'm mad. 'Now you shake hands and say how do you do, OK?'

Bill and May look at each other and burst out laughing.

'Why not?' says May and holds out her hand. Bill takes it in both of his big, capable hands. 'Hello Bill, nice to meet you.'

'Yeah, nice to meet you too, May.'

I'm so pleased with myself as they smile at each other, I want to run round them cheering.

When Bill turns to leave, I fling my arms around him and give him a kiss on the cheek. He laughs and swings me up in the air and as he puts me back on my feet he kisses my forehead. 'Thanks,' he whispers before he lets me go and with a cheerful wave to May he walks out the door.

May is standing there looking at me with a frown on her face. 'So, you and J– Bill. Are you courting?'

I'm about to deny it, but change my mind. 'We might be,' I say. 'Why? You've got Harry, haven't you? Did you want Bill for Nelly?'

'No! Not Nelly and Jock, I mean Bill. He ain't her sort. She likes posh boys.'

'So what's the problem.'

May shrugs. 'Nothing. It's just … Jock? I ain't never thought …'

'Why not? He's lovely.'

'But I've known him all my life. He's like a brother.'

'Well I certainly don't want him for a brother. Maybe if you started thinking about him as Bill, and pretended you've never met him before you might start seeing him differently.'

May shakes her head. 'God help us, you are the strangest person I've ever met, Queenie. How can I do that?'

'Just try, May. You might surprise yourself,' I say as I walk out of the room, leaving her standing there looking totally baffled.

CHAPTER TWENTY

'He's a nice boy,' says May following me. 'Don't you go messing him about, Queenie.'

'Of course I won't,' I say. 'I really like him. I'm surprised he hasn't got a girlfriend already.'

May frowns. 'I dunno. I never thought about him like that. He's always been a mate.'

'My Gran says the best husband is the one who's your best friend too.'

'Huh, I'll bet she never met someone exciting like Harry. Why would you settle for someone like Jock —'

'Bill,' I interrupt.

May rolls her eyes. 'Like Bill,' she says, 'when you could have Harry?'

I don't like the sound of that. 'Well I know she did meet someone just like Harry, and he wasn't half as good as my grandpa.' Before she can asked me how I know I say 'Where is Harry, by the way? I thought you were going to see him.'

'I did. We had tea up town.'

'And?'

'And, what?'

'Come on, May. Spill. I want all the gory details.'

'Mind your own business,' May giggles. 'A girl's gotta have some secrets.'

Yeah, right. Secrets. Spoilers and secrets. Actually I don't want to know what May got up to with Harry. But I've got to make sure that Bill ends up marrying her, end of.

Nelly yells from the kitchen, 'Has he gone?'

'Yes, he's working tonight,' I call back. 'He said the forecast is for clear skies, so there'll be a raid.'

'Right. We'd better get ready to run down the shelter. Turn that heater off in there, now he's gone. We can't afford to burn paraffin if we don't need to.'

May turns it off, which is just as well, because I still don't have a clue how to use the thing. We join Nelly in the kitchen. It's hot and humid in here, as our clothes steam on the racks. It reminds me of our holiday in Thailand last year. I'd never known such soggy heat. It's funny to think, if I'd been born before the war like May and Nelly, I'd never have holidays like that, ever. I just hope I get the chance to have more, but it all depends on whether I can get home or not. And stay there.

'So where's Harry, then?' asks Nelly. 'Didn't he see you home?'

'He had some business up town,' says May.

'He's not getting you involved in no funny business, is he?'

'No, he ain't. Jesus Christ, stop going on, Nell. I ain't a kid, and you ain't my mother.'

Nelly looks stunned. I doubt if May has ever spoken to her like that before. Before the conversation can descend into a full blown row, I step in. 'Whoa, chillax.'

They stare at me, then at each other. May laughs, and Nelly shakes her head.

'Chillax? What's that when it's at home?'

I roll my eyes. It's like speaking a different language sometimes. 'Yeah, chillax. It's Latin. It means calm down and relax. Don't argue, OK?'

'I'm not arguing,' says Nelly. 'I'm worried about her, that's all.'

May opens her mouth, and closes it again.

'Did you want to say something, May?' I ask.

'Get if off your chest,' says Nelly, arms crossed. No way is she chillaxing.

May sighs. 'There ain't no need for anyone to worry about me. I'm all right. And if you'd give him a chance, you'd see that Harry's all right too.'

'That's as may be,' says Nell. 'But we know enough about him to know he ain't earning his money in no proper job, and he ain't showing no signs of joining up like the decent fellas around here, so if you don't mind I'll reserve judgement.'

May shrugs. 'Suit yourself. But while you're fretting over

158

me and Harry, I'll bet you didn't know Queenie here was canoodling with Jock in our front parlour.'

'We were not ... whatever that word is,' I gasp, feeling myself go red.

'Canoodling. Kissing. Wrapped round each other, they were,' May tells her sister. 'They looked right shifty when I walked in there and caught 'em at it.'

'You and Jock?' said Nell. 'But I thought you said he ...'

'He was helping me up. Your sofa swallows you up, so he gave me a hand. I told you, he's really nice, and anyone would be lucky to go out with him,' I say, wishing they'd both shut up.

Nelly frowns. I give her a wink and look at May. Nelly looks from me to May and back. 'Oh, yeah, so you did. But that don't mean you can carry on like that in my front parlour.'

'I won't do it again,' I say, trying to keep a straight face. 'Oh, I left our tea cups in there. I'll get them.'

When I get back to the kitchen, Nelly was alone. 'Where's May?' I ask.

'She's in the lav,' says Nell. 'So you've got about thirty seconds to tell me what the bloomin' heck is going on.'

'Nothing is going on,' I say. 'She just saw me give Bill a hug.'

'*You* gave *him* a hug? Girls round here wait for the fella to make the first move, or they get a bad reputation.'

'It wasn't that sort of a hug. I was just being friendly. I wasn't coming on to him.'

Nell shakes her head. 'I don't know what you get up to in the country, but hugs is hugs round here. If you ain't asking for trouble, you don't go round giving fellas reason to think you are.'

I laugh. 'Bill is cool. We both know it's May he wants.'

'So, why all the canoodling?'

'Maybe to make May jealous? If she sees me with Bill, she might start to see what a nice guy he is.'

'Well, that ain't going to work while she's walking out with flash Harry, is it?'

'No, I suppose not. We'll have to find a way to get rid of him.'

The air-raid siren starts wailing in the street.

'Blimey, they're early today.'

We go into the hall to collect the coats. 'If these raids go on much longer,' says Nelly, 'we might not have to worry about it. Hitler's set on killing the lot of us, I reckon.'

'He'll try, but he won't succeed,' I say, feeling pretty smug. 'We'll beat him in the end.'

'Let's hope you're right, Queenie. I just wish our boys would get on with it. I hate that bloody Anderson shelter.'

It is one of the longest and scariest raids so far. We try to keep our spirits up by playing cards and games. The girls have to teach me most of them because I've never heard of half of them before. We talk about Christmas and plan to make some decorations – paper chains out of old newspapers and magazines, things like that. I remember the lovely tree we have every year at home, with decorations in gorgeous colours, and the lights, and the angel on the top. It seems like another life. Every explosion seems to be getting closer, and the shelter shakes as bombs destroy buildings just a couple of streets away. When the all clear finally sounds hours later we are exhausted.

We stumble out into the frosty night, wanting nothing more than to get inside the house and crawl into bed.

The cold air is filled with the smell of burning. The sky is orange, reflecting the fires that still rage across London. In my room, I leave the light off and peek out through the blackout curtains. God, it's awful. I can see ruined buildings silhouetted against the flames. Beams of light keep searching the sky for stray bombers.

I notice a crack in the window-pane. The glass is held together by the tape criss-crossing it, but I reckon another blast will shatter it completely. I shiver, wondering for the millionth time whether I'll ever get home again. I don't want to die here. I want to see Mum and Dad, and Gran and Great-aunt Eleanor, and my friends, even Jessica.

I wish I knew why Jess did that to me. I mean, she's always saying Simon just plays around with girls. I reckoned he was waiting for me to grow up, but after seeing how stupid May is getting over Harry I can't help wondering if Jess was doing something mad like trying to show me what a tart he is. I mean, what idiot would play around with his best friend's sister? He's either got to be madly in love with Jess, in which case I don't stand a chance anyway, or he's just having a laugh and doesn't care that Luke might not want him messing with his little sister. Oh, I don't know. Am I thinking this way because I'm trying to get May's attention away from Harry and onto Bill by trying to make her see that Bill is sexy? I've known Jess all my life and I reckon she might just be mad enough to think she's doing me a favour by snogging Simon in front of me, knowing how I'd react.

I try to conjure up a picture of Simon in my mind, but can't. He doesn't seem real any more. He's about the same age as Bill, but he seems like a kid compared to him. Actually, come to think of it, Jess's brother Luke is more like Bill. He's a nice bloke. I haven't taken much notice of him because he's Jess's brother. I was so shocked when he asked me out, I've never thought of him like that. Maybe I should take a closer look when I get home? But then again, I'd better sort things out with Jess first. I can't believe I might lose my best friend because of a boy. After the week I've had here, I reckon I'd better get my priorities right.

The next morning there's a knock at the door. It's Bill. He's still in uniform, but it's filthy, covered in soot and grime.

'Bill! What happened? Are you all right?' I ask. 'Come in.'

'No, I won't. I'm just on my way home. I popped over to see if Nan's place was all right. I promised her I'd keep an eye on it while she's gone. A couple of her windows have gone. I'll have to board them up.'

'Do you need any help? We can come over and give you a hand, if you like.' Nell says, as she and May come down the stairs towards us.

'Thanks, but I ain't got enough plywood. I'll get some and come back after I've cleaned up and had a kip. I just wanted to see if you're all alright.'

'We're fine. But you do look tired. Are you sure you don't want a cup of tea or something?' says May.

'Nah, ta anyway. I've been helping fight the fires down at the docks. The WRVS van came down and kept us going with tea and buns all night.'

The Women's Royal Voluntary Service run a fleet of vans which station themselves in bombed areas as soon as the all-clear sounds. They provide food and drink and moral support from street corners. People say the WRVS is a life-saver, and I have to say they were the best thing about coming out of that cellar the other night. That mug of tea they gave me was like nectar – strong and sweet.

'I'm glad they were there for you,' I say. 'Was it awful?'

For a moment, all he can do is shake his head. He looks so tired and miserable. 'It was like I imagine hell is,' he says quietly. I feel my heart squeeze. Poor Bill. 'There's not much of the docks left, that's for sure. Bloody Jerry. They dropped a load of incendiaries on houses, too. God knows how many civilians have been killed. A few of my mates copped it n'all. One of the gun emplacements took a direct hit. Poor sods.'

'Oh, Bill. I'm so sorry,' I say, trying not to cry.

'It ain't your fault. Mine neither. Can't help feeling bad, though.' He takes a deep breath and looks at us. 'Anyway, I'll rest easy knowing you girls are all right.'

'We're fine, Bill,' says May. 'Thanks for thinking of us.'

He hesitates, looking pleased that she remembered to use his name. 'Um, would you mind if I have a quick word with Queenie?'

I glance at the sisters. May looks surprised. Nell looks annoyed.

'Uh, yeah. Of course,' says May. 'Come on, Nell.' She grabs her sister's sleeve and pulls her down the passage to the kitchen. 'See you later, Bill. Don't forget, if you need anything, give us a shout.'

We stand looking at each other, unwilling to talk until the girls shut the kitchen door behind them. The sound of it closing makes Bill flinch.

'Sorry,' he says. 'I'm a bit shell-shocked this morning. Me

ears are still ringing from all the noise.'

'That's understandable. You look ready to drop. Why don't you go and get some rest, Bill?'

'I will. I just wanted … no, needed, to talk to you first.' He pauses, rubbing the back of his neck. His face, under the soot, looks grey with fatigue. 'I meant to tell you yesterday, I tried to talk to Nan about you again. I wanted to get her to tell us how you manage to get home, but I don't reckon she knows anyway. She just said you'll finish what you came here for, then it will all be all right.'

'But what am I supposed to finish? I don't have a clue. God, this is so frustrating!'

'I know. Try not to fret. Here, maybe you're supposed to get May to go out with me,' he grins, but I can see he's dead on his feet, so I doubt if he means it.

'Did you ask her what I'm supposed to do?'

'Yeah, but she keeps muttering on about spoilers. I'll bet that's what you told her before.'

'Well that was particularly stupid of me, wasn't it?' I sigh, resting my head against the door jamb.

'Don't fret. You're a clever girl. You'll work it out. You must do if you've already met Nan before.' He squeezes his eyes shut and shakes his head as though trying to get his brain working again. 'Jesus, I never imagined I'd ever be having a conversation like this. Is this really happening, Rosie? Are you really from the future?'

'Yes and you're really my grandpa, so you've got to make sure you marry May. Don't blow it, Bill. Promise me.'

He sighs. 'Believe me, I'd like nothing better. May's a fine girl. I've always had a soft spot for her. But I can't see how I can make her fancy me. I ain't exactly Clark Gable.'

'I have no idea who Clark Gable is, but that's irrelevant. Just make sure you don't let Harry ruin things, OK?'

Bill scowls. 'That bloody spiv. I've been asking around about him. He's a right sh– shocking piece of work. Seems to me he's only bothered about that bloody dance competition prize money. May's his best bet for winning, so he'll pile on the charm to keep her sweet. But I reckon she won't see none of that money if they win.'

'Well, trust me, she won't thank you for telling her that. No, we've got to think of something else.'

Bill is swaying on his feet. I doubt if he's taken a word I said on board.

'You'd better get some rest,' I say. 'Go on home, Bill.'

'Yeah, sorry love, I can barely keep me eyes open.'

'Why don't you stay at your nan's?'

'Can't. I'll have to sort out some plywood and bring it round and do her windows. Then I'm back on tonight. Me spare uniform's at home. It's not far, just a couple of streets away. You'll have to come round some time.'

'I'd like that. Now go.' I give him a gentle shove. He salutes me and heads home.

CHAPTER TWENTY-ONE

OK, so it's all very well telling Bill he's got to marry May, but seriously have no idea how to get her to see him as a potential boyfriend. And what are we going to do about Harry? I can't just sit around and wait for May to get her heart broken. No, I've got to take drastic action. The trouble is, I have no idea what that might be.

May knows we all hate Harry, but that just seems to make him more attractive, so I can't just keep on dissing him. If I tell her what Bill says about the prize money, she won't believe us and she'll probably blame Bill when it does all go wrong.

I also need to think carefully about how May sees me and Bill. I mean, I really want her to get jealous, to see him as boyfriend material. But if she thinks I'm going out with him, she might just let us get on with it. I need to talk to Bill and make sure everyone knows we're just friends. He needs to be free of romantic entanglements when May finally comes to her senses, otherwise it could all go spectacularly wrong.

'You all right, Queenie?' says May when I go into the kitchen.

'Yes. Why?'

'It sounded like you and Bill was getting mighty serious out there.'

I hope they weren't listening at the door. No, they couldn't have been or they'd be asking me what I was playing at. 'Not really,' I say. 'I just told him he needed to get some sleep, that's all.'

May shakes a finger at me. 'Chaps don't like being told what to do, you know. You'll put him off if you're not careful.'

'Are you serious?' I ask. 'All the boys I know need telling, or they'd sit on their backsides all day.'

'Well, I don't reckon Bill'll take kindly to being ordered

about. You be careful or he'll find himself another girlfriend.'

'I wasn't– I'm not! Look Bill and I are just friends, OK?'

'Friends what hug,' says Nelly.

'If you like. I hug all my friends.'

'You ain't hugging me,' she says crossing her arms.

I laugh. 'Why not, Nelly? You might like it. How about you, May?' I open my arms.

May laughs with me. 'Get on with you, you daft bat.'

I shrug. 'Your loss. Bill doesn't mind.'

'I'll bet he'll be wanting a kiss with all that hugging.'

'No he doesn't. He's a friend. That's all.'

It looks like May wants to ask more, but Nelly changes the subject.

'The washing's dry. I don't suppose your mum showed you how to use an iron, did she?'

'I can use an iron. I'm not stupid.'

'Good, 'cause I ain't got time to do yours n'all.'

She lays a thick blanket over the table, then a folded sheet. May brings out the iron, which was much smaller than the one at home. I'm about to look at it when Nell stands on a chair and reaches up to pull out the bulb from its fitting. Then she connects the iron's plug into the light socket.

'What are you doing?' I shout. 'You'll electrocute yourself.'

Nell raises her eyebrows. 'Ooh, hark at you. I'll electrocute myself, will I? I thought you said you knew how an iron works.'

'I do. But you plug it into the wall, not the light socket.'

'We ain't got many wall sockets,' says May as Nelly climbs down. 'Dad said he'll get some more sorted once the war's over.'

'There's a couple in the parlour, for the radio and the standard lamp,' says Nelly. 'And we can manage in here like this,' she points up to the light fitting, with the wire for the iron hanging down from it. 'We've been using this for years, and no one ain't got "electrocuted" yet.'

For a moment I'm distracted, wondering what Great-aunt Eleanor would think if she remembered the way she talked as a girl. No one meeting her in the future would have any idea that

166

her grammar is so terrible now. I'd love to be around to see how she changes between this time and when I meet her in the future. Hey, hang on. No I wouldn't. I don't want to wait that long to get home!

Whatever happens to Nelly's language skills, there's no denying she's a hard worker. She makes the ironing look easy. I sit at the table watching Nelly ironing while May gets on with her washing. It's pretty obvious this iron isn't the same as Mum's posh steam one. This one's a solid lump, with no steam holes. It's much smaller than a modern iron as well. There doesn't seem to be any temperature control – it's either hot, or it isn't. Nelly is obviously used to it, and uses a damp tea towel between the iron and the cloth when she's dealing with more delicate fabrics.

When she's finished, it's my turn. I take my time. I start with my work overall, which is fairly straightforward, but the blouses are a pain as I have to use the damp cloth and there are so many fiddly bits. Just when I think I've got it sussed I lose my grip on the heavy iron and drop it. I instinctively make a grab for it and catch the side of my thumb on the hot surface.

'Argh! Shit, shit, shit! Ow, that hurts.'

I dance around the room, waving my hand in the air, trying to make the pain go away. Nelly picks up the iron from where it fell on the table and stands it upright. May grabs my arm with damp fingers and drags me to the sink. She turns on the tap and shoves my hand under the cold stream.

'What the bloody hell are you doing, Queenie? Stop fidgeting. Here, Nell, get some butter.'

'What do you want butter for?' I ask, hissing with pain. Even the water hurts.

'For the burn.'

I try to pull my hand out of her grip. 'Are you mad? You can't put butter on it. I'll bloody fry!'

'Stop fussing.'

'Sod off. No way are you putting butter on there.'

'Too right we ain't,' says Nelly. 'We ain't got enough to waste. You'll have to take your chances. And while you're at it, watch your mouth. It ain't our fault you dropped the thing.

We're lucky it ain't broke. I thought you said you knew how to use an iron.'

'I do,' I shout, the pain bringing tears to my eyes so I barely know what I'm saying. 'But you didn't tell me it was some old-fashioned, uncontrollable lump. Why the bloody hell can't you have a decent iron that doesn't weigh a ton and plugs into a proper socket like normal people?'

'We are normal people,' she shouts back 'It's you what ain't!'

I stand in stunned silence, my mouth open, my face wet with tears, as she reaches past me to turn off the tap before the sink overflows.

May gives a nervous giggle as she lets go of my hand and starts fishing her wet underwear out of the water. 'Oh my God, it all happened so quick I forgot me smalls was in there. Thanks Nell.'

'You're welcome, May.' She looks at me. I get the message. I look at my hand. There's a great big welt along the back of my thumb, red and throbbing.

'I'm sorry, OK?' I say. I can't stop my voice from trembling. I think I'm in shock or something. 'This is soooo painful.'

Nelly fills an enamel bowl with cold water. 'Here, keep it in there for a bit.'

I take a deep breath and let it out as I put my hand in. I feel dizzy with the pain. My other hand is shaking. Nelly holds the bowl and urges me towards the table. I sit down, trying not to look at that bloody iron, standing there like a monument to my pain. There's an iron-shaped scorch mark on the sheet. Another thing to annoy Nelly, no doubt. I wait for her to give me another lecture.

Instead she picks up the iron and finishes my blouse, folding it far more neatly than I ever could and adding it to my pathetic pile of clothes. Then she climbs up and unplugs it, then puts it away and clears the table. I feel like a right muppet.

'Thanks,' I say. 'I'm really sorry.'

'What's done is done. Be more careful in future.'

I will. Oh, I will. I nod, too miserable to say anything.

'Aw, don't fret, Queenie,' says May. 'You'll get the hang of it. You just ain't used to what we are.'

Nelly doesn't say anything, but makes a pot of tea while May puts her washing through the mangle and hangs it up. Their quick efficiency as they work around each other in the confined space reminds me of Gran and Great-aunt Eleanor and I'm almost tempted to tell them everything. But as Nelly plonks a cup of tea down in front of me I lose my nerve.

'Here, there's some sugar in it. Good for shock. Let's have a look,' says Nelly, taking my hand with surprisingly gentle fingers. 'Blimey, you don't do nothing by half, do you? That's going to scar, that is.'

I remember Lil examining my hand the other day. She'd said something about a scar. I feel a shiver run down my spine. Up till now I think I've tried to dismiss her story about knowing me in another time as crazy. But suddenly it all seems far more plausible.

I've nearly filled the notebook. In bed I write down everything that's happened today. I wish I'd had the chance to read all this before I ended up here. My hand's throbbing, which makes it hard to hold the pencil. But at least the cold air in here is taking the edge off the pain.

I close the book and leave it on my bedside table, turning off the lamp. It is pitch black, but I can't close my eyes. It's only about nine o'clock, but I was so tired. There hasn't been a raid yet tonight. Nelly says it's because it's raining. The bombers don't like it when there's too much cloud cover. I hope it rains for weeks and weeks.

Downstairs I can hear the faint sound of music from the radio. When I came upstairs May and Nelly were dancing round the kitchen. I remember times when me and Jess would use her Wii Fit dance programmes. We had a right laugh, strutting and posing and pretending we were in Little Mix, or dancing on-stage with Taylor Swift. I bet May would love doing that, once she got used to the music. If ever I get home I'll have try Gran with it. I have to confess though, I'm getting quite fond of the big band sound.

It's weird to think I've gone a whole week without being able to text or watch telly or use a computer. It's only when I'm writing in the notebook or lying here like this that I miss those things. I suppose I've been too busy or too tired to think about them. I wish I had my phone now. I'd give anything to be able to ring someone or take pictures of all this and send them to my mates. Hey, I wonder if you *could* take a phone through time? I mean, I doubt if anyone will take my word for it that all this really happened to me. If I could show people pictures, they'd have to believe me.

Oh well, it's pointless wondering. I haven't got it, end of.

The music stops, I hear the girls coming upstairs. Only, I'm sure that's Gran talking, and Great-aunt Eleanor answers in her posh voice. I lift my head off the pillow, but it feels so heavy I flop back down again. It's so dark in here, the blackness feels heavy around me. My thumb is still throbbing. My arm is resting on the outside of the blankets, to let the cool air get to it. The rest of me is getting toasty warm under the covers and I just can't summon the energy to move. The voices are on the landing now, calling goodnight to each other. In my mind I can see the old women kissing each other on the cheek then going into their rooms. Will Great-aunt Eleanor come in here? I want to put the lamp on so I don't give her a nasty shock, but my body won't take any notice of what my brain's telling it to do.

I should be doing something. I open my mouth to shout, but no sound comes out. The door opens and there's Great-aunt Eleanor, her outline surrounded by light from Gran's hallway. My eyes fill up when I see the magnolia walls and the cactus in the pot on the landing windowsill behind her. Even old Eleanor looks beautiful to me right now.

I blink away my tears and everything disappears, plunging me into darkness. My body suddenly comes alive and I sit up gasping for breath.

So close. I was so close. My heart is beating hard. I can feel my whole body pulsing. I want to scream and throw things. Why is this happening to me? It felt like something was pinning me to the bed, stopping me from doing anything. I couldn't even speak.

I scrub at my eyes, not even fighting the sobs that burst out of me. I hate crying, and I seem to be doing it all the time in this bloody place. I get up and go to the door and open it. Everything is dark and still. It's cold. The damp, faint smell of washing soap lingers in the air. I'm still firmly stuck in 1940.

To rub it in, the air-raid siren starts its long slow wail, building in volume like a scream. I hear Nelly and May moving in their bedrooms, and they both burst out onto the landing within seconds of each other.

'What you doing, standing there like a lemon?' asks Nelly. 'Get some clothes on, you don't want to go down the shelter like that on a night like this.'

'Come on, Queenie. We ain't got time to mess about,' says May, taking me by the shoulders and turning me round. She gives me a little shove into the room. 'Dress up warm, love. It's bleeding brass monkey weather out there. God knows how long this'll last.'

'Don't wait for me,' I say. 'I'll see you down there.'

'You sure?'

'Yeah. No worries.'

'Come on, May,' says Nelly. 'She'll be all right. She knows what to do.'

They clatter down the stairs and I hear them in the hall dragging the big coats off the hall stand.

I put on the lamp and get changed, swearing when knock my thumb. I leave the buttons on my cardigan undone and run down to join the others.

Hours later, I'm wide awake while the girls sleep, snuggled up together on a bench in the shelter. I've come to a conclusion. I'm here for a reason. Until I figure what it is, I can't get back. I have to use my head and figure out why I'm here, and when I do, whatever is holding me here will let me go.

It's as simple as that. I can't go back yet, because it's not finished.

CHAPTER TWENTY-TWO

After a freezing night in the shelter, there's a layer of frost on everything this morning, and the rain-soaked roads have turned icy. I shiver as we leave for work.

'Cheer up, Queenie. It's nearly Christmas,' laughs May as she skips down the road to the bus-stop.

'Bah, humbug,' I say. 'I'm too cold to care.'

'Watch it, May,' warns Nell. 'You'll come a cropper. There's ice all over the place.'

May pulls a face. 'Stop fussing. I'm not a kid.'

'Could've fooled me,' says Nelly. She looks as miserable as me.

May takes no notice and practically dances along the pavement. She's almost at the bus-stop when her heel catches on a broken slab and her other foot slips from under her. She falls with a shriek.

Nelly rolls her eyes and tuts. 'You dozy mare.' I can't help giggling, May looked so surprised as she went down. I offer her a hand and try to pull her up. May's not much help, because she's laughing too.

'Get up, May, we're gonna miss the bus.'

'All right, keep your hair on.' May struggles to get up, slipping again, and nearly pulling me down on top of her. She tries again, I'm not much help because I'm still giggling. Finally Nelly steps forward and grabs her other hand and between us we manage to pull May up. But as soon as she puts her weight on her left foot, May collapses again. 'Ow, me ankle! Oh my God, it don't half hurt.'

'Stop mucking about,' says Nelly.

'I ain't!'

'I don't think she is,' I say. 'Look at her foot.' It's swelling fast. 'Do you think she's broken it?'

'I bloody hope not. That's all we need. God, May, why can't you be more careful?'

'I didn't do it on purpose,' wails May, her face pale.

'Should we call an ambulance?' I ask. 'Where's the nearest phone?'

'We'll have to do something. Oh blimey, here's the bus. We ain't gonna get to work, are we?' Nelly looks really worried. 'We need to call in, or we'll get the sack.'

The bus pulls up and Bill gets off, obviously on his way home after another night shift. He takes one look at us holding up May, her white face streaming with tears, and he turns and lets out a piercing whistle. 'Hold up, mate!' The bus conductor looks out of the back of the bus.

'What's up?' he shouts. 'You ladies getting on?'

'My sister's hurt her ankle. You couldn't drop us off at the hospital, could you?' Nell asks. 'It'll save calling out an ambulance.'

'Yeah, 'course we can. Need any help getting her on?'

'I've got her,' says Bill, picking her up as though she weighs nothing. It's pretty impressive. Even Nelly looks pleased that Bill has taken charge. 'Blimey, May,' he says. 'There's easier ways of getting me to sweep you off your feet, girl. You only had to ask.'

'Be careful, it's icy,' I say. 'That's how she slipped.'

Bill grins. 'Don't fuss. I've got me army boots on. It's them daft women's shoes that do all the damage.' He looks at May, who is shivering with cold and shock. 'Let's get you to hospital, then May. The doc'll soon sort you out.'

We pile on to the bus, thanking the conductor for waiting. 'I couldn't leave you lovely girls on the pavement, now, could I?' he winks at us. 'I still gotta take your fares though, sorry.'

I insist on paying Bill's fare too, while Nelly worries about what's going to happen about work.

'We won't get paid if we don't turn up. And now we'll have to pay a doctor's bill.'

'I'm sorry, Nelly,' says May, looking thoroughly miserable. 'Maybe I should just go home and rest it. You and Rose go to work. I'll be all right. Bill'll help me, won't you?'

'You'll need to get it checked,' I say. 'If it's broken, you might make it worse.'

'She's right,' sighs Nell. 'We can't take no chances. Dad'll have my guts for garters if I don't look after you right.'

'I've got an idea,' says Bill. 'Let me pop her into the first aid station at the barracks. They'll see to her for me, then I can get her home for you. You two don't need to miss work. I'll stay with her, don't worry.'

'But ...'

'Nell, don't argue,' says Bill. 'It makes sense.'

Nelly looks shocked. I don't think Bill's ever spoken to her like that before.

'I agree,' I say. This is a perfect opportunity to give May and Bill some time together. 'We know May's in safe hands, Nelly. And if we can get to work it will stop you worrying about our jobs. They won't sack May if she's been hurt. So long as she gets a note from the doctor, they won't have a leg to stand on.'

'What, like me?' says May, pointing to her swollen ankle. She's obviously still in a lot of pain because she's as white as a sheet and she's hanging onto Bill for dear life. But she's trying to smile, so that's a good sign, isn't it?

We all look at her and burst out laughing.

Me and Nelly leave the two of them on the bus, to go on to the barracks. We make it to work with a couple of minutes to spare.

'I hope we're doing the right thing,' says Nelly as we take off our coats.

'Stop worrying. Bill will look after her. In fact, this is perfect,' I say, feeling smug, even though I had nothing to do with it. 'I hope she realises Harry wouldn't have come to the rescue like that.'

'That puny little runt wouldn't have had the energy or the inclination to pick her up and get her onto the bus like that,' agrees Nelly.

She runs up to the office to report May's accident, and I let Mrs Bloomfield know. When I get to my workstation, Esther gives me a huge smile.

'You look like you've had a good weekend,' I laugh, pleased

to see Esther looking so happy. 'Found yourself a fella?'

She shakes her head. 'No, better than that. I have heard from my parents.'

I feel my heart miss a beat. 'Are they OK?'

'Yes, they are very well. They have reached Switzerland. Some friends helped them, and now they are staying with my cousins.'

I feel my knees give way and I slump into my chair. God I'm so relieved. I'm filling up. 'That is the best news! I'm so happy for you, Esther.'

She gives me a funny look. I suppose she might think my reaction is a bit OTT, but I can't help it.

'Of course I am happy to have heard from them, yes. But I'm afraid this means that we are stuck in different countries and won't meet again until the war is over.'

I hadn't thought of that. I know exactly what it feels like to be far, far away from your parents, not knowing when you're going to see them again. 'Yeah, tell me about it. But trust me, Esther, it's much better to know they're safe and you'll see them again one day. Some people don't know when they'll see their family again, if ever.'

She looks confused. 'I'm sorry, my English ... I think I understand what you say. And I am glad. I just wish I knew when this awful war will end.'

I open my mouth to tell her –.

'Come on, girls,' says Mrs Bloomfield. 'We're down another worker this morning, so we can't afford to waste time on idle chatter. There's a war on, don't forget.'

With a sigh, I close my mouth. It's probably better that I don't say anything anyway. I smile at Esther and get on with my work.

Nell had made Bill promise to let her know what the doctor said, so by lunchtime he'd phoned the office with the news that it was just a bad sprain.

Harry is waiting outside the factory at home time. Nell gives him the evil eye.

'Not working today, Harry?' she asks.

'I've been hard at it, doing my bit for the war effort,' he smiles, pulling at his cuffs.

'You can't have been doing much. You ain't worked up a sweat, that's for sure.'

'That's cause I work with me brain,' he says, tapping his temple and looking far too pleased with himself. He winks at me. I just raise my eyebrows, not impressed. If he's so smart, he'd know better than to provoke Nell.

'Well, mind that brain don't land you in trouble, Harry boy. I hear the recruitment sergeant went round your mum's again last week. Funny how she never knows where you are, ain't it? If you were doing an honest day's work, you wouldn't need to keep it from your own mother, would you?'

He shrugs, looking shifty. 'It's very hush-hush, what I do.'

Nell sneers. 'I'll bet it is. Don't want the coppers finding out, eh?'

'You don't know what you're talking about, Nell, so I'll thank you to keep your mouth shut.'

'Don't you talk to me like that,' snaps Nelly. 'I'll speak as I find.'

'You ain't got a clue,' he hisses. 'I got friends, I have.'

'Yeah? Not what I heard.'

Harry blusters a bit. He clearly can't think of a decent comeback. One point to Nelly, I think.

'Look, I didn't come here to see you. Where's May?'

'Coming to her senses, I hope,' mutters Nelly.

'What? What you saying?'

'She's ill,' I say. 'She's got something really, really infectious. She's covered in spots and everything.' I shake my head. 'It's dead nasty. You'd better stay away, Harry, you might catch it.'

He looks gobsmacked for a minute, but I blow it because I can't help grinning. 'Ah, you're having a laugh,' he says. 'I know you two are trying to break us up. But you ain't going to do it. We're going to win that dance competition, you'll see. You tell her from me. Harry's not going to let no one get in his way.' He waves a fist at us. Bad mistake. Nelly steps forward. Oh my God, she's going to slap him!

Harry – being your basic coward – legs it, nearly knocking an old lady over in his rush to escape.

'Look at him,' I laugh. 'Scuttling away like a little rat.'

But Nelly isn't amused. 'He should have been drowned at birth, that one. Nasty little bleeder. What the blooming hell does May see in him?'

'He never lets her see how truly slimy he is,' I say. 'Seriously, she thinks he's a right charmer.'

'Silly mare,' says Nell. 'She ain't got no sense when it comes to fellas. We'll have to be careful and make sure he don't turn her head. He's nothing but trouble, that one. Come on, let's get home and see how she is. I just hope there ain't a raid tonight. Getting her down the shelter will be a right pain.'

CHAPTER TWENTY-THREE

At the house, we find them in the parlour, both fast asleep, May stretched out on the sofa and Bill in one of the armchairs next to the fire. Ah bless!

Nell looks at the mantel clock and frowns. She shakes Bill awake. 'You'd better get a move on,' she says quietly. 'You'll be late for duty.' May sleeps on. 'It's nearly six.'

He yawns and rubs a hand over his face. 'It's all right, Nell. I saw me sergeant and switched. One of the lads needs time off tomorrow for a funeral, so I'm doing a double shift then.'

'Well, that's a relief,' says Nelly. 'I didn't want you getting in trouble after everything you've done for us today. Thanks, Bill. You'll stay for tea, won't you? I managed to make a lovely cottage pie with our mince ration and those spuds you brought round. It only needs heating up.'

'I'd like that, thanks,' he says. 'Tell you what, Nan left some tins at hers 'cause she couldn't carry them. She won't mind if we have some of them. There's tinned pears and some evaporated milk. How about I bring 'em over for pudding?'

'That would be very nice,' she says. 'Are you sure Lil won't mind?'

'Nah, she told me to use 'em up.'

'But they'll keep. Why don't she want to save them? She'll have to something in the pantry when she comes back.'

He shakes his head. 'You know what she's like. She's got some daft idea the house ain't going to be there for her to come back to. She made me take a load of stuff round to our house 'cause she said it'll get lost otherwise.'

'Well, she's always been worried about being bombed, ain't she? I'm surprised she hung on round here as long as she did.'

'Yeah, I suppose.' He looks at me and away again quickly. What's that all about? 'Anyway, I'll go and get those tins.'

'I'll go and put cottage pie in the oven,' says Nelly.

When she's gone, I slip into the hall and catch Bill at the door. I step outside with him so we can talk in private.

'Is everything all right?' I ask him. 'What's up with Lil?'

At first I think he's going to deny it, but then he sighs. 'She said you warned her to get out the house 'cause it's going to be blown up.'

'I never did!' What is he on about? 'I swear I did not say anything like that to Lil. How could I? I have no idea what's going to happen.'

'Don't you? You've told me plenty.'

'Not really. Hardly anything. I can't, can I? It might change the future.'

'Well you're doing your best to change my future, ain't you? I mean, I never dreamed I had a chance with May until you started going on about it.'

'That's different,' I say. I don't have a clue what he's so upset about. 'You and May are meant for each other.'

'We'll see, won't we? In the meantime, I don't think you should've got Nan all worked up like that.'

'But I didn't! Honestly, Bill. I never said a word. I don't know anything about ...' Oh hell! Standing here on the pavement, looking at Lil's house I realise that when I stand outside Gran's house in the future, it looks different. Instead of the unbroken line of terraced houses, there's a break. Right where Lil's house is now, in the future there's a couple of more modern houses in amongst the older ones. I'd totally forgotten all about that. Now it's staring me in the face. But that doesn't mean Lil's house got blown up, does it? Oh crap, who am I kidding? But how could I have possibly said anything to Lil? 'Maybe it was me in another time,' I say, thinking aloud. 'It definitely wasn't me now.'

'Bloody hell, Rosie, I don't know what to think about all this blinking time travel lark.'

'Tell me about it,' I say. 'It's totally doing my head in. But I definitely haven't said anything to Lil about her house. Not in this time.'

I must look really pathetic, because he pulls me into a bear hug. 'Aw, come here. What's done is done. For all I know, you've done us a favour. I'm sorry I had a go at you.'

'That's OK,'

He puts me away from him. 'Time will tell, eh? I'd better get those tins.'

'Yeah, OK. See you in a minute.' I go back indoors and sit in the parlour with the sleeping May. I suppose I should go and see if Nelly wants some help, but I just want to be alone with my thoughts for a while.

I'm almost dozing off when May wakes up.

'Where's Bill?'

Well it's got to be a good sign if he's the first person she thinks of.

'He's just popped over to Lil's to get something. He's going to have supper with us. How do you feel?'

May sighs and raises her bandaged ankle. 'I won't be dancing for few days, that's for sure. The doc strapped it up tight, and told me to stay off it. I've got a pair of crutches to help me get about. Bill put 'em behind the settee for me. What happened at work? I ain't got the sack or nothing, have I?'

'No, don't worry. They're too short-staffed to get rid of you. Daisy wasn't in either. Someone said her house was hit. She was under the stairs with the children.'

'Oh no! Are they …?'

I shake my head. 'No, thank goodness. They're all alive, although Daisy's broken some ribs, and one of the kids has a broken arm.'

'We've been telling her to evacuate those littl'uns, but she's so bleeding stubborn. Well, I hope she's learned her lesson now, and gets the little mites out of London before they all get killed.'

'It must be hard, though, sending your children away.'

'Better that than seeing 'em killed, I reckon. We're all in the same boat, missing family. I wish our Dad wasn't away. He's all we've got.'

'He'll be back, May. I know it.'

May sighs. 'You keep saying things like that, Queenie, but you ain't God. You just don't know. None of us do.'

Not for the first time, I really wish I can tell May the truth, but don't dare. 'Maybe I've got a bit more faith than you have,' I shrug.

There's a knock at the door. 'I'll get it,' I say. 'That'll be Bill.'

It's not. It's Harry. He's obviously bathed in another barrel full of aftershave, his hair is extra slick, and under his arm is a box of chocolates. 'Hallo, Queenie, love. Tell May I'm here, will you?'

I want to slam the door in his face. 'She's really not well, Harry,' I say instead, giving him a totally insincere smile. 'If those are for her, I can pass them on, and tell her you called.'

He looks at me through narrowed eyes. 'You wouldn't be winding me up, would you? 'Cause I don't take kindly to being mucked about.'

'Really, Harry,' I say, trying to look wide-eyed and innocent. 'Why would I do a thing like that? Shall I get Nelly? She'll tell you the same as me, I guarantee it.'

He only just manages to hide his alarm. Then he turns all cocky.

'Well, it's understandable – you wanting to keep May out the way. I saw the way you was looking at me at the dance the other night.' He smirked. 'I ain't daft. I could see you liked me.'

Yeah, right. You wish. I want to tell him exactly what I think of him but I keep my mouth shut. He takes my silence for agreement.

'Well you don't need to fret your pretty little head, Queenie. I might be paying a bit of attention to May right now, but it don't mean I ain't got my eye on you n'all.'

'Really?' I say, trying to keep my true feelings off my face. What I really want to do is kick him where it hurts. 'So it's not serious with May, then?'

'Nah, 'course not. I promised her I'd partner her for a dance competition at the Palais next week, and I reckon we can win it. The money's always handy. But me and May?' He shakes his head and moves closer. I fight the urge to move back. 'She's all right for a laugh, but I know class when I see it. You're the sort of bird I'm looking for long term. Don't you worry, I just need to keep May sweet for a bit longer, then I'll be round to see you. I'll show you a good time.'

Oh. My. God. I think I'm going to throw up. I can't believe his nerve, the slimy toad.

'That sounds like fun,' I say, all the while thinking 'NOT!' He really is an arrogant, stupid little rat-bag and I really want to punch him on the nose.

'Yeah, don't it just,' he says, sliding a hand round my neck and pulling me towards him. He kisses me on the mouth. I want to gag, especially when he pushes his tongue into my mouth. He tastes of cigarettes and bad breath. His sickly aftershave is making me feel faint.

I twist, trying to get him off me, but he's holding my head and moves with me. Out of the corner of my eye I see a movement. May! Oh hell. I close my eyes. This is a nightmare.

I clamp my teeth on Harry's tongue in frustration. He groans, but doesn't let me go. I'm tempted to bite him really hard, but the thought of getting his blood in my mouth stops me. God knows what I'd catch from him.

'Harry? What the bloody hell's going on?' May yells.

I unclamp my teeth and Harry staggers back, right into the arms of Bill, who has just walked through the door. Nell comes out of the kitchen as well, just in time to see what's happening.

'Bloody hell,' said Harry.

'Why were you kissing her, Harry?' Nell asks in her scary, don't-mess-with-me voice.

'I'll tell you why,' cries May. 'He's a bloody two-timing git, that's why. I'm all right for a dance or two, but Queenie here's got the 'real class', ain't she, Harry?'

I want a great big hole to open up in the floor and swallow me up. I have never been so embarrassed in all my life. Why didn't I just knee him in the privates and yell rape or something?

'May, darlin',' says Harry. 'I didn't mean nothing by it. It was just a joke. Look, I bought you these.' The box of chocolates is looking crumpled and sad. 'Special sweets for my sweetheart.'

May glares at him. 'Well I ain't laughing. So you can take those and shove 'em where the sun don't shine. Now sod off!'

'But ...'

'You heard the lady,' says Bill. 'Now shove off.'

Harry looks at Bill, and sneers. 'Don't worry, Jocky me lad, I'm off. They're a bunch of bloody witches that lot. Mind they don't turn you into a frog.'

'Right, that's it.' Bill grabs him by the lapels and lifts him clear off the ground. Harry drops the chocolates. 'Listen here, you piece of dog turd, if I see you around any of these girls again, I'll knock your bloody block off.' He manhandles Harry round and pushes him hard. Harry lands in the gutter, shrieking like a girl. Bill wipes his hands, as though getting rid of any dirt he's picked up from Harry, then turns back to us.

He grins. 'Close your mouths, girls, or you'll be catching flies.'

Nell's the first to move. She runs past me and picks up the chocolates, then throws them at Harry. They land on his head and he howls, 'Oi! Sod off!'

'No,' yells Nell. '*You* sod off, and take your black market rubbish with you. I'll be telling the coppers about you. I hope you rot in jail.'

I want to cheer. This is great! We've seen off horrible Harry, and Bill is a hero. May's bound to see him differently now. I turn to look at May, but she's gone back into the parlour. I follow her, leaving Nelly and Bill to watch Harry run down the road.

'May? It's all right, he's gone.'

'Yeah, I heard. Why don't you go after him?'

'What? Are you kidding? I don't want ...'

'Well, you could have fooled me, you ... you ... bloody tart!'

I freeze, hardly breathing. I know I shouldn't be surprised by May's anger, but I am. Surely she must realise I didn't want to kiss him, that I would never do anything to hurt her? 'You don't understand.' Oh my God, that's exactly what Jess said to me when I caught her snogging Simon! Of course she wasn't trying

184

to take him from me, she was trying to save me from making the biggest mistake of my life. And like May, I completely lost it. I should have known better. I didn't trust her but I know I can trust Jess with anything. She's the best friend a girl could ever have.

I wasn't thinking straight. And now May isn't either. She's hurt and angry and it's all my fault.

'I ... I'm sorry,' I say.

'Sorry you got caught, more like. God, I was worried you were going to mess Bill about, but I had no idea what a greedy little cow you are. One fella's not enough for you, is it? Oh no, you have to make a play for mine n'all.'

'I did not!'

'Oh yes, you did. I heard every word.'

I feel my heart sink. May has no idea what I was trying to do, so of course she thinks I was after Harry. 'Honestly, May, it wasn't what you thought. You don't understand ...'

'Oh, I understand all right. Well, at least Bill's seen through you now, Miss High and Mighty. He's too good for the likes of you.'

Bill, standing in the doorway, coughs. I can't look at him. I hope to God he understands what's going on. I can't bear it if he thinks I'm really like that.

'You're right,' I say, my voice shaking. 'He's far too good for me.'

Bill coughs again. 'Nelly says the pie's ready. Come and eat.'

The thought of food makes me feel sick. How can I be expected to eat when everything's so horrible?

'May, listen,' I say.

'I ain't listening to nothing you've got to say, Queenie,' she says. 'I wouldn't believe a word of it.' She picks up her crutches and hobbles out of the room.

I sink down onto the sofa.

'Come on, Rosie,' says Bill. I brace myself to look at him, not know what to expect. He gives me a sad little smile. 'She'll come round. May don't hold grudges.'

'But Nelly does,' I say, remembering how Great-aunt

Eleanor reacted when she recognised me as Queenie.

'Chin up,' he says. 'At least it got rid of Harry. I reckon that's got to be a good thing. Now, come and have some food. You can't hide in here all night.'

'You go ahead. I won't be a minute.'

He leaves me alone and I sit there, trying to get everything straight in my head. This must be what Gran and Eleanor were talking about, when they thought I'd stolen May's boyfriend. If it is, then this is the night I disappear. For a moment I can't breathe, I feel fear wash right over me. Is this the night I die?

CHAPTER TWENTY FOUR

I can't sit here all night. I've got to face them, even if no one's talking to me.

As I enter the kitchen there's an awkward silence. Bill gives me a nod, but the girls ignore me and carry on eating. There's a plate of cottage pie at my place. I sit down and pick up my fork. I take a mouthful, but I'm so stressed I can't taste anything and when I swallow it feels like a stone in my throat. I close my eyes, fighting back tears. This is awful. I don't know what to do.

The air-raid siren cuts through the air, making us all jump.

'Come on, May, we'd better get you down the shelter,' says Nelly. 'Bill, can you get her crutches?'

'I'll carry her,' he says. 'It'll be quicker.'

'Right. Good idea. I'll get the coats.'

Bill picks May up and she gives him a shy smile as she wraps her arms round his neck.

'Thanks, Bill. I'm sorry to be such a pest.'

'It's no trouble, May. I'm glad to help.'

The look they share brings tears to my eyes. That's my Gran and Grandpa, falling in love. And you know what? I don't care how horrible things are, or what might happen to me, because I've just witnessed the most beautiful thing in the world. I stand up, really wanting to hug them both.

Big mistake.

May glares at me as Nelly comes in with May's fur coat and Bill's army coat. She's already got her Grandpa's great coat on.

'You'd better get a coat, Queenie,' says Nelly. 'Hurry up.'

'I ain't going down the same shelter as her,' says May.

Bill frowns. 'We can't leave her out.'

May shakes her head, her eyes cold. 'It's her or me. I can't stand the sight of her right now.'

Bill hesitates. I can't let them argue, not now.

'It's all right,' I say. 'You go ahead.'

'He's right, May,' says Nelly. 'I ain't happy with her either, but we can't shut her out.'

I shake my head. Tonight's the night. I can't be with them. Somehow or other I'm leaving 1940, dead or alive. A strange sort of calm washes over me. Bill is May's hero now. My job here is done.

'I'll find a public shelter. There must be one round here somewhere.'

'Turn left out of here, second right. It's near the pub,' says Nelly.

May nods. 'That's settled then.'

'Here, hang on a minute,' says Bill. 'We can't send her round there. It'll be full of drunks.'

I shrug. 'I'll be OK.'

'No you won't,' he says. 'Look, there's an Anderson in Nan's back yard. Go down the alley next to number thirty-three and round the back. Her house is four doors up from there. The back gate ain't locked. There's a lamp in the shelter.'

'Are you sure Lil won't mind?'

'Don't be daft. She'd skin me alive if I let you go near the pub shelter.'

'OK, thanks.'

'Get a move on then,' says May. 'And good riddance.'

'We'll see you later,' says Bill.

'Not if I see her first,' she says, earning a frown from Bill.

I want to say goodbye, but I know I can't. They won't understand. Instead I take a deep breath to stop myself from making a complete fool of myself, and walk away.

Nelly follows me out in the hall.

'Is it still all right if I borrow a coat?' I ask.

'I suppose.'

Poor Nelly, she wants to kick me out on my bum, but her sense of duty is forcing her to do the right thing.

'I'm sorry Nelly. It wasn't what you thought, but I can't explain. Maybe one day you'll understand.'

'I won't never understand you, Queenie, and it don't matter.

I might not have approved of Harry, but you didn't have to treat May like that. I'll never forgive you for hurting my sister.' She opens the front door. 'Now get out.'

I walk out and she slams the door shut behind me. As soon as the light from the hall is gone I'm plunged into darkness.

It's not the first time I've been out on the streets during a raid, or been alone in an air-raid shelter. I know I should be scared, but I'm feeling kind of numb. It took me a while to make my way across the street and to find the alley. There was a bit of light from the search beams in the sky to help me, but when I got into the narrow path between the houses it was pitch black and I had to feel my way along the wall. It was better when I got to the back of the houses, but only because I could see fires a few streets over. So it wasn't better, was it? What kind of a monster am I? Those lights were people's homes and lives going up in smoke.

Now I'm sitting here, in Lil's little armchair in Lil's shelter. I wonder if she realises she's my great-great Grandmother? I wish she was here now. There's so much I want to ask her, so much I want to tell her. But that's selfish, isn't it, wanting her here, when she's safe at her daughter's. God! I've made such a mess of things!

OK, I admit it, I'm crying. I'm blubbing like a baby. I can't stop. I know I haven't been here long, but I really love them, you know? May and Nelly – yes, even Nelly. The girls at the factory. Bill and Lil.

Bill and Lil? I let out a hiccup of laughter. I've never put their names together before. They sound like they should be a characters on CBeebies or something. I start crying again, because they're not puppets, they're real people, and I don't think I'm ever going to see them again.

The raid is going on and on. The constant drone of the planes, the ack-ack-ack of the guns, the whoomps and roars as the bombs land and explode. Every night. Every bloody night. Even though I know it won't go on for ever, that we're going to win, it's grinding me down. It's unbearable for the others who

189

don't know what the future holds.

I'm exhausted. I really should try to sleep. That way, if I'm going to die, I might not see it coming. But my brain won't let me rest.

I keep thinking about May and Nelly and Bill. I hope they'll forgive me in the end. I think May will, because Gran said Queenie had done her a favour, didn't she? And I know how happy she was being married to Bill.

Bill's disappointed with me right now, but I think he'll realise that I wouldn't deliberately hurt May. And I definitely wouldn't fancy Harry. God, what a total loser!

But Nelly won't. Look how she talked about me when we found the suitcase at Gran's. If I can just get back to them I can explain. She might not believe me, but I can at least try. *If* I get back. *If.*

The raid just won't quit. The lamp stops working, I can't see a thing. Without any light it seems to get noisier. I think it's getting closer because everything seems to shake with every explosion. Debris falls onto the shelter roof and a couple of times it feels like it's bowing under the weight of whatever's landing there. I feel the pressure of it pushing down on me, then it pushes the door outwards with a bang. I try to pull it shut again, but the doorframe is warped and in the end I give up. I sit down again and watch.

The sky is filled with light – beams searching for the enemy; tracer dots from their guns; a plane with an engine alight streaking across the sky, trying to get away; the fires on the ground, orange and blue flames eating houses and shops and everything in them.

Why are they doing this? This is so horrible. Nothing but hate and destruction. I don't care what people say, war is wrong. You can't do this to people.

It's so cold I can't stop shivering. I pull my knees up and hug myself. If I'm going to die, I hope it's quick. I don't want to burn. Oh God, what am I thinking? I don't want to die! All I want is to get back to Gran's, to my own time. I want to see her and Great-aunt Eleanor, and Mum and Dad, and even Jess. Yes, I've got to make it up with Jess. I know she did to me what I did to May. I'm sure of it. I've got to tell her. I'm not bothered about Simon any more. He's not worth it.

He hasn't changed. I have. I don't need to make a fool of myself over some vain, cocky sod who thinks he's God's gift. I need to find a chap like Bill, or, or Jessie's brother Luke. A nice guy who makes me laugh and who'll really care about me.

And things will be different with Mum and Dad too. I've grown up. I can't believe how stroppy and lazy I was. I'll never take them for granted again, I promise. They're always telling me I'm capable of doing things, and I've always ignored them. Being here with May and Nelly I've seen it for myself. I'm better than I thought I was, thanks to them.

The bombs are falling closer. I can see along the gardens of the houses, and suddenly there's a *whoomp* and all the windows blow out. The back wall of next door starts to crumble in slow motion. I can see a bed sliding into the garden, surfing down the collapsing wall and landing with a crash just a few yards away from me. A cloud of dust fills the air, I choke and cough, my lungs burning, my eyes stinging.

What am I doing here? Sitting and waiting to die? Forget it! I'm out of here!

I need to get back to the house. I don't care if the girls hate me, I've got to talk to them. I can't leave it like this. I'll make them understand. I refuse to let them live for seventy years thinking I was a tart or a spy or dead. I don't care if I change the future. They have to know the truth!

Still coughing, I head back to the house, praying it's still there.

CHAPTER TWENTY FIVE

As I reach it there's an almighty explosion behind me. I fling myself at the front door and it swings open. I land in a heap in the hallway. I can't believe Nelly left it unlocked. That's just not possible. I'm sure I heard her lock it behind me.

I stand up and in the light from the street I see Harry creep out of the parlour.

'What are you doing here?' I ask.

He swears. 'Why ain't you in the shelter with the others?'

'It's none of your business. You shouldn't be here, Harry. What are you up to?'

'Just get out the way, Queenie, and you won't get hurt.'

I suppose I should be scared, but I'm not. He's sweating and looking over his shoulder into the parlour. A pale whiff of smoke spirals out.

I move closer, blocking his escape. He grabs my arms and pushes me back against the wall. I feel his smelly breath on my cheek. 'You wouldn't hurt me, would you Harry?' I say, pretending to be scared, when in reality I'm so angry I'm shaking.

'I might. You don't know what I'm capable of.'

It's hard not to smile at his tough guy act when you remember he ran off down the street whining like a *girl!* 'I've got a good idea, Harry,' I say.

'Well then. I'm going to let you go, then I'm going to walk out of here, and you're going to keep schtum, all right?'

'I'm sorry Harry, I don't actually know what schtum means,' I say, widening my eyes trying to look all innocent. 'I come from the country, remember?'

He growls, looking over his shoulder at the smoke, which is getting thicker. I've got to stop it. He can't get away with this. I've got to use my head.

'Have you ever been to Glasgow, Harry?'

'Eh? No, 'course not. What you on about?'

'So you've never had a Glasgow kiss?'

He looks nervous. 'You want to give me a kiss?'

I grin. 'Oh yeah, a really special one. I saw it on a film about Scottish gangsters. You're going to love it. I've been dying to try it.'

'Don't give me that. You bloody bit me last time.'

Damn, I'd forgotten that. I flutter my eyelashes. 'I'm sorry you didn't like it, Harry. That's how we kiss in the country. I only did it because you're special.' And if he believes that he deserves everything he gets.

'Is that right? Well, all right then. But no tongues, all right?'

'All right. Now close your eyes.'

He smirks and shuts his eyes. As Gran would say, what a plonker! I screw my eyes shut, and slam my head into his face. He lets out a groan and drops to the floor, out cold.

Ow! Ow! Ow! God, that hurt! I shake my head, seeing stars.

There's a crackling noise from the parlour. I kick Harry's prone body out of the way and run into the room. The sofa's on fire. It's not too bad at the moment, but there's a lot of smoke and any minute now it's going to spread. I run back out into the hall, looking for something, anything I can use to douse the flames. I look at the coat stand. No, I can't use the fur, Nelly will kill me. I pull it off and hang it up.

Think! I've got to think! Lil said 'use your head', but I've gone and headbutted Harry and now I can't think straight.

He groans. I kick him, hard, and he groans again, still stunned. He's wearing a big coat. That'll do. I grab it and roll him so that I can pull it off.

I run back into the parlour and throw it over the sofa. The smoke makes me cough again but I don't stop beating at the flames until I'm sure the fire's out. At last it's done. I turn on the light to make sure, and lean against the wall choking and spluttering.

I hear Harry moaning again. I pick up his coat which is all scorched and smoking, and as I do something drops out of a pocket. It's a small box. I open it and gasp, which sets me coughing again. Inside is a ring. *My Gran's ring.* I've known it all my life. Gran wears it all the time. She told me it was her Mum's.

I quickly search through the other pockets and find loads of stuff that doesn't belong in an honest man's pockets – a table lighter, a little silver pot, and a small leather bag containing a tie-pin. I know that too. Dad calls it his inheritance – it was his Grandad's and he wears it on special occasions. I see red. Harry's going to pay for this!

He's on his hands and knees, trying to get up. I kick his hands away and he falls on his face, his bum up in the air like some great big stupid baby.

'Where do you think you're going, Harry boy?'

I jump on his back, reach round, undo his belt buckle and pull the leather strap off him. He's so beaten up he doesn't even fight me. It doesn't take long to pull him arms back and wrap the belt round his wrists.

'Let me go, you mad bitch,' he whines.

'Now why would I do that? The girls will want to see you, Harry. And I reckon after they've finished with you, you'll be grateful for some police protection. I expect there's a nice safe cell down the station with your name on it.'

What am I like? Oh God, this feels great! It's like being in your own action movie.

He squirms beneath me and I push his face into the lino. 'Don't make me hurt you again, Harry.' He goes limp. Ha! What a wimp. 'Now, I'm going to get up, and you're going to get up, but you'd better not try anything because I'm a black belt in origami, right, and you don't want to know what that really means, OK?'

I hold onto the belt binding his wrists and we stand up. I'm ready to bash him again if he tries to run, but as he straightens the hall lights up. I blink. Who turned the light on?

'Rosie! Is that you darling?'

'Gran!'

She's standing there in front of us, a rolled umbrella in her hand. Behind her I can see the magnolia walls and beige carpet up the stairs. Great-aunt Eleanor comes to stand beside her, looking fiercer than ever.

'It's all right, Rosie, you can let him go now,' she says. 'He won't give us any trouble, will you Harry?'

I can feel him tremble as I let him go. He sags a bit, as though his knees are going to give way, but he manages to stay upright. 'Who ... who the bloody hell are you?' he asks, his voice squeaking with fear.

Eleanor looks at him over her glasses. 'We, young man, are the ghosts of Christmas yet to come.'

'G-g-ghosts?'

'And we don't take kindly to little toe-rags messing with defenceless girls,' says Gran, shaking her brolly at him.

'Defenceless? She's nearly killed me!' he cries.

Gran gives him a poke in the stomach with the brolly. Harry falls to his knees. 'Please, missus! I didn't mean no harm.'

'Like hell,' I shout, slapping the back of his head. 'He nicked your ring and Dad's tie-pin, and tried to burn the place down.'

'Oh dear,' Eleanor purses her lips. 'What are we going to do with you?'

'Lock him up and throw away the key!' says Gran.

Harry whimpers.

Eleanor shakes her head. 'There's no time for that.' She nudges Gran with her elbow. They both look up. I follow their gaze and realise that the line between the girls' hall and Gran's hall is going wobbly. The portal is about to close. 'Stand up, boy. Rosie, your work here is done. Open the door.'

I do as I'm told. There's no time to lose.

'Now, young man. We know who you are and where you live. If you continue with the life you've been leading you will never be safe, do you understand? We are avenging angels who will be watching your every move. You will leave this place and never return. If you know what's good for you, you'll join up and become a man. Do you understand?'

Harry nods.

'Well, go on then you snivelling little rat, be off with you!' Gran waves the brolly again and he heads out the door, his hands still tied behind his back. I pick up his smouldering coat and throw it at him. He shrugs it off and legs it. We watch him run a few yards before his belt-less trousers fall round his ankles and he pitches forward onto his nose. He lets out a scream and keeps moving, trying to get away from us. 'That's it, slither off on your belly like the snake you are,' yells Gran as she slams the door shut.

She turns and grabs my arm. 'Come on Rosie. We can't hang about.'

I look at Eleanor and she's fading. 'Take my hand,' she says. As soon as I do she pulls us through and we all land in a heap on the carpet. *Carpet!*

I'm laughing and crying at the same time as I help Gran and Great-aunt Eleanor to their feet.

'Well, I never did,' says Gran, laughing with me. 'What a turn up for the book!'

'You saved me, Gran!' I hug her, so happy. 'I've been trying to get back for ages, but I couldn't. How did you do it?'

'God knows, love. We heard you take a tumble just now and when we came out to see if you were all right, there you were with Harry.'

'You mean – I've only just – but –'

'That appears to be the nature of time travel,' says Great-aunt Eleanor, brushing soot off her skirt. 'You tend to return to the moment from which you left.'

'Come on, Rosie love, let's see if there's any tea left in the pot. I expect you'll be wanting a biscuit with that n'all.'

I follow them into the kitchen. The fitted oak units and stainless steel sink are back, the old water heater and monstrous cooker gone. It's exactly as I left it over a week ago.

'Sit down, darling. What an adventure! Thank God we managed to get you back. I'd never have forgiven meself if you'd been stuck there.' Gran fusses, checking the tea in the pot. 'Oh, this is stewed. I'll put the kettle on for a fresh one.' She pushes the biscuit tin towards me. I pick a chocolate digestive and eat it in three bites. Oh wow, that tastes epic! I take another one and nibble it slowly. If I'm not careful I'll polish off the whole tin. The sugar rush gets my brain working again.

197

'Hang on,' I say. 'Did you know this was going to happen?'

'Of course,' says Eleanor, sipping her tea. 'We've been aware of Queenie's true identity since before you were born.'

'But how –?'

'Bill,' says Gran. 'Bless him, he couldn't keep it secret once we was married, now could he?'

Bill. My friend. My Grandpa. I'm never going to see him again.

'Ah, bless, don't cry, love.' Gran pats my hand, and I flinch. 'Oh! Of course, you burned yourself on the iron, didn't you? Come here, I've got some proper cream for that now. Lucky you never let us put any butter on it, ain't it? Blimey, we had some daft ideas in them days, didn't we? I'd better get a flannel for your face n'all, you're all dusty. Is that a bruise on your forehead? Oh you poor love, you have been through it, haven't you?'

I put my hand up and feel a great big lump where I head-butted Harry.

'I don't understand,' I say. 'Why didn't you tell me before? You acted like – I don't know – '

'We acted like a pair of batty old women,' says Eleanor.

'Exactly. Why?'

She smiles. 'Spoilers.'

I put my head in my hands. 'Lil.'

Gran laughs. 'We thought she was dotty, for years and years, God rest her. I even thought my Billy was taking after her when he started talking about you being our grandaughter, I can tell you. But in the end, it all started to make sense. And when you was born, of course, there weren't no denying it.'

'I thought she was dotty too. In fact, I hoped she was. She said she met me before. I thought I was going to be stuck in the wrong time for the rest of my life.'

'No love. Billy said you would get back, and here you are, thank God. But he didn't know it would be me and Nelly what rescued you though. He'd have loved that, wouldn't he? Did you see Harry's face?' Gran laughs so hard tears run down her face. 'No wonder we never saw hide nor hair of him again! Oh, Nelly, you was amazing, weren't she, Rosie? 'We are the ghosts of Christmas yet to come.' I thought Harry was going to wet himself.'

'Totally,' I say, grinning.

Eleanor shrugs. 'As the incident occurred close to Christmas, I took my inspiration from Dickens. However, Harry was never going to be difficult to deal with. I've had a lot of practice with recalcitrant children in my career.' She's looking stern, but her eyes are sparkling.

'Nelly,' I say. 'You were fabulous.'

'My name is Eleanor,' she says. 'A strange young woman I met a long time ago told me it was a nice name. Only my stubborn sister persists in calling me by that ridiculous nickname.'

'She must have been something special for you to take any notice of her,' I say.

'She had her moments,' she says and we all laugh.

'Seriously though, some of the stuff Lil told me doesn't make sense,' I say. 'I mean, she said she met me when she was a girl, and then I apparently met her daughter.'

Gran looks at her sister. 'Is it all right to tell her, Nell?'

'Mmm,' says Eleanor. 'I suppose we ought to. Lil and I had some interesting conversations with her after the war. You could say she sparked my interest in history. And then of course there are the diaries.'

'What diaries?'

'The one that you wrote in this house, for starters. Did you really think that a teacher of my experience would be unable to decipher simple text-speak?'

I feel my cheeks go hot. God, I hope I didn't say anything too nasty about Nelly! I'm sure I didn't, but sometimes I just wrote stuff down without really thinking.

'And then Bill's Aunt Ethel gave us some more,' says Gran. 'I couldn't make head nor tail of them of course, so I handed them over the Nelly.'

This doesn't sound good.

'You might well look concerned,' says Eleanor. 'It seems that your adventures are far from over. But don't worry. I have had many years to study the diaries and the history of the times.

I will ensure that you are at least properly equipped to deal with whatever you encounter.'

'Can I read the diaries?'

'I don't think that's wise, do you?'

'But you said –'

'That I would prepare you. That doesn't mean you should know everything, young lady. To use your own phrase – we must beware of spoilers.'

'It's not my phrase. It's from *Doctor Who*.'

'That explains a lot. Young people today take television far too seriously. But it does not change the fact that if you know what is going to happen you may try to change it, and that could be disastrous.'

'Or I might change the future,' I sigh.

'Exactly.'

I take another biscuit and eat it. This sucks. Eleanor knows exactly what's going to happen and I'm left to stumble around in the dark.

'Do you at least know *when* it's going to happen?' I ask. 'I mean, not just where I'm going, but when it happens in our time?'

'Don't worry,' she says. 'We have a little while yet before your next adventure. But we've a considerable amount of work to do, so we must get on.'

'Not tonight, Nell, surely?' says Gran. 'Look at the poor girl, she's in no fit state. What she needs is a decent meal and a good wash.'

'Ooh, yeah! Can I have some fish fingers, Gran?'

'Course you can, darling. With chips?'

My mouth is watering. 'Ah Gran, you're the best!'

She laughs and gets on with the cooking while I run upstairs to May's old room, now a gleaming modern bathroom, and have a quick shower.

When I come down, I sit and watch her. I'm so happy to see Gran again. It was great to meet her when she was younger, and I'm going to miss May. But this is my Gran, and I love her. And Nel - er – Great-aunt Eleanor. Now I've known the Nelly that Gran grew up with, the old one isn't nearly as scary as I thought she was. It's dead easy to talk to her now, and we chat about what I've been doing over the past week.

'What I don't understand,' I say to her, 'is *why* it happened. I mean, it shouldn't be possible, should it? And why me? I'm nothing special. Just an ordinary teenager. And what about that suitcase? Where did that come from?'

'Indeed. I have wondered about that myself. But that seems to be one mystery we aren't going to be able to solve. Whether the real Miss Smith sent her things on in advance and then met with an accident, I don't know. But no one ever claimed it.'

'I suppose it's stuck in a time loop now. I find it here, it goes back to 1940 with me, I leave it there, you guys keep it, and I find it again years later.'

'Mmm. Who knows?' Eleanor shrugs. 'It was certainly a lucky coincidence that it did arrive.' She looks thoughtful. 'Unless ...'

'Unless what?'

'Oh, I don't know. Perhaps I should have asked Lil about it. I'm beginning to think that there's far more to this than we might imagine.'

'And what does – did - Lil have to do with it?' I still can't get my head round the fact that it's not 1940 anymore.

'I can't be sure, but I suspect you are not the first person in the McAllister family to have travelled through time.'

'Seriously? Are you saying it's genetic or something?'

'I have no proof, but Lil often became confused, and sometimes she mentioned incidents that didn't seem to relate to you. When I questioned Bill, he confirmed he had heard the same stories about family members, usually female, who claimed to have met their ancestors. He'd dismissed them as myths, assuming these women were hinting at clairvoyance or some such nonsense, as we all did. But after meeting you, of course, he began to think quite differently.'

No wonder Bill believed me. If Lil had been feeding him stories like that, what I told him would have made some weird sort of sense.

'This is doing my head in,' I sigh, rubbing my eyes. 'Does that mean I could come face to face with other time travellers, and we'll be related?'

'Possibly. But maybe not. It will be interesting to find out.'

'Well not tonight it won't' says Gran putting a plate of fish fingers, chips and beans in front of me. 'Get that down you love. You've lost weight, ain't you? We'll soon get you sorted.'

'Oh Gran, this is …' I try not to cry. No more spam fritters. No more corned beef hash. No more sterilised milk. 'Fantastic. Bloody fantastic.'

She hands me a knife and fork and I dig in. Mmmm! It's soooo good.

'And what about the fresh pot of tea you threatened us with?' Eleanor asks Gran. Before Gran can answer, she raises a hand to stop her. 'No, I'll do it,' she says, standing up stiffly. 'A woman could die of thirst waiting for a cup of tea in this house.'

I nearly choke on my chips. God, it's good to be home!

THE END

With Special Thanks to

The Accent YA Blog Squad

Alix Long

Anisah Hussein

Anna Ingall

Annie Starkey

Becky Freese

Becky Morris

Bella Pearce

Beth O'Brien

Caroline Morrison

Charlotte Jones

Charnell Vevers

Claire Gorman

Daniel Wadey

Darren Owens

Emma Hoult

Fi Clark

Heather Lawson

James Briggs

With Special Thanks to

The Accent YA Blog Squad

James Williams

Joshua A.P

Karen Bultiauw

Katie Lumsden

Katie Treharne

Kieran Lowley

Laura Metcalfe

Lois Acari

Maisie Allen

Mariam Khan

Philippa Lloyd

Rachel Abbie

Rebecca Parkinson

Savannah Mullings-Johnson

Sofia Matias

Sophia

Toni Davis

With Special Thanks to

The Accent YA Editor Squad

Aishu Reddy

Alice Brancale

Amani Kabeer-Ali

Anisa Hussain

Barooj Maqsood

Ellie McVay

Grace Morcous

Katie Treharne

Miriam Roberts

Rebecca Freese

Sadie Howorth

Sanaa Morley

Sonali Shetty

THE SEA SINGER

SHOME DASGUPTA

There was a voice once that sang the ocean to sleep…

March is born in April, just as the sun is setting. A singing baby who cannot sleep, she sets Kolkaper on edge. The Town Council orders scientists to take her away and study her at the Cave Forest, a place for freaks like her. Acting quickly, March's parents send her away to the distant town of Koofay. But March's destiny is tied to that of Kolkaper.

She must return to save the city from itself.

An enchanting fable about love and faith and accepting the odd ones among us.

Luca, Son of the Morning

Tom Anderson

The water is warm … but can you be in too deep?

Luca loves reggae, hates his parents' rum habit, and wishes his dad could get a proper job. He also loves Gaby (though he'd never admit it to her face) so upsetting her is enough to push him into a dark place. Retreating to the local beach, as he always does when he can't sleep, watching the waves gives his life some sort of rhythm.

One night, as he lets the tide lull him, a group of figures emerge from the water and walk past him, unseeing. Spellbound by these impossible sea-men, Luca holds nightly vigils at the beach. Until one night the sailors beckon him to follow them back into the sea…

THE DEEPEST CUT
natalie flynn

'You haven't said a single word since you've been here. Is it on purpose?' I tried to answer David but I couldn't ... my brain wanted to speak but my throat wouldn't cooperate...

Adam blames himself for his best friend's death. After attempting suicide, he is put in the care of a local mental health facility. There, too traumatized to speak, he begins to write notebooks detailing the events leading up to Jake's murder, trying to understand who is really responsible and cope with how needless it was as a petty argument spiralled out of control and peer pressure took hold.

Sad but unsentimental, this is a moving story of friendship and the aftermath of its destruction.

For more information about **Alison Knight**

and other **Young Adult** titles

please visit

www.accentya.com